SOMEONE TO STAY

THE SKYLARK SERIES

MICHELLE MAJOR

Dear Reader:

If you've been to Skylark before, welcome back. If this is your first visit, I'm so glad you're here. To be honest, I've been obsessed with Felix Barlowe since he first walked onto the page in Someone To Love (Book 1). He's swagger and charm with a heart he's convinced isn't worth much. Pairing him with Piper, who's just as stubborn and twice as guarded, is the kind of slow-burn, banter-filled story I love to right.This is a story about two people who've been left too many times learning to stay. I hope it makes you laugh, swoon, and maybe reach for the tissues once or twice.

Big hugs from Colorado

Michelle

1

PIPER

I came to this cabin in the Colorado wilderness outside Vail because I needed an escape from life. The kind that only a secluded, way-too-big-for-one-person mountain retreat can provide. My brother-in-law Ian bought the thirty-acre property when he moved to Skylark after retiring from the NFL. I guess being quarterback royalty includes a six-thousand-square-foot log-and-stone "getaway" for when you want a break from small-town Colorado life.

I'm not complaining.

I also came alone because I didn't want any witnesses to my spectacular life implosion. While my plan involved wallowing in the—well, I wouldn't call it misery, more like the terrifying uncertainty of my current situation—I did *not* come to be murdered in the middle of the night by a high-country killer.

Yet, here we are.

I'm not ready to die. Not even at my lowest did I feel that desperate.

Not when I saw my ex-fiancé Bradley at the hospital yesterday, smugly cozying up to his new bride. The one he'd started dating approximately five seconds after I called off our wedding last summer. The wedding I walked away from in the middle of the rehearsal dinner because I finally realized he's a condescending douche canoe who treated me like an accessory rather than a person.

I didn't get the memo that he'd returned to our shared hometown of Skylark, Colorado. And I sure as shit didn't know that he and the new Mrs. Bradley Carlson, a nurse like me, would be working at our small-ish community hospital where I couldn't avoid them if I tried.

I can't blame my entire meltdown on Bradley. That would be giving him too much power over me, and I vowed never again to let a man take my power that way. But it's been a rough month—longer if I'm being honest. Seeing them together in the break room, a diamond the size of a small planet on her left hand, was the last straw. I quit on the spot, packed a bag, and fled to Ian and Sadie's cabin before the Skylark rumor mill could start churning.

So I'm alone as I creep down the darkened staircase, my bare feet silent on the hardwood steps and my would-be killer rattling the front doorknob, wielding a tennis shoe in one hand and my e-reader in the other.

One to use as a weapon, the other as a potential shield. Because—once more for the bitches in the back—I don't want to die tonight.

Although I'd really hate to lose my new Kindle, the fancy one with the warm light setting. I highly doubt whether it could stop either a bullet or a knife swipe, but it seemed like a better option than a feather pillow from the guest bedroom where I'm sleeping. To be fair, the pillows are those fancy European ones that probably cost more than my monthly student loan payment, so who knows what they could do in a pinch.

If I make it through this night, I swear on all that is holy, I'll go back to leaving my phone on the nightstand when I sleep. I've been reading too much about blue light and beta waves, or whatever the hell it is that a phone emits, and while I'm not going to don a tinfoil hat any time soon, I figured keeping the phone in the kitchen would be a smart choice.

Being able to call 911 would have been preferable at the moment, but it is what it is.

My Jeep is parked in the attached garage, so if I can get to it before the intruder gets inside, maybe I'll have a chance at escaping. The keys are on the hook by the mudroom, because I'm organized like that.

I hear the soft snick of the door opening, and a deep voice mutters something about fucking light switches.

So much for getting out before he gets in. Back to Plan A, whatever the heck that was.

"Don't move," I shout, pitching my voice low like I'm the threat. Which is ridiculous because I'm currently scared out of my mind *and* pants-less.

"The fuck?"

The killer doesn't sound particularly cowed or predatory. More like...annoyed?

There's a sliver of light coming in the front window—the June moon is nowhere near full—and all I can see is the hulking outline of one giant of a man.

Adrenaline spikes, and I think about how much I have to live for. Topping the list is the fact that I'm right now growing a tiny human inside me. A baby who deserves better than to have their mom taken out by a home invader.

"Yippee-ki-yay, motherfucker!" I shout as I hurl the tennis shoe in the man's direction. Apparently, when faced with death, I channel *Die Hard*.

I played soccer and volleyball in high school—I wasn't exactly All-State material, but I made varsity in both sports all four years and have decent aim. The shoe connects with a satisfying thwack, followed by a string of curses that would make a sailor blush.

This is my chance. I bound down the rest of the stairs and turn the corner toward the back of the house just as the lights flip on.

The sudden brightness is blinding, and I blink rapidly, trying to adjust.

"What the fuck, Piper?"

Nearly to the kitchen, I stop mid-stride and whirl around, which knocks me off balance. I windmill my arms to keep from face-planting. That would be bad given the potential for general humiliation plus the pesky detail of me not wearing pants.

And suddenly I'm facing the last man—potential murderer, notwithstanding—I want to see right now.

Relief washes over me, my body not quite on the same page as my brain, and my knees give out as Felix Barlowe, my brother-in-law's huge, handsome, star NFL wide receiver brother stalks toward me. All six-foot-four inches of him. With his stupid perfect jawline and his stupid dark hair that looks like he just rolled out of bed. The same hair I ran my fingers through that night in Denver when we...

Nope. Not going there. That was tequila and temporary insanity and a mistake we agreed to forget.

"Are you trying to give me a fucking heart attack?" I demand through raspy breaths. My heart is doing this weird galloping thing that I'm attributing entirely to adrenaline. It has nothing to do with how his gray T-shirt stretches across his chest. The same chest I...

Stop it, Piper. This is *not* the time.

"You nearly took my damn eye out."

His annoyingly piercing—and entirely unharmed—eyes do a slow perusal of my current state, and I swear the temperature in the room jumps ten degrees. Just like it did in that bar in Denver when my friend's bachelorette party collided with his celebration for signing with the Denver Grizzlies franchise. When we'd had too many shots and ended up pressed against each other on the dance floor.

And then in the elevator.

And then in his hotel room

And then...

Focus, Piper.

"I thought you were here to kill me."

"Only in my dreams," he mumbles. And there's that smirk, the one that makes smart women do stupid things. The one that made *me* do stupid things when hours of trading insults somehow turned into foreplay. "Why did you throw a shoe at me?"

"Um, I thought you were a whack job coming to kill me. Maybe you should knock next time? Or, I don't know, text? Call? Send a carrier pigeon? Literally anything other than breaking and entering?"

"Ian gave me a key." He rubs his forehead where my shoe made contact. "Nice arm, by the way."

"High school volleyball. Not that you'd remember anything about me that doesn't involve shit talk."

The look he levels at me shoots sparks up my spine. "I remember plenty that doesn't involve talking," His voice drops a fraction, and, oh God, he's thinking about it too. The first weekend of April. Denver. The hotel room. The way we agreed the next morning that it was a terrible lapse in judgment. That we hated each other, and it would never happen again. And that no one, especially not Ian and Sadie, would ever know.

"Forget whatever you're remembering." I resist the urge to place a protective hand on my stomach, which is stupid because I'm not showing yet. And I have no idea what the hell I'm going to do about my baby's father being a man who can't stand me, and who told me to my face he doesn't want kids.

"Put some fucking clothes on," he says through gritted teeth, as if I'm the one being unreasonable.

I glance down at my faded T-shirt with "Night Shift Nurse: We Can't Fix Stupid, But We Can Sedate It" printed across the front. It hits at mid-thigh, well below the danger zone, and I'm wearing my comfiest cotton bikini briefs, not even a thong.

I cross my arms, which—oops—makes the shirt ride up higher.

"It's not like you haven't seen it before," I tell him, and then immediately want to die because that's not going to help either of us forget that night.

His eyes go wide, and I suck in a breath that has nothing to do with the adrenaline comedown and everything to do with the way he's looking at me. Like he's remembering exactly what's under this shirt.

"I'm referencing legs in general, you asshat. You've seen plenty of female body parts." On plenty of women who aren't his brother's sister-in-law, or carrying his secret baby. Women he actually likes.

"I'm not here to murder you, Hart," he says, his cadence painfully slow. "And I'm trying to be respectful." He pauses, his jaw working like he's physically forcing himself to keep his eyes on my face. His gaze drops for just a second before snapping back up. "Put on a bra, while you're at it," he commands. Like he has a right to demand anything where I'm concerned.

I clutch the Kindle closer to my chest. The device might not protect me from bullets, but it's definitely shielding me from Felix's opinion of my braless state. "How about I go back to bed and you turn around and go back to whatever whore hole you crawled out of?"

The murderer accusation clearly bothered him, but the man-whore comment makes his lips twitch. Interesting. Either way, I've gotten under his skin, which pleases me to no end. He's been under mine since April. Literally and figuratively.

"I'm not going anywhere." He glances over his shoulder as if he's just remembered something, and then takes a step away from me. "I've got someone in the car, and—"

"Fuck off, Felix." Why should I care if he brought a woman up here? It's not like we're...anything. We had one stupid, tequila-fueled, admittedly mind-blowing night that meant nothing. Even if the result means everything to me. I need to tell him, obviously. But that's a conversation I'm not prepared to have at the moment.

What I am prepared to do is kill my sister for not warning me he was coming. She knows I came here to escape drama, not to have it delivered to my door in the form of a six-foot-four football player with commitment issues and the ability to make me forget my own name with just a kiss. Not that we're kissing ever again. That was a one-time thing. Felix Barlowe is a gorgeous, athletic, surprisingly tender mistake who's brought another woman to the cabin where I'm trying to figure out my life.

I sigh and give him my best glare because the truth is he has as much right to be here as I do. His brother did marry my sister, after all. We're family. Sort of. In the most technical, non-blood-related, we-accidentally-made-a-baby-together way.

"At least do me the courtesy of keeping her quiet." I aim for casual indifference and land somewhere around bitter resignation. Because I'm not at all looking forward to hearing him with another woman while my hormones are doing whatever the hell they're doing—which feels a lot like wanting to fangirl all over him.

"Wear earplugs," he says, that smirk widening into a full-blown grin as he disappears out the front door. But not before I catch him muttering something that sounds suspiciously like "who needs sedation" and shaking his head.

I stand there for a full minute, Kindle still clutched to my chest, dignity hanging out on the floor with my shoe. The secret of my pregnancy sits like a stone in my stomach as I wonder how my peaceful mountain escape just turned into...whatever this is.

The universe has a twisted sense of humor. And right now, the joke's on me.

2

PIPER

I TRY to go back to sleep. Really, I do. But even with an earplug jammed into each ear, I can still hear noises. Strange ones. Not sex noises. It sounds like whimpering, but the voice is too young, and it's not the kind of whimpering I'd expect from a woman spending the night with Felix. Not the sort I did that one stupid, regrettable, drunken night in Felix Barlowe's bed.

I mean, unless there's some kind of perverted role-playing going on, it definitely sounds like a child crying. But that's impossible, because Felix doesn't have kids. He doesn't want kids. It's a point he made that crystal clear at Christmas dinner last year when he told Ian in no uncertain terms that kids weren't in his game plan. Ever.

Which is why the secret I'm carrying, the one that's going to make him a father in about seven months, makes my stomach pitch wildly. And finally propels me out of bed. I want to know what the hell is going on out there.

I put on a bra and some loose sweatpants. Not because he told me to, but because I'm afraid my nipples are going to betray me again, perking up the way they seem to whenever he's within a fifty-foot radius. My body hasn't gotten the memo that Felix Barlowe was a one-and-done for this girl.

I'm in one of three guest bedrooms on the second floor, and I can see a light coming from the partially cracked door of the room at the far end of the hall. The primary bedroom is on the main floor of the cabin, and I'm a little surprised he didn't take that since Ian and Sadie aren't here. I know firsthand that Felix sleeps like a starfish—arms and legs spread wide, taking up every available inch of mattress.

The crying has mostly subsided, but there are still little hiccupping sounds coming from his bedroom. I'm probably going to regret this when I get an eye-full of more than I bargained for, but my spidey senses are tingling. I'm a pediatric nurse, primarily NICU—or at least I was until I walked off the job—and I can't ignore the sounds of a child in distress.

God, I hope he's not into some weird diaper kink.

I knock on the door and wait for Felix to growl at me to "go the fuck away," but he doesn't respond. Neither does the woman who's in there with him. Then I hear the noise again: not quite a cry, not exactly a whimper, and definitely not an adult.

I push open the door and peek around the edge of it toward the bed, bracing myself for whatever scene I'm walking into. Only nothing could have prepared me for the sight of Felix, fully clothed and propped up against the headboard, with a child in his arms.

Based on her size and the length of her hair, the girl is between two and three years old. She's sleeping fitfully against his chest, squirming every few seconds and letting out those tiny sounds of distress that tug at my heart. Felix's massive hand nearly spans her entire back, and there's something achingly tender about the way he's holding her, like she's made of spun glass.

"What the—"

The words are meant to stay in my head, but I must have spoken them out loud, because Felix's eyes pop open. They're a startling, clear blue—the color of the bright sky above a snowy peak—and it takes a moment for him to register me standing there. He was definitely sleeping more deeply than the kid, but sensing my presence, he jolts up with a start, jostling the child. Her eyes blink open for a moment before they squeeze shut. Her face crumples, and she lets out a wail.

"Shh, it's okay, sweetheart," he says as he stands, his giant hand keeping her secure against him as he bounces, his movements almost endearingly unpracticed.

"Dude, come on," he says to me, his tone uncharacteristically put upon. "I just got her to fall asleep. She cried the whole drive up here from the airport in Denver."

"Don't *dude* me, Felix." I take a step forward. "What the hell have you done?"

"Don't swear in front of her." His voice is soft. Clearly, he doesn't want to upset the child in his arms any more than she already is, but his gaze is fierce.

"You need to tell me what's going on," I demand, pitching my voice to a whisper.

The little girl—who has wispy curls of sandy blonde hair, the widest brown eyes, and is wearing pink pajamas with donuts all over them—cries and squirms, but Felix holds her tight. Almost too tight. Like she's a ball he needs to protect until he gets her to the end zone.

"What does it look like?"

"It looks like you kidnapped a child and brought her to a remote cabin in the wilderness."

"Pump the brakes, Olivia Benson," he tells me, and the reference to one of my all-time favorite television characters gives me a moment of pause. Does he know I binge-watch *SVU*? Let's put a pin in that for the moment.

"Did you take someone's baby?"

"Of course I didn't *take* her," he says through gritted teeth. "She was given to me."

That admission stuns me. I know football fans can be devoted to their favorite players, and since the announcement a couple months ago, it's been the talk of the town around Skylark that the great Felix Barlowe is going to be playing for Denver's beloved Grizzlies. But I don't think even the most rabid superfan would give him a baby, would they?

"Felix, I swear to God, if you don't start making sense—"

"I can hear you thinking, Piper, and whatever explanation you've come up with in that beautiful blonde head of yours—there's no way you've guessed the truth."

I take a step closer and automatically hold out my arms. I love babies, and although I know Felix is trying, his awkward attempts at soothing this one aren't working.

"You're not going to run off with her, right? You're going to let me explain?"

"Jury's still out and it better be a good one," I say.

He hands over the girl with a relieved—and quite possibly exhausted—sigh. I didn't notice the dark circles under his eyes downstairs, but this isn't the high-energy, Tigger-coded Felix I know and don't love.

"Who is she?" I ask as the little girl settles against me, warm and smelling like baby shampoo.

"Her name is Ellie. And since mid-May, I've been her legal guardian."

I'm not sure I could stop my mouth from gaping open if I tried.

I shake my head.

"Who would leave you…"

I trail off before the rest of that sentence leaves my mouth. Since we met last summer, Felix and I have turned giving each other shit into an art form. But given the situation and the sweet little girl in my arms, what I was about to say feels too cruel, even for our toxic dynamic.

But I said enough. Felix knows the rest.

"Who would leave me a child when I'm the last person on

earth who should be responsible for one?" The smile he flashes isn't angry or defensive. It's genuine, and so damn defeated.

"I didn't mean—"

"It's fine, Hart. For once we're in complete agreement." He chuckles softly, then grabs the carrying bag for what looks like a portable crib I hadn't noticed resting against the wall.

"Are you okay holding her while I put this together? She wouldn't let me set her down, and doing it one-handed is—"

"Go ahead." The weight of the child feels right in my arms, and I try not to think about how in a few months, I'll be holding another baby. One with Felix's blue eyes, maybe.

"Her dad was my best friend in college. We came in together in the same recruiting class. Troy Wallace."

He looks at me almost expectantly, and I shrug as I sway back and forth, Ellie peacefully conked out against my shoulder.

"I don't really follow football."

"You wouldn't know Troy. He was supposed to be the best defensive lineman the league has ever seen. But he took the ass end of a dirty hit midway through our senior year. Went down hard and broke his back."

I flinch at the mental image, causing Ellie to stir. I adjust my hold, and she settles again. Felix watches us for a moment before returning to crib assembly.

I'd like to tell you I don't notice his strong hands or the tattoos snaking up his arms or how capable and efficient his movements are. But I'm only human. And it appears my pregnancy hormones have decided that Felix Barlowe assembling baby furniture is the hottest thing I've ever seen.

Awesome.

"It took a lot of rehab, but he walked again. Not a chance of him playing football after."

He pauses before continuing, and I expect him to tell me how Troy got hooked on painkillers, and his life went off the rails from there.

"The wild part is, I don't think he had any regrets." Felix smiles, glancing at me, then back down at the crib. "He met Julie, his wife, because she was his physical therapist. She kicked his ass five ways to Sunday. Made him work for his recovery. He got his teaching certificate, then a job as a fourth-grade teacher at the local elementary school, and took over coaching high school football where they lived in Mississippi. He was happy. A lot happier than a lot of guys who have multimillion-dollar contracts but no one to really give a shit about them."

I wonder if he's talking about himself, but that's none of my business, so I don't ask. Although the hollow look in his eyes suggests maybe he is, and maybe I should.

"He was so damn happy when Julie got pregnant. They told me together after a game in Atlanta. Troy and I celebrated by drinking entirely too much brown liquor, and he asked me to be the godfather."

The crib is together now, and he pulls a sheet from a duffel bag sitting at the foot of the bed.

"You said yes?"

He nods and runs his hand over his jaw, which is sporting at least three days' worth of stubble.

"I didn't think anything of it. I'm Riva's godfather. The fun uncle. And I'm f—" He glances at the sleeping baby, then corrects himself. "I'm darn good at it. I spoil my niece rotten. I figured I could do that again. Send ridiculous gifts on her birthday, dump a bunch of money into a college fund."

His big hands tighten on the sheet, and the soft fabric looks like he could tear it without trying.

"He never mentioned putting me in their will as her guardian." When his eyes meet mine, the devastation in them knocks me back a step. "Why would he?" His voice is so quiet it's like he's asking himself more than me. "They were young and healthy, and..."

"What happened?" I whisper, because I have to know. And as

much as I have to know, I get the feeling Felix needs to talk about it. He might not want to, but he needs to.

"It was a car accident," he says, turning away to fit the sheet around the thin mattress. "They'd gone out to dinner for their anniversary."

"Was Ellie—"

"No." He cuts me off. "She was at home with a babysitter. One of the other teachers at the elementary school where Troy worked." His head tips back and he stares at the ceiling for a moment like he's replaying a scene that haunts him even though he didn't actually witness it. "Troy ran off the road. It was raining, and he'd had a few drinks at dinner. His blood alcohol level was above the legal limit. He took a turn too fast and overcorrected when the car started to skid. They went over an embankment, and the car flipped." He shakes his head like he still can't believe it. "Both he and Julie died on impact. They didn't suffer."

The room falls silent except for Ellie's soft breathing against my shoulder. Felix smooths the sheet one more time, then straightens up, his hands hanging helpless at his sides.

"So she's yours," I say softly.

He lets out a dull laugh. "For now. I'm looking for other relatives. Troy grew up in the foster system, and Julie's mom died a few years ago. She didn't know her dad. But there might be cousins, aunts, uncles. Someone who actually knows what they're doing with kids and wants her."

"Right." The word comes out sharper than I intended. "Because you don't want kids."

His eyes snap to mine. "You can't seriously believe I'm the right person to raise her?"

"Your friend Troy believed in you."

"He was wrong."

My hand unconsciously drifts to my stomach before I catch myself. "So you're just...what? Playing house until you can pawn her off?"

"That's not what this is." He runs both hands through his hair, making it stick up in ways that shouldn't be adorable but somehow are. "I want to do the right thing for Ellie. Troy trusted me with his daughter. I can't fail him again."

"Again?"

He looks away. "I should have been there more. I got caught up in the whole NFL machine. I let our friendship slide. He never held it against me, but I did. I do. And now..." He gestures helplessly at the child sleeping in my arms. "Now I have to figure out how to take care of his little girl until I can find her a real family. She deserves to be loved the way Troy and Julie would have."

"Does anyone else know?" I ask, shifting Ellie's weight as she burrows deeper into my neck.

"No." The admission seems to cost him something. "Not even Ian and Sadie."

That stops me cold. "You haven't told your brother or my sister?"

"I couldn't. Not yet. Ian would try to fix it. And Sadie..." He shrugs. "Sadie would mother hen me to death. I needed some time to figure this out on my own."

"Except you're not on your own," I point out. "I'm here."

"Yeah, well, that wasn't exactly the plan either."

A yawn escapes before I can stop it, and Felix steps forward, already reaching for Ellie.

"Here, give her to me. You should get some sleep."

Our hands brush as we transfer the sleeping child, and I swear I feel that same electric jolt I felt that night in Denver that led to the secret I'm carrying. Felix must feel it too because his eyes darken, his gaze dropping to my lips for just a moment.

"Thank you," he says quietly, and the sincerity in his voice catches me off guard. "For helping. For not running screaming when you found us."

"Yeah, well." I take a step back, needing distance between us before I do something stupid. Like tell him the truth. Or kiss him. Maybe both. "I've always been a sucker for kids."

Something flickers across his face that looks suspiciously like longing, but it's gone before I can identify it.

"Piper—"

"I should go," I say quickly, already backing toward the door. "Back to bed. Separate beds. In separate rooms. You know what I mean."

Real smooth, Pip.

"Right," he says. And is it my imagination, or does he sound disappointed?

I'm almost out the door when his voice stops me.

"Piper? This stays between us, right?"

I look back at him, this giant of a man cradling a tiny girl like she's the most precious thing in the world, and my heart does something complicated in my chest.

"Your secret's safe with me," I promise, the irony of those words not lost on me. After all, I'm keeping a much bigger secret.

I close the door softly behind me and lean against it for a moment, hand pressed to my stomach where our baby grows. Felix Barlowe doesn't want kids. He's made that crystal clear—twice now. But watching him with Ellie, seeing that tenderness he tries so hard to hide, I can't help but wonder if maybe he's wrong about himself.

Or maybe that's just the wishful thinking of a woman who's about to have his baby.

Either way, things just got a whole lot more complicated.

3

———

FELIX

I WAKE up the next morning to the sound of...holy shit, is that silence?

Actual, honest-to-God silence. No crying or whimpering or tiny fists and feet beating against the mattress.

I turn my head to confirm that Ellie is still sleeping, careful not to move any other part of my body and accidentally make a noise that might shatter this miracle.

Only...

Jesus fucking Christ, she's gone.

I launch out of bed like the goddamn mattress is on fire, my heart doing a spot-on impression of a jackhammer against my ribs. "Ellie!" I shout as I race for the door. "Piper! Are you—"

"We're in the kitchen," Piper calls up, her voice soft as the morning light spilling in through the edges of the blackout curtains. "Everything's okay."

Everything's okay. Sure, sure.

Everything except the way I just lost a decade off my life and my dignity in approximately three seconds flat.

I stand there in my boxer briefs, one hand pressed to my chest like I'm trying to keep my heart from escaping, and consider my options. I could stomp down there and unleash the verbal hurricane that's been building since Piper launched that shoe at me last night. Tell her exactly what I think about people who steal babies from their beds without warning.

She'd take it. Piper Hart might look like something straight out of a fairy tale—rosebud lips, curves in all the right places, and rich brown-green eyes that see all the way to a person's soul—but she also has edges. Sharp ones. The kind that cut through the bullshit I like to dish out without breaking a sweat.

And, man, I could do with letting off a little steam. Not just our patented verbal sparring either. The other kind. The kind that involves a lot less talking and a lot more—

No. Absolutely not.

I know she doesn't want that from me, and I can't want it from her. Unless I want my older brother to string me up by my toenails and use me as a piñata at the next family gathering.

Besides, I think as I duck back into the bedroom, this is the first time in weeks—since I fired the most recent nanny—that the morning has started without Ellie's heartbreaking symphony of tears.

I don't blame her for crying. Hell, I'd cry too if I was in her position. Orphaned and stuck with a guardian who can't tell if she needs a snack or a nap most of the time.

I take a quick shower, letting the hot water beat some sense into me, then throw on a pair of athletic shorts that have seen better days and one of the training shirts the Grizzlies' front office keeps sending me. I finger-comb my hair, because using an actual brush would require giving a shit, and head downstairs.

"She loves blueberries," Piper says from where she's sitting with Ellie in her lap at the massive granite island. Light streams through the east-facing windows, turning her hair into spun gold.

I nod but don't say anything in response, because I might have just swallowed my tongue.

I've never seen anything more beautiful than Piper Hart

actually smiling at me, like she's forgotten to hate me for a few seconds. Like taking care of a traumatized two-year-old is the best way she can think of to spend her morning.

Ellie grins and bounces excitedly when she notices me standing there, revealing a mouthful of half-chewed blueberries. The sight hits me like a blindside tackle, and the ginormous ball of tension that's been lodged in my chest since the day I got the call from Troy's estate attorney—telling me my friends were gone and I was now responsible for a tiny human—shrinks ever so slightly.

"Thanks for getting up with her. You didn't have to do that."

Her smile dims like I just told her Christmas is canceled, and I don't know what I said wrong, but I'd take it back in a heartbeat if it meant restoring the light to her eyes.

"I was already up," she tells me, cradling Ellie a little closer. "And I heard her."

I rub my hand over the back of my neck, guilt shooting up my spine. "She was crying, right? And I slept right through it. Guardian of the year over here."

Piper's eyes go gentle again, doing annoying things to my stomach. "She wasn't crying, just talking to herself. You know the little morning noises babies make. The door was open and..." She pauses, studying me with those bleached-sky eyes that see too much. "You seemed tired last night."

"Fuc—" The word tries to escape before I can catch it. Ellie stares at me with curious eyes. I clear my throat and try again, this time with the kid filter on. "Fudging exhausted."

Piper's eyes sparkle with barely suppressed laughter. "Fudging. That's a good one, Felix."

"Yeah, well...I'm trying." And failing spectacularly. I haven't slept more than a couple of hours in a row since becoming an instant parent. Even on the rare occasion Ellie manages a full night, I lie awake wondering how the hell Troy thought I was the right choice for this.

"Why don't you have a nanny?" Piper asks, shifting Ellie so the girl can grab another blueberry.

The question hits a nerve. "I fired my third one a few weeks ago."

Her eyebrows climb toward her hairline.

"I came home from a meeting with the estate attorney and found the nanny naked in my bed." I pause for emphasis. "Uninvited, in case that needed to be said."

"Oh my God."

"Which is the second time that's happened, and this round I specifically requested a woman old enough to be my mother. Potentially my grandmother."

"Are you hiring nannies off Tinder?" Piper asks, and there's that edge, sharp and teasing.

A surprised laugh escapes me. "That's not a thing."

She rolls her eyes, and the ball of tension shifts a little, making room so I can take a deep breath for the first time in weeks.

I like the way Piper dishes it out. She doesn't treat me as if I'm sports-celebrity special. To be honest, I like a lot of things about her. Way too many things.

I pivot toward the coffee maker like it holds the answers to all the questions I can't answer on my own. "Mind if I grab a cup?"

"Help yourself. There's creamer in the fridge."

"I take mine black. Like my soul."

"Like your soul," she says at the exact same time, and when I turn to look at her, she's fighting a smile.

Edges indeed.

"What happened to the one nanny who managed to keep her clothes on?" She dabs a napkin to Ellie's chin, which is covered with drool and bits of blueberry peel.

"The one who didn't attempt to seduce me suggested I give Ellie a little nip of brandy. Said her grandmother swore by it to quiet a crying baby."

"What the fudge..." Piper mutters, and I bite back another laugh.

"Anyway, that was back in Mississippi when I was packing up Troy and Julie's house." The words still feel like shards of glass in my throat.

"Tell me you had better luck with movers than you did with nannies."

"Yeah, but I did most of the work myself." I needed to touch their things, pack their memories, and try to understand why they thought I could do this. I don't say that to Piper, of course. No need to completely expose my soft underbelly. "Like I said, no one knows about Ellie. I don't want the press getting wind of it or having my personal life drama take away from the focus on football leading up to the season."

I see Piper's walls go up as she straightens her shoulders. "Oh yeah." Her voice drips with sarcasm. "Heaven forbid an orphaned child take attention away from the precious football season."

"It's not like that." I drain half the mug of coffee in one go, then refill it before turning back to face her. "I'm looking at options, but I want them vetted. My attorney has strict instructions not to reveal my identity if he finds a family member who might be a good fit. Not at first, anyway. I don't want them to take Ellie just because..."

"They could bleed you dry?" Disappointment flickers across her face.

"For all I care, Ellie can have everything I own," I say, and it's the damn truth. Every penny, every trophy, every stupid endorsement deal. Anything that would get rid of the guilt that's been eating me alive since...

I shake my head to block that train of thought. "I don't want someone taking her for reasons other than love. She deserves everything her parents would have given her along with a person who knows what the hell they're doing."

The kitchen goes quiet except for Ellie's happy babbling.

Piper's eyes shimmer like she's fighting back tears.

"Please don't cry," I say, panic rising in my chest. "If there's anything worse than a baby crying, it's a woman crying. Especially if I'm the asshole who caused it."

"I'm not crying because of you," she snaps, brushing a hand over each cheek. "It's just..." She blinks hard and swallows.

"I get it." I nod, sagely. The fact is, I'm kind of an expert on women. "You're crying because it's your period."

Piper blinks, then glares as if evolution hit pause when it got to me, my knuckles still scraping the sidewalk when I walk. "For fudge sake, Felix, it's not my period."

"It wasn't a criticism," I quickly amend.

"Shut up and let me talk."

"Roger that." I mime zipping my lips shut and earn a nod of approval.

"I never knew my dad." Piper places a soft kiss on the top of Ellie's head. "And I was twelve when my mom died. I mean, I had Sadie to raise me, and, as you know, she's amazing. But I understand what it's like to grow up without your parents. And you're right, she deserves to be loved the way her mom and dad loved her."

I wait for her to say something—anything—to confirm what we both know. That I'm clearly not the right person for this. But she doesn't. Maybe there's no need to state the obvious. Or maybe, just maybe, she sees something I don't.

I want to believe there's a chance that someone believes in me the way I can't believe in myself. And right now, against all logic and history between us, I want that person to be Piper.

Neither of us speaks, but the unexpected connection between us pulses in the silence like a heartbeat.

I clear my throat to break whatever spell we're under and take a step forward. "I can take her now."

She frowns like she doesn't want that, but stands and hands the baby to me.

Ellie pats my cheek with her sticky fingers, and I pat hers right back. When she's not crying, the kid is cute as hell. She's cute as hell when she's crying, too, but I definitely prefer her like this.

"How long are you staying here?" Piper asks, wiping blueberry residue from the counter with a napkin.

I shrug. "A few weeks. Maybe longer. I don't have to be at training camp until late July, and the house I bought won't be ready until right around then. I'm having a bunch of renovations done."

"In Denver?" Her tone is neutral, but I catch something underneath it. It could be hopefulness or it might track closer to disappointment. Piper is a bit of a mystery to me, and I'm surprised how much I want to figure her out.

"Yeah, Denver," I confirm. "My trainer's coming up tomorrow. Tyler will whip me into shape before team workouts start." I gesture toward the stairs leading to the lower level. "Ian's got an insane setup in the basement. It puts most pro gyms to shame."

Piper's eyebrows draw together. "And who will be watching Ellie while you're working out?"

The question hangs in the air like the steam rising from my coffee cup. I adjust my grip on Ellie, who's now trying to grab my nose.

"I'm working on a plan."

"Working?" She doesn't sound convinced.

"I'll figure it out. Don't worry about me."

"It's not you I'm worried about." She crosses her arms, and I know that look. It's the same one she gave me at Christmas last year when I wrapped up an actual lump of coal and gave it to her as a surprise gift.

"What about you?" I deflect. "What's with the lone wolf routine? No book club besties or high school friends keeping you company? Coming to a cabin alone isn't exactly your style."

Something flickers across her face that could be panic or guilt before she schools her features into that air of casual dismissiveness she's so good at with me.

"I just needed to get away for a bit." She moves to rinse her mug in the farmhouse sink, effectively giving me her back. "Clear my head."

"From what?"

"From life, Felix. Not everything needs a detailed explanation or can be managed with tequila."

I study the rigid line of her shoulders, the way her fingers grip the edge of the sink. There's definitely something she's not telling me. "So you'll be heading back to Skylark after the weekend?" I shift Ellie to my other arm. "Since you're just here to clear your head and all."

She goes still for a moment, then turns the water off with more force than necessary. "I haven't decided yet."

"But you have a job to get back to. The hospital—"

"I'm taking some time off." The words come out clipped, and it's clear she's in her feelings about whatever's going on.

Piper loves her job. She's one of those people who actually found their calling, unlike some people who just happen to be good at catching balls and running into other large men at high speeds.

"Piper—"

"I should get dressed." She turns, not quite meeting my eyes. "I'm going to go for a hike before it gets too hot."

I want to keep her here with Ellie and me, but she's not mine to hold onto. I watch her walk up the stairs, but she pauses at the landing. When she looks back at me, her expression has softened.

"You know, Felix, your friends made you Ellie's guardian for a reason." Her voice is quiet, but the words slam into me as if she's screamed them. "Maybe instead of looking for someone else to love her, you should figure out why."

Piper might not know much about football, but she just landed a perfect hit, completely leveling me. By the time I find my voice, she's gone, leaving me standing in the gourmet kitchen with a sticky toddler in my arms and more questions than answers.

Ellie pats my face again, reminding me that I need to find time to shave, and makes a sound that might be "Fee" but sounds more like "flee." Which feels appropriate at the moment.

Because Piper Hart just dropped a truth bomb in my lap, and every instinct I have is telling me to run. The problem is, I have no idea where I'd go.

4

PIPER

THE TRAIL WINDS upward through aspens and pines, and I'm grateful for the excuse to breathe hard. At least I can blame the altitude instead of the emotional tornado that's been spinning in my chest since Felix Barlowe showed up at the cabin last night with a toddler in tow.

A child who isn't his, as opposed to the one growing inside me.

I pause at a switchback, pressing my hand to my stomach where our baby—*his* baby—is barely the size of a raspberry. I've been able to blame my mild morning sickness on other things so far. But the exhaustion has been hitting me like a freight train, which is another reason I want an escape from Skylark.

That and my ex-fiancé's smug face. Not to mention having to say goodbye to my sweet Max three weeks ago. Sadie and I adopted him a few months after our mom died. His silly puppy antics were the only thing that made me smile when my grief felt like it might swallow me whole. He was the goodest good boy up until the very end, and my childhood home has felt way too quiet without him.

I guess I can also add quitting my job in a moment of spectacular self-destruction to the list of reasons I needed to get away. And being completely, utterly alone for the first time in my life.

Only, I'm not alone. Felix might not be the man I'd choose to have a baby with—okay, clearly some tequila-soaked part of me *did* choose him that night in Denver—but he's a bigger mess than I am right now. Which is...oddly comforting. Maybe it makes me an asshole, but not being the only person whose life is a dumpster fire tamps down the flames a bit. Between moving to a new team, the sudden guardianship, a series of nanny disasters, and the barely concealed panic that flashes in his gaze every time Ellie makes a noise he can't interpret, his life is off the rails in a much more visible way than mine. And it has me thinking...

What if I stay up here for a while? I could offer to watch Ellie, which would give me a chance to watch Felix with her for a few weeks. That could help me figure out what to do, right?

At least it might help me know what to expect when I finally tell Felix about our baby. Will he be angry? Freak out? Will he throw money at me like this pregnancy is a problem to solve? Or will he surprise me the way he did this morning, looking at that little girl like she was a real-life unicorn?

The trail levels out at a spot that overlooks Vail Village below, and I stop to catch my breath. Skylark sits at about 6,000 feet, but the cabin is at closer to 9,000 feet. Enough of a difference to make me dizzy when I push too hard, which apparently, I just did. I bend forward, hands on my knees, waiting for my racing pulse to slow.

A branch cracks behind me.

My head snaps, and then I go completely still. I'm alone in the middle of the woods, about a quarter mile from the cabin. It could be a bear or a mountain lion. Please not a mountain lion. First a possible murderer last night, now a potential mauling by a wild animal? The universe really has it out for me at the moment.

"You okay, Hart?"

I spin around so fast, the world tilts sideways. Felix appears around a bend in the trail, Ellie bouncing happily in a hiking backpack on his shoulders, her chubby hands gripping his hair like reins.

"Jesus, Felix." Relief floods through me, followed by a wave of dizziness that makes the trees blur together, the ground shift, and—

The next thing I know, I'm cradled against something warm and solid, moving through dappled sunlight. Felix's soap—which I guarantee has a name like One-Eyed Snake Swagger or Hot Boy Summer—fills my lungs with each breath.

"Did I just—"

"Scare the living sh—sugar out of me again by fainting? Yeah." His voice rumbles through his chest where my cheek is pressed. "I give you an eight out of ten for wilderness drama."

"Put me down." I try to sound commanding, but it comes out breathy.

"Not a chance."

"I can walk, Felix."

"Clearly you can't, since you just face-planted into the dirt."

"Pretty sure it was more of a graceful swoon."

"You dropped like a sack of potatoes. Lucky for you, I've got good hands."

I'm acutely aware of those hands right now. One is under my knees while the other supports my back. "What about Ellie?"

"She's loving life."

A delighted giggle from behind his head confirms this. I crane my neck to see her grinning at me, those honey-hued curls bouncing with each step.

"This is ridiculous. You can't carry us both when—"

"Shut it, Hart. You weigh about as much as my gym bag." He adjusts his grip, pulling me closer to his chest. "Less, probably."

"Your gym bag wouldn't appreciate being manhandled down a mountain either."

"You *fainted*."

The concern in his deep voice makes my chest tight. "I'm fine," I whisper against his shirt. "The altitude got me for a minute."

He makes a rumbly sound low in his throat. "What did you have for breakfast?"

"Blueberries." And only a few. My stomach can't handle a big breakfast these days.

That elicits a snort. "The perfect fuel for a mountain hike at nine thousand feet."

He's moving fast, although oddly I don't feel jostled. Just...safe and held. I close my eyes and sink into the feeling because it's kind of nice. More than kind of if I'm being honest. We're approaching the cabin now, a quarter mile covered in what feels like seconds in his arms. For a guy who thinks he needs to work on getting in shape for training camp, he's not even breathing hard.

"I can walk from here," I protest as he navigates the porch steps.

"Humor me."

He deposits me on the massive leather sectional in the great room with surprising gentleness, then swings Ellie down from the backpack. She immediately crawls up next to me, patting my cheek with concerned little fingers.

"Pi 'kay?" she asks softly.

My heart melts. "I'm okay, sweetheart."

Felix disappears into the kitchen and returns with a glass of water and a protein bar. "Drink. Eat. Don't argue."

I take the water and protein bar while Ellie snuggles into my side. Felix hovers like he's not sure what to do with his hands now that he's not carrying me.

"I have a proposition," I say, then immediately regret my word choice when his eyebrows shoot up. "Not that kind of proposition, you jacka—lope."

"Lope, lope," Ellie repeats in her sing-song voice.

"Jackalope?" Felix's wide mouth curves up at one end. "That's as good as fudge."

"Sorry I scared the *sugar* out of you." I offer up a world-class eye roll even as I'm fighting my own smile.

"Whatever. You were about to proposition me," he says, taking a seat in the overstuffed chair next to the sofa. Ellie babbles something about butterflies, oblivious to the tension suddenly crackling between us.

I clear my throat. "I want to be your nanny."

Felix blinks. "Come again?"

"I can stay here with you for the month, or until your house is ready."

"What about your job?"

"Yeah, about that." I take a quick sip of water before wiping the back of my hand across my lips. Those butterflies Ellie's babbling about take up residence in my stomach when Felix's intense gaze holds on my mouth. "I actually quit my job at the hospital."

"Why?"

"I needed a break," I say, then quickly continue, "And you need someone you can trust with Ellie who won't end up naked in your bed."

Felix shifts his weight as if he's reacting to the image that popped up in his mind at my words, and I drain the rest of my water. "Suffice to say, I'd like to be somewhere that isn't Skylark right now."

He studies me with those impossibly blue eyes, and I can see him working through what this might mean for both of us. "What about Max? I assume you'll want to pick him up from Sadie. I can't believe he isn't here—"

"Max died a few weeks ago." The tears come before I can stop them. Stupid hormones. "We came home from a short walk, and he laid down on his bed and then he was gone."

"Piper..." His voice goes soft in a way that makes the tears fall faster.

I bite down on the inside of my cheek and draw in a deep

breath. "I know it's stupid to cry about losing my old dog when you and Ellie are dealing with—"

"It's not stupid." He sits forward, close enough that our knees almost touch. "Max was your boy."

"My best boy," I whisper. "But I didn't deserve him." The admission slips out before I can stop it. "I'm glad I got to be with him in the end, but I should have taken him with me when I moved after college. Bradley didn't like dogs, and Sadie was so good with him. But I should have been a better dog mom."

"Pi, feel bettr," Ellie says as she swipes at my cheeks with her chubby hands. "No cry."

I take her face in my hands and kiss her on the tip of the nose. "You're right, Ellie Bean. No more crying."

She grins. "Happy Pi."

I force my gaze back to Felix and flash a tight smile, embarrassed by my display of emotion. "You know what? Forget it. This was a stupid idea. You don't need me, and I should go back and face my life instead of hiding out." I start to stand, but Felix catches my hand. His calloused fingers feel warm in a way that makes me want to climb into his lap and curl into his broad chest again.

I seriously need to get out of here.

"Stay."

"Felix—"

"The truth is, you'd be saving my ass, Piper." He runs a hand through his hair, which is sticking up at adorably odd angles thanks to Ellie. "Tyler is a fu—fudging drill sergeant, and I can't watch Ellie and train properly. I need...someone. And she already loves you."

As if on cue, Ellie burrows into my lap, her head resting against my chest like she belongs there, which is exactly how I felt with Felix's arms around me. And *exactly* why this was a terrible idea on my part.

"One month. That's all I've got." More accurately, it's all I've got until I'm unlikely to be able to hide my pregnancy from him any longer. Of course, I'm planning to tell him sooner than later. Just...not yet.

"One month." He nods, then that dangerous smirk appears. "Think you can keep your hands off me that long?"

"Do I get a bonus if I manage it?"

He laughs. "You might get a bonus if you don't."

"I hate you."

"No, you don't."

He's right, and that's the problem. I don't hate Felix Barlowe. I might actually like him, which is a thousand times worse. Because in seven months, I'm going to have his baby, and he's made it crystal clear he doesn't want kids. Even the one who I watch climb off of my lap and into his like she belongs there.

"This is only about Ellie," I say, needing to establish some boundaries before I do something stupid. Like tell him the truth. Like kiss him again. Like fall for him when I know how that story ends.

"Yep." He nods, then lifts Ellie above his head like she's an airplane. The toddler lets out a delighted squeal that makes me wince slightly. Felix, who doesn't seem to miss a thing where I'm concerned, chuckles and swoops her back and forth, making her shriek even more. "Welcome to the cabin of chaos, Hart. Hope you're ready for it."

I'm not. Not even close. But as Ellie dissolves into fits of giggles, and I try not to imagine Felix holding our child in those strong arms, I realize I'm already in too deep to back out now.

God help me, what have I gotten myself into?

5

———

FELIX

"DUDE, are you sure you know what you've gotten yourself into?"

I pause mid-deadlift, sweat dripping off my chin, and glare at Tyler Bron. My longtime personal trainer stands a few feet away, hands on his lean hips, wearing baggy shorts, an athletic shirt, and a know-it-all smirk that makes me want to knock him into next Tuesday. And I could, too. He's toned, but I'm bigger.

"Stop making this more complicated than it needs to be, Ty."

He shakes his head, his dark eyes glinting with amusement. "This is Piper Hart we're talking about. The woman who's lived rent-free in your head forever."

"Hardly forever." I grab a towel and wipe the back of my neck. "I met her at Ian's wedding last summer." I should never have told him how much she gets under my skin, or about our one-night stand.

"Right, your *sister-in-law*," Tyler says, like I've somehow proven his point.

"She's not *my* sister-in-law. She's my brother's sister-in-law. We're not related. Not family." I toss the towel aside, annoyed at having to explain this again. "And she doesn't live rent-free

33

anywhere." Trust me, there's a cost to the mental real estate Piper Hart occupies. One I'm determined to ignore.

"If you say so."

"I don't get why you care." I return to my position for another set. Outside of Ian, Tyler's my best friend. But he's going a little heavy on the helicopter mom vibes, if you ask me. "If she hadn't offered to help, you'd be running me through these workouts holding a two-year-old in your arms."

The initial plan had been for Tyler to stay with me at the cabin until I figured out childcare for Ellie. Two men and a baby, minus the Hollywood ending. But once I mentioned Piper being here, he insisted on staying at his family's condo near the ski village instead. They only rent it out during ski season, so it sits empty all summer.

When I told Piper about the change in plans, she'd seemed disappointed. As if she'd been counting on a buffer between us. I tried—and mostly failed—not to take offense. It's not like I want to play house or pretend this is something more than it is—a lucky break for me and an excuse for her to avoid whatever's waiting back in Skylark.

I still don't have the whole story there, and I shouldn't be so damn curious, but I am. What would make her quit a job I know she loves? It can't just be grief over Max, though I'm not dismissing her loss. She and Sadie adored that old dog. And even though Ian and I didn't have pets growing up, I get that kind of devotion. Pets weren't Dad's thing. Not much else other than football could hold his attention.

"I care about your focus, and obsessing over Piper isn't going to help you keep your eyes on the prize."

"I'm not fucking obsessed," I growl. So what if I haven't been able to get her—and since April, that one night we spent together —out of my mind? I'm not about to admit it to Tyler, but I'd be lying if I told you I haven't thought about what might happen if she did turn up naked in my bed.

Even if joining her there means enduring the wrath of my older brother. Ian was built for monogamy, even when he thought he wasn't, so he wouldn't appreciate me blowing off steam with the woman he now considers his little sister.

Me, on the other hand...I was all about commitment. Until committing to the wrong women resulted in my heart being trampled not once, not twice, but three times. First in high school, then college, and most recently with Veronica Bolton, the woman I thought would be my partner in starting our own little football dynasty of baby Barlowes. That dream was crushed when I found her getting railed by my teammate and supposed friend, Cincinnati's marquee quarterback, Russ Farmington.

Russ and I were magic on the field. We had the kind of connection the pundits love to talk about. But it all fell apart last season. Every time I saw Russ's hands on the ball, I also saw his hands all over Ronnie. So when the opportunity in Denver presented itself, I didn't hesitate.

A thump overhead interrupts my thoughts. What if Ellie fell? Or Piper fainted again? That shit scared the hell out of me yesterday.

My chest tightens, the protective instinct I can't seem to tamp down flaring. It's the kind of caveman-coded shit Piper would rake me over the coals for, but I can't stop the word that pulses through my veins. *Mine.*

Only Piper and Ellie aren't mine. Not to protect or keep or anything.

"Focus," Tyler murmurs as he studies me. "You still here?"

"Yeah. Let's keep going," I say and grab the weights again.

"How much longer, Felix?" Tyler asks as I grunt through another set.

"At least thirty more minutes."

"I mean, how much longer are you staying in the game?" He inclines his head. "You don't have to put yourself through any of this."

"You know I've got something to prove this season."

"What more could you possibly need to prove? You've got Super Bowl rings, money, a clear path to Canton and the Hall of Fame."

"I need to show everyone I can do it without Russ." Most importantly, I need to show myself.

"The magic between you and Farmington was mutual." Tyler shakes his head. "He and Ronnie did you dirty, but that's on them. It has nothing to do with you or your ability to—"

"To what?" The weights I'm holding hit the floor with a bone-jarring clang. "Keep my girlfriend happy so she doesn't crawl into bed with my friend?"

"To catch a ball and make plays and be the fucking hero on the field you seem to think you have to be. You're more than the game, Felix, and there's life after it. Look at your brother. Ian's doing great."

"Ian had a reason to leave." My brother chose to retire in order to take a more active role in parenting his now thirteen-year-old daughter. "Riva needed him."

"You've got reasons, too."

"Name one."

"Ellie." Tyler says her name softly, but it's like being smacked upside the head with a two-by-four.

"Fuck you," I whisper, "for bringing her into this. You know it's not permanent. I'm going to find her a real family."

"Troy made you her godfather for a reason." His dark eyes hold steady on me.

"Yeah, because I'm rich and generous. A fun honorary uncle."

"That wasn't—"

"Neither of them could have possibly considered an accident that would take them both. Nobody leaves their kid to the funcle."

"Troy and Julie chose you."

"They didn't think it through." I scrub a hand over my jaw. "No parent believes they're going to leave their toddler an orphan.

Troy probably figured I was the backup plan they'd never have to utilize."

He throws me a towel. "Good parents prepare for worst-case scenarios. And they still picked you, Felix."

"Can we stop fucking talking about Ellie?" I mutter. It's the same argument Piper made, and I don't appreciate it any more now. "I pay you to train me, not to psychoanalyze my life choices." Never mind we've been together since I got drafted. He's been with me through the highs and lows of my career and my personal life, always grounding me in addition to kicking my ass.

Tyler moves forward to spot me as I position myself on the bench.

"I throw in the psychobabble free of charge."

"Save it for somebody who gives a shit."

He grins and adds extra weight to each side of the bar. But he could load it up with every plate in this gym at this point. I've got enough—let's call it energy versus emotion—pulsing through me to bench-press an elephant right now.

"Easy there, old-timer," he says as I heft the bar with more force than is necessary or smart.

"Screw you," I answer.

"Right. So since you're not interested in Piper beyond her nanny skills, you wouldn't mind if I ask her out?"

The bar nearly slips from my grip as I bite back a growl. "Why the fuck would you want to do that?"

"Why not? She's beautiful, fun, and gives you shit like a pro. That's a winning trifecta in my book."

The incessant drumbeat pounds through me again. *Mine.*

But I know what he's doing. This is some reverse psychology bullshit.

"Go for it. You two would be fucking adorbs. Shout me out as your matchmaker when you go Instagram official." Given his success with the ladies, I could too easily see it happening.

Tyler's grin widens. "Will do."

I know he's bluffing. Tyler has a type: dark-haired and girl-next-door sweet. And while Piper might be the literal girl next door to my bedroom at the moment, anybody who makes the mistake of calling her sweet would end up gargling their nuts.

"What nights does she have off?"

"She works every day that ends in a Y." The words escape before I can stop them.

"That's what I figured." His smile widens.

"Shut up and spot me."

Ty and I are friends, but I also respect the hell out of his training methods and pay him good money to whip my ass. And the old-timer comment might have been a joke, but I'm not as young as I used to be. I give him a lot of credit for keeping me competitive in the league this long.

I give him more credit than my former quarterback and backstabbing friend, that's for damn sure.

We go hard for another forty-five minutes, then I hit the sauna Ian installed next to the weight room. By the time I head upstairs, I've sweated out most of my pent-up frustration. Or so I thought.

I have a reputation around the league as a man who loves women. And I do. All shapes and sizes. And grandma nanny notwithstanding, I rarely discriminate on age either. But since having my heart trampled for a barely believable third time last summer, I've put a moratorium on dating. And more specifically, on fucking. A ban I've only ignored once.

With Piper.

Voices drift from the family room, and I'm annoyed to realize one of them belongs to Tyler, who should be long gone by now. My jaw clenches. Unless he was serious about wanting to date her.

Damn it, I don't care. Ty and Piper can date and do whatever else to their hearts' content.

And no, I'm not gritting my teeth so hard it feels like I'm going to crack a molar when I find the two of them cozied up in the family room. Tyler stands behind the couch while Piper sits on the floor with Ellie, who's gnawing on a block instead of stacking it. They look comfortable together. Too comfortable.

"Fee!" Ellie shouts, spotting me. Her face lights up as she waves the soggy block and lifts her hands into the air.

Yeah, the kid is damn cute.

I try to ignore the sharp pinch in my heart at the thought of that attorney calling and telling me he found a family member willing to adopt her.

"Fee up," Ellie demands.

I lean down to kiss the top of her head. "I need to shower first, Bean. Uncle Felix is a stinky mess."

"Fee up! Fee up!" She reaches for me, not seeming to care that I stink.

Tyler chuckles. "You always did have a way with the ladies."

"Not all ladies," Piper mutters, but there's warmth in her eyes when she glances at me. She likes that Ellie likes me. I can see it in the soft way she watches us together.

"Tyler was just telling me about the children's art center and a couple of good playgrounds around Vail," Piper says, standing and brushing off her jeans. "Ellie might enjoy some toddler-friendly outings."

"My sisters have scouted all the kid-friendly activities in the valley," Ty confirms.

Of course. They're talking about kid stuff, not planning a date. The relief that floods through me is embarrassing.

"I should probably head out." Tyler glances at me, then checks his phone. "Same time tomorrow?"

"Yeah." I watch as Piper scoops up Ellie, settling her on one hip with practiced ease.

"We'll walk you out," she tells Tyler. "This one loves to watch the hummingbirds go at it in the feeders out front. Don't you, sweet girl?"

Ellie claps her hands. "Hummies!"

"Come on then." Piper leads my trainer toward the door

without looking back at me. Like I'm not even part of the equation. "Thanks for the kid tips, Tyler."

"You bet. Maybe we can grab coffee sometime? I can tell you about all of Felix's most embarrassing moments."

Piper laughs, the sound hitting me in the chest. "I'd love that. The cringier the better."

They're at the door now, Piper shifting Ellie in her arms while Tyler opens it for her. She moves out of sight, and he turns back to me with a wink and a thumbs-up.

My hands curl into fists as the door closes behind them with a soft click.

I move to the window like an idiot, sweating my ass off as I watch my trainer and Piper walk down the front steps side by side. Tyler says something that makes her tip her head back and laugh, while Ellie points excitedly toward the hummingbird feeders hanging from the porch's rafters.

They look natural together, like a little family unit.

The thought makes my chest burn with something that definitely isn't jealousy. Because I don't get jealous over women who aren't mine. Particularly women who can barely tolerate me on a good day.

Except, Piper didn't seem to *barely tolerate* me that night in Denver. And the way she melted into me yesterday when I carried her halfway down the mountain felt like anything but tolerance.

"*Fuck*," I mutter, heading for the stairs.

Tyler's either being friendly or trying to get under my skin. He isn't going to try to date her. She's off limits. He has to know that. Even if I haven't explicitly said so and have no claim on her whatsoever.

Even if watching them together makes me want to punch something.

I strip off my clothes and crank the shower to cold, stepping under the icy spray with a hiss. It's none of my business. Piper can date whoever she wants. Tyler can flirt with whoever he wants. I'm just the guy who happens to be sharing a house with her for the next month while she helps with Ellie.

I just have to survive one month without doing something stupid. Like telling Piper Hart I haven't stopped thinking about her since April. Or admitting that having her here feels right in a way nothing has in a long time.

Or clocking my best friend for making her laugh.

The cold water beats down on me, doing absolutely nothing to ease the heat still flaring through my veins. Because all I can think about is the sound of her laughter floating back through the door, and how badly I want to be the one making her smile like that.

I'm so completely fucked.

6

———

PIPER

As the sun beats down on the back porch the following afternoon, I'm curled up in one of the oversized Adirondack chairs under the shade of the pergola with a thick paperback balanced on my knees. Ellie's been down for her nap for about twenty minutes, and the afternoon is quiet.

Well, except for the rhythmic thwack of an axe hitting wood near the edge of the property.

I try to focus on the page in front of me. It's a particularly gruesome scene in the true-crime inspired thriller where the detective discovers the third victim, but my brain keeps drifting. Iris's selection for this month's book club meeting is freaking me out, especially up here in the middle of nowhere. I mean, yes, technically I'm not alone anymore, but still.

I grab my phone and pull up the book club group chat.

Me: I want to formally lodge a complaint. This book is terrifying, and I'm reading it in a remote cabin in the woods. Can we go back to Taylor's smutty romances? Those made me uncomfortable in a fun way.

The responses come fast.

Taylor: That's what you get for running away to the wilderness by yourself! 😄

Molly: Seriously, Pip. You picked the worst possible reading environment.

Avah: Maybe don't answer the door if anyone shows up asking to use your phone.

Iris: In my defense, I warned you the story borders on horror. It's SUPPOSED to be unsettling.

Sloane: Next month we're reading a cozy mystery. Promise.

The familiar back-and-forth with Sadie's book club friends—my friends now, too—has me smiling despite the creep factor of the novel. But Taylor's comment about running away makes me wince a little. Even though she meant it playfully, the words sting. Because that's exactly what I did, isn't it? I ran away from Skylark. From my empty house. From Bradley's smug face.

From my imploded life.

Me: There's a difference between running away and strategically regrouping.

Avah: Is there though?

I type out a response, delete it, try again. But nothing feels right, and suddenly I don't want to keep joking about it. I toss my phone onto the side table and pick up the book again, determined to push through at least one more chapter.

But before I get my eyes on the next word, I make the mistake of glancing up.

Felix is at the woodpile about fifty yards away, and he's decided to go shirt optional in the summer heat. His skin is bronzed and glistening with sweat as he swings the axe overhead. The movement is fluid and powerful, the muscles in his back and shoulders flexing as the blade comes down with a satisfying crack, splitting the log cleanly in two.

Sweet baby Jesus in a manger.

His tattoos—a geometric pattern that wraps around his left shoulder and down his bicep and lower arm—seem to move with each swing. It's like watching a very attractive, *very* muscular Viking doing manual labor, and my brain short-circuits like it's taken in too much data. Too much Felix Barlowe, that's for sure.

He tosses the split pieces aside, grabs another log, and positions it on the stump. The motion makes his abs contract, and as I try to figure out if he's got a six or an eight pack, my mouth goes dry.

Get it together, I silently command my hormones. I should be reading about serial killers, not ogling Felix Barlowe like he's a Lumbersnack Monthly centerfold. My ovaries pay no attention, staging a full-scale revolt.

He pauses to wipe his forearm across his forehead and glances up to catch me staring. Even from here, I can see his smirk.

Shit.

I immediately drop my eyes back to the book, my face burning hot enough to fry an egg. Maybe if I focus really hard on the murder scene, I can pretend the last thirty seconds didn't happen.

My phone buzzes with a text from Sadie.

Sadie: Hey, when are you coming home? How are you feeling? Do you need me to come up there?

A knot of emotion tangles in my chest as I stare at the message. Part of me wants to say yes and have my big sister come rescue me from this increasingly complicated situation. But that's part of my problem. I keep letting Sadie rescue me. From raising me after Mom died, to taking care of Max when I couldn't, to transferring the house to me and helping me get a job at the hospital when I moved back to Skylark.

I'm twenty-three years old and I've never actually stood on my own two feet.

Me: I'm good. The altitude is helping clear my head. I'll head back in a week or so.

I hate lying to Sadie, but I can't keep expecting her to save me. I'm a grown-ass woman who's going to have my own child to take care of soon. I shouldn't need rescuing.

Sadie: You sure? I can take a day and drive up. We could hike or just hang out. I miss you.

The offer is tempting because Sadie is good at taking care of people, me especially. But not with Felix here. Not with this whole situation I haven't fully explained to anyone yet. Besides, I want to figure out how to save myself.

Me: I'm fine. Enjoying the peace and quiet. I'll call you in a couple days.

I add a heart emoji, but guilt sits heavy in my stomach. What am I supposed to say? *Actually, Felix Barlowe is here with an adorable toddler and we're playing house and I'm kind of falling for him while pregnant with his secret baby?*

Yeah, that would go over well.

The doorbell rings, echoing from the front of the house. I glance at the baby monitor on the side table to make sure Ellie's still sleeping, then head inside. That sweet girl could typically sleep through a punk concert, but I don't want to chance her nap being interrupted.

Through the front window, I see a delivery truck in the driveway. A guy in a brown uniform is standing on the porch next to three massive boxes.

I open the door. "Can I help you?"

"Delivery for Piper Hart." He glances at the scanner he's holding. "I need a signature."

"I didn't order anything."

He shrugs. "Your name's in the system."

I lean closer to look at the first box, and my heart does that stupid flutter thing I should be used to by now. There's a picture on the side of a miniature kitchen set, complete with toy appliances, plastic food, and tiny pots and pans. It's pink and white and absolutely adorable.

Realization dawns. Felix ordered this for Ellie, and he put it under my name so his wouldn't be recognized.

"Where do you want them?" the delivery guy asks.

"Um, just inside the door is fine." I sign his scanner in a daze while he makes quick work of hauling the boxes into the entryway.

"Have a good one," he says, then heads back to his truck.

Standing here staring at the boxes, I'd bet money this play kitchen costs more than my monthly rent in Kansas City used to. Why does my heart melt at this tangible proof that Felix is thinking about Ellie's happiness and making her feel at home?

"She loves being in the kitchen."

I jump about a foot in the air and whirl around to find Felix standing behind me. Praise the Lord for small favors, he's wearing a shirt. After all, I'm only human. His hair is damp like he dunked his head under the outdoor spigot, and I can't seem to wipe the image of him swinging that axe from my brain. Right along with a vision of him swinging me over his shoulder and carrying me...

For the love of all that is holy, can I stop fantasizing about my baby daddy for a hot second?

"I thought she'd like one her size," he continues, moving closer to examine the boxes. "I paid for rush delivery."

"She'll love it," I say, my voice hoarse.

Am I a total idiot with this nanny arrangement? It was supposed to give me a better handle on how Felix might be as a dad, not make me feel things I have no business feeling. Now he's being thoughtful and sweet and unexpectedly fatherly, and it's doing dangerous things to my carefully constructed emotional walls.

My awareness of how close he's standing, his T-shirt clinging to his still-damp chest, and his eyes dropping to my mouth makes the air feel thick. All I want to do right now is step closer, get sweaty with him and ignore the walls between us or knock them down.

"I'm going to shower," he says after a moment, his voice rougher than normal. "Then I'll put this together. Shouldn't take long."

"Okay." The word comes out breathy, like I've just summited a fourteener.

He holds my gaze for another heartbeat, and the connection I didn't expect to feel for him crackles between us. Then he heads for the stairs, and I'm left standing in the entryway with three boxes and a heart that's beating way too fast.

I need something to do with my hands, so I decide to tackle the basket of Ellie's clean laundry that's sitting on top of the dryer. I'm folding tiny leggings and miniature T-shirts when the monitor lights up and I hear the soft babbling that means she's transitioning out of sleep.

I turn for the door, then hear Felix's voice. "Hey, munchkin. Did you have a good nap?"

Ellie's response is garbled but enthusiastic, and his answering laughter rumbles through me.

"Let's get you changed. We've got a surprise downstairs."

"Prise?" Ellie's voice is excited.

"Yep. But first, diaper change. Not your favorite, I know. But Uncle Fee's getting pretty good, aren't I?"

It feels like I'm eavesdropping on an intimate moment. But I can't seem to make myself turn off the monitor or stop listening to Felix's patient, playful tone as he talks Ellie through getting changed, or her delighted giggles when he apparently makes a funny face.

This is the Felix no one else sees. Not the cocky NFL star or the charming flirt or the guy who trades barbs with me at every family gathering. This is the man underneath all that armor. And he's so much better than he thinks he is.

By the time they make it downstairs, I've finished the laundry and composed myself. Mostly.

Felix has Ellie on his hip, and she's pointing at the boxes with wide eyes. "Big box!"

"Really big," Felix agrees, carefully setting her down. "Want to help me open them?"

She bounces on her toes and gives me that toothy grin. "Ewwie and Pi help."

My heart clenches again, and I head to the kitchen for a knife to cut through the packing tape. For the next twenty minutes, we work together to unpack and assemble the play kitchen. Felix reads the instructions while I sort pieces, and Ellie "helps" by sitting in the middle of the chaos, banging toy pots and pans together like she's leading an enthusiastic one-toddler band.

"Hand me that panel?" Felix points to a piece of pink painted wood. "The one with the oven door?"

I pass it over, and when our fingers brush, the familiar but still unsettling shock zips up my arm. I pull back quickly, nearly dropping the oven door. He catches it smoothly, his eyes meeting mine with a teasing glint that says he knows I'm not thinking about toy furniture at the moment.

Focus, Piper.

"This is about a thousand times nicer than the kitchen in my house," I joke, needing to break the tension. "Which hasn't been updated since my mom died, so the bar's pretty low."

Felix looks up from where he's attaching the sink unit. "Yeah?"

"Scuffed cabinets, laminate countertops, floral wallpaper." I tick off the list. "It's classic."

"Nothing wrong with that." He fits another piece into place. "It just means it has character."

I chuckle. "A generous way to say it's outdated."

"I want my forever house to have character. To feel like people actually live there." He adjusts the cabinet door. "I've had too many friends and teammates with sterile showroom houses."

The phrase "forever house" hits me square in the chest. Felix Barlowe thinking about forever anything feels significant, even if he's just talking about real estate.

"I bet your decorator in Denver loves you as a client," I answer, switching to what feels like a safer topic.

"Everyone loves me." He grins, and I realize now that I know it's part of his mask, the cocky expression I used to find annoying feels charming. "I'm extremely lovable."

Apparently not safe at all. "Keep telling yourself that, Barlowe."

He winks, and my toes curl. "Spittin' facts."

Sure, sure.

He finishes tightening the last screw and sits back on his heels. The kitchen is even more gigantic than it looked in the photo on the box. There's plenty of room in the cabin, of course, but it's almost comical to watch Ellie exploring her new toy.

"How did you decide on this kitchen?" I ask, trying to hide my smile.

"I Googled 'what's the most expensive play kitchen you can buy' and ordered it."

I blink at him. "You what?"

"Go big or go home, Hart." He shrugs, like dropping a stupid amount of money on a toy is no big deal. "Ellie Bean deserves the best."

My throat goes tight. "Felix—"

"Don't give me grief unless you want to talk about how I caught you watching me chop wood earlier."

My face flames. "I was reading."

"You were drooling."

"I was not—"

"Practically panting."

"Oh my God, you're impossible." But it's true, and we both know it.

"Impossible to resist?" He waggles his eyebrows in the most ridiculous way.

I throw a plastic carrot at his head. He laughs and catches it one-handed, and a warmth unfurls in my chest that feels strangely like happiness.

Ellie chooses that moment to toddle over to her new kitchen, running her hands over the tiny oven door with reverence. "Mine?"

"All yours, Bean," Felix says softly.

She looks up at him with pure adoration, then at me, and it's like the three of us are doing more than playing at being a family. Like this could be real if we wanted it to be.

But Felix is trying to find Ellie a "real family" because he's convinced he's not father material. And I'm carrying his baby, a secret that grows heavier with each passing day. Each sweet domestic moment makes me stupidly hope that just maybe he could want this, too.

"Pi hungy?" Ellie asks, holding up a tiny pan in my direction.

"Yeah, sweetie. I'm so hungry."

She beams and immediately sets to work "making dinner," chattering away in her toddler language.

Felix and I clean up the packaging in silence, but I'm hyper-aware of his big presence, all that heat and strength. When we finish, he straightens and looks at me with an intensity that makes my breath catch.

"Piper—"

"Fee! Fee!" Ellie interrupts, holding up a play hamburger. "Eat!"

He shakes his head as he studies me for another long moment before turning to crouch down next to Ellie. As he marvels over how yummy her dinner is, I escape to the kitchen, my heart racing.

This whole situation was supposed to be simple. A month of helping with Ellie, figuring out what kind of father Felix could be, then telling him about the baby and dealing with whatever came next.

But I'm quickly discovering that nothing about Felix Barlowe is simple, and I realize I'm not just evaluating him as a potential co-parent.

I'm falling for him.

And I have absolutely no idea what I'm going to do about it.

7

FELIX

Two days after setting up Ellie's dream kitchen, I come pounding down the trail and into the clearing behind the cabin, lungs burning like I've just sprinted up Mount Doom with Frodo in my arms.

I double over, palms on my knees, pulling in sharp gulps of air and praying my legs don't give out underneath me. High altitude training: the gift that keeps on punishing.

I glance up at the house where I know Piper and Ellie are, but there's no movement behind the windows. Not that I expected her to be waiting for me to get back, or even want her to be. That would be a little too domestic and couple-y for our situation. Except...I kind of want exactly that.

Fuck.

"Dude," Tyler pants as he flops onto the grass at my feet. "Stop staring at the house like a fucking creeper. You're down bad."

"You know the fact that I left your ass in the dust back there on the trail wasn't by accident." I nudge his leg with my foot. "I was sick of hearing your yapper flapping."

"What's the big deal? You like your sister-in-law. You're not breaking any actual laws."

"She's *Ian's* sister-in-law," I say through clenched teeth. "Not mine. And I don't *like* her."

Tyler shades his eyes with his hands as he stares up at me. "You're joking, right?"

"Sure, I can admit she's hot. But that's straight facts and has no bearing on—"

"There's more to it."

"There's not." My jaw is so tight it's a wonder I can speak at all. "And she's not *just* hot," I blurt before I can stop myself. Tyler's brows shoot up, and I instantly regret opening my mouth. "She's more than...I mean, the way she looks is not the point."

"I get the point." Tyler's slow grin infuriates me. "When's the last time you got laid, man? Scratch that. When's the last time you *wanted* to get laid?"

I roll my eyes. "You need a hobby."

"Poking the Barlowe bear *is* my hobby." He gets up and dusts off his shorts. "Anyway, we should hit the bars in Vail this weekend. You need a release valve before you blow your top. There's always a girls' trip or bachelorette party—"

"No bachelorette parties," I say darkly. That's how Piper and I ended up in bed together in the first place. Lightning doesn't need to strike twice.

He snorts. "How about you just swipe right on someone normal and—"

"Why is my dick and what I do with it any of your business?"

"Because it's screwing with your focus." He lowers his voice. "And probably your sanity. I've never seen you wound this tight. You need to chill, Felix. Chilling is your superpower. Whatever it is you're trying to prove on the field this season, it might be easier if you didn't have a ticking time bomb of unresolved sexual tension sleeping down the hall."

"I bet Gronk's coach never told him to chill."

"First, you're not Gronk, and second, I'm saying it as much as your friend as your trainer." He softens his tone. "I know this situation with Ellie is a lot to deal with."

"You have no idea," I say. I mean for my tone to come across as scathing, but it sounds more like bone-deep desperation. "You can't possibly know."

"That's fair. But—"

I shake my head. "No more, Tyler. It is what it is, and I'm doing my level fucking best here. I'm hoping to get Ellie settled with her new family by the time I have to report to training camp in late July. But only if the attorney finds people who are a good fit for her. Either way, we're going to be fine."

Saying the words out loud should make them feel true. It doesn't.

His brows lower. "You're sure that's the right way to go?"

"It's the only way," I insist, even though I'm not sure of anything at the moment.

Well, I'm certain that Piper looks like a literal angel in the morning light, and Ellie's laugh makes my chest feel like it might crack open. I'm also pretty sure I've stopped sleeping through the night because I lay awake thinking of them both.

None of which I'm about to admit to Tyler.

Piper is great with Ellie, which is no surprise, and her help gives me a lot more time for training. But she's also got me spun up in about a million different ways. As irritating as I find it, Tyler might be right. Maybe letting off some steam is the right call.

It certainly worked in that Denver hotel room.

"Looks like you have a visitor," Tyler says as we get closer to the house.

I follow his gaze to where a compact SUV is parked in the cabin's circular driveway. My heart stutters like I'm some teenage kid about to get in trouble. No one knows I'm here. And according to Piper, only her sister and the book club gang know she's run away to the cabin.

If Sadie's here, there's a good chance Ian's with her. The last thing I want is my know-it-all older brother finding out about Ellie before I have things worked out for her future.

If it's not someone we know, then who the hell is it? What if something's wrong? What if Piper needed help and I wasn't here?

I take the stairs to the back porch two at a time, busting through the door to the house with all the tact of a bull in a china shop.

"Who's here?" I demand, coming around the corner toward the kitchen, my heart still doing that weird hammering thing.

Piper frowns and holds one finger up to her lips. "Ellie just went down for her nap, and she's not going to stay that way with you bellowing."

The relief that floods through me is embarrassing. She's fine. They're both fine. Of course they are. I'm being ridiculous.

I don't recognize the other woman in the kitchen, but Piper doesn't seem bothered, and that's what's important. In fact, there's a smile playing around the edge of her mouth like my mini-freak out amuses her. And as long as she's okay, I'll sing and dance and do back flips to keep the smile on her face.

Shit. When did Piper's comfort become the barometer by which I measure my own?

I run a hand along the back of my neck. "Hey." I nod at the woman, silently hoping she'll get around to shutting her mouth, which is gaping wide at this point.

"Maybe you want to put a shirt on," Piper suggests conversationally as she glances between me and our houseguest. But there's something heated in her gaze that makes my skin feel too tight.

Get it together, Barlowe.

I left the house wearing a shirt, but it was hot with the sun beating down, so at some point I shucked it and tucked it into the back of my shorts. I pull it on, hyperaware of Piper's gaze tracking my movements, just as Tyler enters the kitchen.

"Hey, Piper, who's your friend?" he asks, which sounds way more normal than my Neanderthal entrance.

What is it about Piper Hart that short-circuits my brain?

"This is Mindy McMurry." Piper raises a brow in my direction, clearly agreeing that I need to get it together. "She owns True Kitchen, a meal delivery service in Vail. Felix apparently ordered meals from her."

"Fuck," I mutter. That's right. I'd contracted with the home chef I found online because there are things I like to do in the kitchen—not *those* kinds of things, get your mind out of the gutter—but making healthy meals is not one of them. And Piper needs to eat. She barely touched her dinner last night, pushing the chicken around her plate like a kid avoiding vegetables.

"Nice," Tyler says, moving forward and reaching out a hand. And there's more of that social grace that I apparently left on the trail. "I'm Tyler Bron, Felix's personal trainer. Did he talk to you about his nutrition plan for the next few weeks, macros, and the protein he—"

"I talked to her about everything," I bark, probably sounding like an ass. Again. "Thanks, Mindy. I forgot you were coming today. If everything's unloaded, I think we're done here. You can go."

She blinks and then nods slowly. "Oh, okay."

"Why are you acting so weird?" Piper interrupts, glaring at me, hands on her hips.

Because everything about this situation is weird, including some of the instructions I gave to the home chef, and I want her out of here before she shares any of those embarrassing details.

Tyler jabs a finger in my direction. "Are you trying to get rid of her so she doesn't reveal that you requested a bunch of chicken wing fat bomb meals?"

"I bake my chicken wings," Mindy says, sounding affronted.

Tyler's ears go pink. "Sorry, no wing shade intended. It's just that Felix—"

"My meal plan is on point," I cut in. "I'm sure Mindy has other things to do."

"Every one of the meals adheres to the nutrition guidelines Felix gave me." She's not paying attention to me, suddenly locked in a stare-down with Tyler that reminds me of two defensive linemen sizing each other up. "Which, as he explained in his email, adheres to the guidelines *you* gave him."

"That's great," Tyler sputters. "But it doesn't explain why—"

"I also prepared food for Piper and Ellie." Her gaze flicks from Tyler to Piper, her features softening slightly. "Felix was way more concerned about your meals than his own choices."

Oh, no. She didn't just say that out loud.

Piper's head whips toward me, eyes wide.

"I don't mind the same food on repeat." I raise my hands, palms facing out like I'm ready to ward off an attack. "It's not a big deal. I've been doing it for years."

But the thought of Piper living on toast and orange juice when she's clearly not feeling well is another thing keeping me up at night, so I may have sent Mindy an extra email. Or ten.

"You didn't need to order anything for me," Piper says. Her voice has gone soft, like she's handling something delicate. That something might be me. Or not. "I can take care of myself."

"Toast isn't a food group," I tell her, hating how much I sound like I want to take care of her. Even though I do, way too much.

"I eat stuff besides toast."

"Not since I've been here."

"I like toast." She lifts her chin in that way that makes me want to either kiss her or argue with her, maybe at the same time.

"You need a balanced diet. Protein and shit. I'm sure Mindy has it all set up." I throw the meal-prep lady a glance. *Bail a bro out, sister.*

"I do, in fact." Praise the Lord, Even though I don't appreciate her watching Piper and me like we're the entertainment portion of her afternoon, I do appreciate Mindy picking up what I'm laying down. "I was just about to go over how it's organized in the refrigerator when you came in."

Tyler appears a lot less pissed than he did moments earlier when he thought I was trying to veer from the nutrition plan he has me on. Smug is not a good look for him.

"I'm sure we can figure it out," I say quickly. I do *not* want to go over this with an audience. I definitely *do* want to wipe the smirk off of my personal trainer and *former* friend's face.

"I think you'll find the meals to your liking," she tells Piper gently, "and they'll be easy on your stomach."

Christ. Could she be any less subtle?

"Felix went over your preferences in detail, so—"

"How do you know my preferences?" Piper demands as she turns to me again. It sounds an awful lot like an accusation. As if I've committed some kind of crime by paying attention to what she eats.

"We've had plenty of meals together."

She raises a brow. "Plenty?"

"Plenty might be an exaggeration," I admit, running my hand through my hair. "But enough that I know you like chicken breasts but not thighs. You don't eat red meat, you're iffy on mushrooms, and you have a mild shellfish allergy. Most importantly, if a person could survive on bread and pasta alone, that would be your choice."

Her mouth opens and shuts a few times, and once again, her lips are driving me to distraction. "That's disturbingly accurate," she says quietly.

Mindy, bless her, senses the vibe and heads toward the door. "Like Felix said, I'm sure you can figure it out. Call or text with any questions or to reorder."

"I'll walk you out." Tyler is already falling into step beside her. "I'd love to get some more information on your business and how things are structured. We'll be up here a few more weeks, and the truth is I'm not much of a cook myself."

They disappear toward the front door, and Piper stares after them for a long beat. "Did you inadvertently play matchmaker by being rude and insufferable?"

"I'm neither of those things, and I played get-the-hell-out-of-our-kitchen."

"I didn't need you to order food for me," she repeats, but there's less heat in it now. She's looking at me like whatever's pulsing between us is a puzzle she can't quite solve.

Join the club, Hart.

"You could just say thank you," I prompt, although watching her struggle with gratitude is strangely endearing.

"Thank you." Those two whispered words sound like they were painful. I get that. Vulnerability isn't easy for either of us.

She's quiet for a moment, then moves to the fridge. "Mindy found something in the fridge and wasn't sure how it got there."

"That sounds...ominous."

"Just odd," she clarifies, opening one stainless-steel door. "What exactly is this?"

She pulls out a glass mason jar, and I bite back a groan. *Shit*. I thought I'd hidden it better.

"It's nothing."

"Mindy said it's sourdough starter."

I shrug, trying for casual and probably landing somewhere closer to guilty teenager caught sneaking out of his girlfriend's bedroom window. "Maybe Sadie left it up here."

Piper rolls her eyes. "My sister doesn't bake sourdough, and Mindy said it's been fed recently, whatever that means."

Busted.

"Felix, are you a bread baker?"

"You don't have to make it sound like you discovered my porn stash." Honestly, that would have been less embarrassing at this point.

"Nice deflection. Sourdough," she says again, and there's something in her voice I can't quite place. Possibly amusement, but maybe respect? "You have to order meals, but you bake fresh bread?"

"My deep dark secret is out." I stalk forward and grab the jar from her hands, trying not to notice how soft her fingers are when they brush mine. Trying not to remember how they felt on my skin that night in Denver. "I like to bake bread. It's a hobby, obviously. I have a regular job."

"Yes. NFL wide receiver. I'm well aware." She's fighting a smile now, and it's doing dangerous things to my self-control.

"I started after Ronnie and I broke up last summer," I admit, not sure why I'm telling her this. Maybe because I've completely lost control of this conversation—and my mind, where Piper is concerned. Maybe because I don't want to keep secrets from her. "I needed something to do with my hands that wasn't throwing things or punching walls."

"So you punch dough instead?"

"Kneading isn't the same as punching. The truth is, it's wildly therapeutic." I set the jar back in the fridge, then pick up a kitchen towel from the counter, suddenly very interested in the fingerprints marring the shiny stainless steel. "I like the science of it. Feeding the starter, watching it grow, waiting for the perfect rise. Everything in my life is fast and violent, but bread takes time. Patience. It's good for my mental health, you know?"

When I finally look up, she's staring at me like she's never seen me before.

"What?"

"Nothing. Just..." She shakes her head, smiling in a way that makes my stomach do loop-de-loops "You're full of surprises, Felix Barlowe."

"Yeah, well, don't get used to it," I warn, but there's no heat in the words. "And if you tell anyone—"

"Your secret's safe with me." Her smile widens, hitting me square in the chest. "Add it to the list."

Right. The list of secrets we're keeping. Ellie. That night in

Denver. Whatever this thing is that's building between us, despite our best efforts to ignore it. I should step back and create distance between us. Go take a cold shower. Do literally anything except stand here staring at her like a lovesick idiot.

"I should check on Ellie," she says, but she doesn't move.

"She's sleeping."

"Right."

Neither of us moves.

"Piper—"

"Don't," she says softly. "Whatever you're about to say, don't. We agreed this was a bad idea."

"The worst," I confirm, taking a step closer despite myself. "Terrible judgment all around."

"Your brother would kill you."

"Probably." Another step. "Ian's got a mean right hook."

"And we don't even like each other."

"Not one bit." I'm close enough to see the pulse jumping in her throat and smell her shampoo. That fruity scent that lingers even when she's not in the room and has been driving me crazy. "Except...maybe we can be friends."

She swallows hard. "Not the kind with benefits."

"I don't want benefits," I agree, and we both know it's a lie. Maybe it started that way, but somewhere between the shoe throwing and the breakfast routines and watching her with Ellie, things shifted. My heart shifted.

"Same," she whispers, but her hand comes up to rest on my chest, right over my heart, which is doing its best to break free from my rib cage.

I cover her hand with mine, holding it there. Can she feel how hard my heart is pounding? Is hers doing the same thing?

"This is such a bad idea," she breathes.

"The absolute worst." I slide my hand up her arm until my fingers tangle in her hair at the nape of her neck. She shivers. "We should definitely not do this."

"Definitely not."

But the way she's tilting up her head feels like an invitation. Her eyes darken, and those lips I can't stop thinking about part slightly.

Somewhere in the back of my mind, my better judgment is screaming at me to stop. Reminding me of all the reasons this is complicated. But Piper Hart is looking at me like I'm something worth having. Like maybe she sees me as more than a flashy meat stick of a man who catches balls for a living. And I want to believe we both see that there's more here, and it's worth exploring.

Besides, I've never been good at following rules.

I lower my head slowly, giving her every chance to pull away. She doesn't. Instead, she grips my shirt and pulls me closer, eliminating the last few inches between us.

When our lips finally meet, it's nothing like Denver. That night was desperate and frantic, fueled by tequila and straight-up physical need. This is different. It's deliberate, with both of us making a choice we know we probably shouldn't.

The kiss starts out tentative, as if we're testing the waters. But then she makes a small sound in the back of her throat, and the control I'm gripping with white knuckles snaps. My arm hooks around her waist, pulling her tight against me as I deepen the kiss. She responds in kind, her fingers sliding up into my hair and tugging just hard enough to make me groan.

She tastes like the juice she was drinking earlier, sweet and tangy, and I want more. I want to memorize the way she feels pressed against me, the soft sounds she makes, the way her body fits perfectly with mine—like maybe we were designed for each other.

The thought should terrify me, but it doesn't.

She breaks the kiss first, gasping for air, her forehead resting against my chest. "We can't—"

"I know."

"This is—"

"I know."

"But—" She pulls back enough to look at me, her pupils blown wide and her cheeks flushed with desire. "Maybe just one time?"

"Just this once," I agree, and it's the biggest lie I've ever told.

Because even as I kiss her again, backing her against the kitchen island, I know one time won't be enough. It can't be. Not when she feels this right in my arms. When her laugh makes my heart skip a beat and her smile makes me want to be better than I am.

"Fee!" Ellie's cry rings out from the monitor on the counter, tinny but insistent.

We spring apart like guilty teenagers, both breathing hard and trying to look anywhere except at each other.

"I should—" Piper gestures toward the stairs.

"Yeah."

She starts to leave, then pauses in the doorway. "Felix?"

"Yeah?"

"This can't happen again."

I nod slowly, willing the ache in my chest—and in other, less publicly acceptable places—to settle.

She brushes her fingers across her mouth like she's trying to erase the kiss. Or maybe keep it. I can't tell.

"Definitely not," I agree, and she disappears.

I stand there for a long moment, one hand pressed to my mouth like I can still feel her lips on mine, wondering what the fuck I've just done. And why I'm not more worried about it.

Because I know I've started falling for Piper Hart. And I have no clue how the hell I'm supposed to stop.

8

PIPER

I WAKE up thinking about Felix Barlowe's mouth.

Specifically, the way it felt pressed against mine yesterday in the kitchen. He kissed me like I was oxygen after he'd been holding his breath for far too long, and I'd responded in the exact same way.

"Not going there," I mutter into my pillow. "Absolutely not."

But my traitorous body has other ideas, and the pregnancy hormones currently hijacking my system make a strong case that Felix Barlowe is the answer to all the questions I'm too afraid to ask. Particularly the smutty ones.

I'm ready to force myself into a cold shower, but I sit up and draw in a deep inhale as the most amazing smell drifts up from downstairs. Could that be actual fresh-baked bread at—I check my phone—six-thirty in the morning? Felix seemed embarrassed that his covert identity had been revealed, but even with the freshly-fed starter in the fridge, I didn't truly believe he was a bona fide bread baker. Based on the way my stomach is growling instead of churning with its typical hormone-induced nausea, I think I'm about to be proven wrong.

I throw on baggy sweats and a sports bra under my T-shirt, bypassing the closed door to the bedroom that Felix moved Ellie into as I follow my nose downstairs. I find Felix at the kitchen island, joggers hanging sinfully low on his hips and a faded T-shirt with the sleeves cut off stretched over his toned chest. His tattoos and muscles make my mouth go dry in a way that has nothing to do with morning sickness. His hair is rumpled, and there's a smudge of flour on his unshaven jaw. A mountain of a man who accidentally stumbled onto the set of a TV baking show.

My ovaries cheer wildly.

"Morning," he says as he slowly slices something golden-brown in the pan on the counter in front of him. "You want a glass of juice?"

"You seriously baked?" The question comes out more accusatory than I mean, but I'm thrown off by all of it. The muscles, the rumpled hair, the unexpected intimacy of the moment. And that heavenly scent...

"A cinnamon-sugar focaccia," he confirms, finally glancing up at me. His expression is careful, like he's trying to gauge where we stand after yesterday's kitchen incident. Neither of us mentioned the kiss last night, and I plan to keep avoiding the topic. "The recipe uses sourdough discard, so it only takes a couple of hours." He pauses, then adds with a slight smile, "Now that my baking bro secret's out, I'm working on a real loaf for you to try. Fair warning, though, sourdough takes time."

"The best things do," I murmur, tempted to place a hand on my stomach, then move to the sink for a glass of water, trying not to bump into him. The area between the counter and the island isn't exactly narrow, but Felix takes up a lot of space, and my body is very aware that we're alone. In fact, my nipples seem to have their own ideas about this whole situation. Praise the Lord for a padded sports bra. "What time did you get up?"

"Before five. I couldn't sleep." He plates a piece of the bread and holds it out to me. "Try this."

"I'm not really hun—"

"Just try it, Hart. Don't make things weird."

Ignoring the fact that everything about this is weird, I take the plate. Our fingers brush for half a second. Even that brief contact sends sparks shooting along my skin, which is ridiculous. But I bite into the bread and—oh my God.

It's perfect. Still warm from the oven, and practically melts in my mouth. I might make a sound that's not entirely appropriate this early in the morning. Or anytime anywhere out of the bedroom.

Felix's blue eyes darken just a fraction. "Good, right?"

"This is genuinely unfair," I say around another bite. "You can't have washboard abs and also bake something that makes me want to eat the whole pan in one sitting."

"You like my abs?" He lifts his shirt to reveal said washboard, and I just about forget my own name.

"I like your focaccia more," I lie.

He grins. "Sure you do. But you have plenty of talents. The most impressive one is getting a two-year-old to eat her veggies without throwing a fit." He takes a bite of his own piece of bread, and I try not to watch the way his throat works when he swallows. "That's actual sorcery."

"I'm used to giving kids shots. Veggies are a cake walk in comparison." I take a seat at one of the island's high stools. To my surprise, my stomach seems to have no problem with me shoveling in the bread like I haven't eaten in weeks. Felix takes the carton of juice from the fridge, pours me a glass, and slides it in my direction. The fact that this man, who I don't want to like, seems intent on taking care of me is beyond weird. It's disconcerting, disturbing and it feels dangerously domestic. "Ellie's easy compared to some of the toddlers I've worked with."

"She screamed for an hour straight when I tried to give her a bath the first night I had her." His voice hitches in that way that does complicated things to my chest. "I thought I'd broken her."

"You aren't going to break anything. I'm sure she was scared and confused." I take a sip of juice. "You've done an amazing job with her, Felix. Really."

He looks away, his jaw working like he's physically holding back his response. The moment stretches between us, taut with all the things neither of us is willing to say.

"Fee! Fee!" Ellie's voice crackles through the monitor, followed by a delighted giggle. "Pi!"

"Duty calls," I say, grateful for the interruption before I blurt out that watching him take care of Ellie makes me want things I shouldn't. Things like having him be a father to our baby. But I'm going to have to tell him the truth soon.

"I'll get her," Felix says, already heading for the stairs. "You need to eat more. Protein ideally. Breakfast is the most important meal of the day."

"Yes, Dad," I call after him.

"That's Zaddy to you," he answers with a low chuckle, and there go my ovaries again, cheering like we're at the Super Bowl and Felix has just caught the winning touchdown.

By the time he comes down with Ellie, who's wearing her donut pajamas, hair sticking up in a way that oddly mirrors Felix's, I've managed to pull myself together. Mostly.

"Pi!" Ellie reaches for me, and after sliding the eggs I've scrambled onto a plate, I take her, settling her on my hip. She smells like sleep and lavender shampoo, and my heart does that stupid squeeze it's been doing lately whenever I hold her.

This is what it could be like, I think. Me and Felix and Ellie and a baby. Except he doesn't want to be a father, and I haven't told him, and—

"You okay?" Felix asks, studying my face with concern. "You're pale again."

"Fine. I need some protein, like you said. Ellie and I are sharing the eggs." She's going to eat them all, because pregnant me still thinks eggs are disgusting. But I'm not mentioning that to him. I kiss the top of her head, using her as a shield against his scrutiny as

I place her in the booster seat Felix had delivered. "What's your plan for today?"

"Tyler's coming over this afternoon for leg day." He pulls out ingredients for what looks like an elaborate smoothie. "I was thinking this morning we could take Ellie to a playground like you talked about with Ty. I looked online, and there's one near Vail Village that has bucket swings and a sandbox."

"Swing," Ellie agrees, then shoves a bite of egg into her mouth.

"You want to go to a public playground?" I raise an eyebrow. "What about flying under the radar?"

"I'll wear a hat."

"Yeah, because that's going to keep people from recognizing you."

"I doubt the playground will be popping with rabid football fans." He dumps a few fresh blueberries onto Ellie's plate. "She needs to see more than just this house, and honestly, so do I. Plus, you could use some fresh air in a way that doesn't involve fainting on mountain trails."

"One time, Felix."

"Once is enough." He cocks a thick brow. "You up for a field trip?"

I should say no. I need to maintain distance and boundaries and all the things that went out the window when I agreed to be his nanny. But Ellie gives me a heart-melting grin as she ignores the eggs to shove blueberries into her mouth, while Felix is looking at me with as much hope as a golden retriever bestows on the treat jar, and I'm apparently incapable of denying either of them anything.

"Sure," I agree. "But maybe skip the Grizzlies merch. And you're on sandbox and swing duty. I'm claiming a bench."

"Deal."

Two hours later, I'm sitting on said bench, watching Felix push Ellie on the baby swings, and my heart is flinging itself against my ribcage like it wants in on the action.

He's wearing a CU Buffaloes cap pulled low, aviator sunglasses, and a plain gray T-shirt that does nothing to hide the way he's built. Every time he pushes Ellie, she shrieks with joy. His laugh, deep and genuine, makes my heart go even more haywire.

"Higher, Fee! Higher!"

"That's as high as we go, munchkin," he tells her, grinning as widely as the toddler. "Don't want you flying to the moon."

"Moon!" she shouts, her arms shooting into the sky like she's riding a roller coaster.

As Felix predicted, we have the playground to ourselves for most of the visit. After a while, a mom pushing a stroller as she follows two rambunctious older boys stops near the edge of the rubber mulch. She smiles at me, then does a double-take when her gaze lands on Felix. At first, I chalk it up to the typical reaction people have to a man of his size. I don't know much about pheromones, but I'd bet money Felix emits them in tsunami-sized waves.

He grins at the boys, who start clambering up the geometric dome climber in the center of the space, then glances over to the mom and offers her a polite smile. She must be a football fan because I see the moment actual recognition hits. Her eyes go wide, her mouth forms a little 'o', and she reaches into the diaper bag strapped onto the handle of the stroller like she's going for her phone.

"Nice morning for a *private* family outing," I say as I stand and move toward Felix and Ellie.

The woman freezes like I've just read her Miranda Rights. "Is that...?"

"A giant human pushing a toddler in a swing?" My voice is sweet as spun sugar but there's no mistaking the warning beneath my words. "Yes, it is."

"We're huge Grizzlies fans," she answers, almost apologetically. Felix's focus has returned to Ellie, so he's clueless about being spotted.

I should have trusted my instinct about him being recognized and feel kind of bad because Felix Barlowe has a reputation for being available and down-to-earth with his fans. From everything I've read online (yeah, I've Googled him more than once), he manages to retain a "guy you could meet at a BBQ" vibe while being a superstar athlete. But with Ellie in the mix and his desire to keep a low profile, there's going to be more of a balancing act between being approachable and maintaining personal boundaries.

Our playground outing was fun while it lasted.

"Honey." I slip my hand into his and feel him go rigid. That's an interesting reaction, but I ignore it. "I think someone needs a diaper change."

Felix glances at the woman, registers her starstruck expression, and immediately lifts Ellie from the swing. "Right. Thanks, babe."

Babe?

"Have a great day," he tells the woman as we head toward the parking lot.

"Go Grizzlies," she says in a breathy voice.

To my surprise, he holds onto my hand until we're at the vehicle.

"I can't believe I got Mom IDd," he says, buckling Ellie into her car seat. "Her boys didn't spare a second glance."

"She was going for her phone," I say as I climb into the passenger side, trying to ignore how much I liked the weight of his hand at the small of my back when he'd guided me away from the woman. How natural it felt to have our fingers linked together.

"Close call and fast thinking, Hart."

I blow out a breath and glance over at him. "You called me 'babe.'"

"You called me honey." He backs out of the parking space, lips twitching. "I thought we were committing to the bit."

"The bit where we're what, exactly?" My voice is sharp, but I'm not angry at him. I'm angry at myself for how much I liked it.

How, for just a second, I let myself pretend we were exactly what the stranger thought we were—a family. "We aren't..." I shake my head. "Anything."

The words taste like ash in my mouth. Because we're something, aren't we? Something undefined and complicated and getting messier by the day. But saying it out loud would make it real, and I can't afford real right now. Not when I'm hiding a secret that could destroy whatever this fragile thing between us is.

Felix's fingers grip the steering wheel more tightly, his knuckles going white. "I didn't mean anything." He adjusts the brim on his ball cap like he's shielding himself from something. "I get that you were helping me avoid a scene, and I appreciate it."

"Right." I look out the window, a ball of emotion I can't quite identify lodging in my throat. "Just two people pretending to share custody of a toddler who isn't ours while we avoid a fangirl mom moment. All part of the deal."

A heavy silence stretches between us, and I want to take the words back, or soften them somehow, but I don't know how without revealing too much.

"Piper—"

"We should grab lunch." I cut him off, desperate to move past this moment. "How about that café Mindy recommended? She said they have the best chicken noodle soup and great sandwiches. I can run in and order carryout while you stay with Ellie."

He studies me for a moment, like we have way more important things to talk about than sandwiches. Then Ellie starts singing about twinkling stars from the backseat, and he nods slowly.

"Give me the name, and I'll put it in the GPS."

Twenty minutes later, I return to the car with soup, sandwiches, and sides, and we drive back to the cabin in near silence. The only sound is Ellie's happy babbling and the occasional ding of the turn signal.

The lunch feels awkward in a way things haven't been since

that first morning. We make ridiculously polite small talk, and when Felix reaches for a chip at the same time I do, we both jerk back like we've been burned.

"Sorry," we say in unison, then look away from each other.

This is taking weird to a whole new level. By the time we finish eating, the tension is thick enough to cut with a knife. Tyler shows up just as I'm placing the leftovers in the fridge, and the personal trainer seems blessedly oblivious to the uncomfortable energy, which I use as an excuse to escape.

"I'll put Ellie down for her nap," I say as I lift the girl from her high chair. "You two can do your thing."

Felix quirks a thick brow. "What exactly is *our thing*?"

I throw Tyler a desperate glance. "You know what I mean, right?"

"I want to hear your answer, Hart," Felix clarifies with a smirk.

"Leg day, *Barlowe*," Tyler says and offers me a slow wink. "I'm going to wreck him."

"Totally support that," I tell the trainer and give Felix a one-finger salute behind Ellie's back. He laughs, the sound rolling through me like thunder.

Damn, I'm in bigger trouble than I realized.

I carry Ellie upstairs, grateful for the distance. I need to pull myself together. The cabin is thick-walled and well-insulated, so I can't hear anything from the basement gym. But I can imagine it way too vividly. Felix will be loading weight plates onto the bar, his muscles flexing as he positions himself on the bench. The focused intensity of his face, the way his body moves as those muscles that haunt my mind flex. I shake my head, forcing the images away as I settle Ellie in her crib.

She fights sleep for a few minutes, babbling about the "swing" and "Fee," but eventually her eyes drift closed. I watch her for a moment, this perfect little girl who somehow feels like she belongs to me even though she doesn't. Just like Felix doesn't, and won't. Because nothing about this situation is permanent or real.

Neither of them should mean anything to me. But they do, and I don't know how to make it stop.

I slip out of her room and into mine, intending to read or maybe finally respond to the text messages I've been ignoring from my sister and the rest of the book club. Instead, I lie down on the bed, just for a minute.

The bread Felix made—warm and sweet and perfect—settled my stomach instead of making it worse. Even the soup didn't bother it. I'm still tired, but for the first time in days, I haven't felt the constant low-grade nausea. I can't help thinking my relief is about more than just the focaccia. It has something to do with my mountain of a man.

Except...nope. He's not mine. I'd like to go back to that place where Felix Barlowe annoys the hell out of me with his giant muscles and giant personality. That would be a lot simpler, especially given the complexity of the secret I'm carrying. The one I need to tell him about, even though it scares the hell out of me. I can't hide it forever, and I can't hide away from life for much longer either. It's time to pull up my big girl panties and deal with everything I'm trying to ignore.

I lay back against the pillow and place a hand on my stomach, letting my eyes drift closed. Maybe just a tiny nap first.

9

______

PIPER

WHEN I WAKE, the light has shifted, late afternoon sun slanting through the windows and causing my heart to leap for different reasons than Felix Barlowe does.

I grab my phone from the nightstand. It's nearly six. I've been asleep for three hours?

Uh, oh.

Stumbling out of bed, I make my way into the bathroom. This baby might be tiny, but his or her effect on my bladder is significant. I also take a second to splash cold water on my face, which does nothing to lessen the pillowcase crease on my cheek.

Is it possible that Ellie's still sleeping? The sound of voices drifts up from downstairs as I check her bedroom and find an empty crib, which means I'm a sucky nanny, vegetable whisperer skills notwithstanding. I hurry down the stairs and into the living room, then stop short.

Felix, Tyler, and Ellie are sprawled on the massive sectional, all three of them staring up at the giant TV screen mounted above the fireplace where two animated dogs are doing something with a xylophone.

Bluey. They're watching *Bluey.*

"For real life?" the cartoon dog asks, and Ellie giggles, clapping her hands.

"I didn't mean to sleep so long," I say as Felix glances up at me. "I'm so sorry. I was supposed to be watching her, and I blewy it."

"Epic fail," Felix agrees solemnly before rolling his eyes. "I'm joking, Hart. No biggie."

It feels like a biggie. Because what if Felix and Tyler hadn't heard her and I slept through her cries without the monitor in my bedroom? What if I fall asleep and inadvertently ignore my baby crying? Is that the kind of mother I'm going to be?

Whoa, cue the nausea. Only I don't think I can blame it on hormones this time.

"How long did she sleep?" I ask, trying to sound casual and not like I've decided I'm the worst mom-to-be ever.

"About thirty minutes. I tried the whole going in and rubbing her back until she fell asleep again thing, but she wasn't having it." He lifts Ellie to stand on his legs and she starts bouncing and jiggling like she's on the dance floor. "Girl is ready to par-tee," he says with the besotted smile Ellie brings out of him.

"He's thrilled leg day got cut short," Tyler adds, standing and stretching. "But I put him through a decent amount of torture before the munchkin takeover."

"I'm so sorry," I repeat, mortified. "Taking care of her is literally my job, and I—"

"We managed just fine," Felix cuts me off, his voice gentle. "You must have needed the rest. Tyler will be back to kicking my a —" He wrinkles his nose at Ellie, who's watching him with wide eyes. "...Bum... all over the gym on Monday."

Ellie giggles again. "Bum!"

Felix points to the television. "Bluey bum."

Ellie shrieks with delight then drops onto his lap, curling against him. And despite my internal guilt trip, I can't help but smile.

Tyler grabs his gym bag from the floor. "As much as I'd love to continue bingeing the adventures of painfully annoying cartoon dogs, I'm out." He jabs a finger in Felix's direction. "Show up tonight."

"Not likely." There's an edge to Felix's voice I can't quite identify.

"What's tonight?" I ask, not sure I really want to know.

"I'm meeting up with Mindy and some of her friends at a bar in town. Live music, pool, darts, people. All of which are normally right up Barlowe's alley. Only now, he's a hermit."

"You know why," Felix says through gritted teeth.

"You have Piper to stay with Ellie." Tyler pulls out his phone, tapping the screen. "I'm texting you the address. Come out, man. It's Friday night. You need to let the old Felix out of his cage for a few hours."

Felix rolls his eyes. "Fudge you, Ty."

"You're not my type." Tyler's tone is dry, but he turns to me with a smile. "If he stays in, you're welcome to join us instead. I guarantee a good time."

Felix makes a sound low in his throat that sounds an awful lot like a Roy Kent-style growl, which is surprisingly hot. But he doesn't say anything or tell me I can't go.

"Thanks," I say, even though the idea of hitting a bar makes me exhausted all over again. "I'll think about it."

As Tyler heads for the door, I walk to the kitchen and grab a glass of water before returning to the family room. Bluey's family is playing some elaborate game that involves the entire house, and Ellie is transfixed. Even with the sound from the TV, the cabin feels too quiet. Too intimate.

"I should feed her dinner," I say, needing something to do with my hands. "Do you want—"

"I'll handle it." Felix places Ellie on the sofa next to him then stands.

"I can do it, Felix. I'm capable of handling dinner."

"I know you are." One thick brow lifts. "But if you're meeting up with Tyler and the gang, you might want to start getting ready."

"How bad do I look that you think I need hours of prep for a night out?" I try to make the question sound like a joke, but the truth is his words sting more than they should. "And why aren't you going?"

"You don't look bad." His jaw clenches, and he glances out the picture window that frames the valley. "Tyler's right. I'm wound too tight, and now I'm projecting on you. Maybe I need to go out and get my head straight."

We both know it's not his head that he's talking about, and something twists in my chest at the thought of Felix with another woman. Like I have any right to act or even feel possessive. So I plaster on the widest smile I can manage. "You should definitely go out."

I move to the sofa and take a seat next to Ellie, gathering her in my arms. Felix and I stare at each other for a long moment, engaged in some silent battle of wills neither of us wants to acknowledge.

"I'm going to take a shower," he says finally.

"Great." I force a brightness into my voice that coats my tongue in acid. "Maybe you'll meet a nice single mom fangirl who can help with your *head*."

His eyes flash with something that, if I didn't know better, I'd call hurt or anger, but he just shakes his head and disappears upstairs.

The episode ends, and I carry Ellie into the kitchen, my thoughts churning as I heat up her dinner. This is good. It's what Felix and I need—space, distance, and a reminder that this isn't real. We're just two people stuck together by circumstance...and a series of poor decisions on my part.

By the time I finish cleaning up the mess left from the toddler mealtime tornado—sweet potato everywhere—it's clear that, thanks to her abbreviated nap earlier, Ellie's exhausted. She loves the bath, so I figure an early one will burn up some time before bed and also prep her for—fingers crossed—a good night's sleep.

I assume Felix will slip away without saying goodbye, but as we reach the hallway, his door opens. He's wearing dark jeans and a fitted gray T-shirt. His hair is damp from the shower, and he smells like soap and something woodsy and expensive. He also looks like he stepped off the cover of a magazine, and my stupid, hormonal body responds accordingly.

"Have a great time," I say, trying to keep my voice neutral.

"I—" He stops, looking first at me and then Ellie. Her face is buried against my shoulder like she's about as pleased as I am. When he looks back at me, his gaze is dark and slightly wild. "Do you have a problem with this, Hart?"

"Not in the slightest. One of us needs to get out of the house." I shift Ellie on my hip, using her as a buffer between us. "I'm happy right where I am."

I move past him toward the bathroom, but his voice stops me.

"Piper—"

"Seriously, Felix. It's fine. Ellie's fussy, so I'm going to give her a bath and try to put her down early. You don't need to stick around for that."

I don't look back at him. If I do, I might do something stupid. Like ask him to stay.

Instead, I close the bathroom door between us and start running water for Ellie's bath.

An hour, three rounds of *Goodnight Moon,* and two lullabies later, Ellie is clean, pajama'd and finally passed out in her crib.

I'm already plotting my own early night when I smell fresh-baked bread.

Totally ignoring the fact that Felix is gone—so this could be the start of a doughy horror movie—I make my way downstairs, following the scent like a cartoon character floating toward a pie on a windowsill. Once again, instead of a villain, I find Felix in the kitchen. He's changed out of the jeans and back into athletic shorts and a looser fitting shirt.

I command my booing ovaries to hush and watch in rapt fascination—or maybe that's hunger—as he pulls a golden loaf from the oven.

"I thought you were going out," I say.

He sets the bread on a cooling rack, not quite meeting my eyes. "Changed my mind."

The kitchen island is set for two, with plates and silverware and what looks like two of Mindy's prepared meals ready to go on the counter.

"You made dinner."

"I *heated* dinner," he corrects with a smile that looks almost shy and totally out of character for larger-than-life Felix Barlowe. "But the bread is mine." He moves to the sink to fill two glasses with water. "Figured we both need to eat."

"Felix—"

"Sit down." He points to a chair at the island. "It's dinner, not a marriage proposal."

As if I needed that reminder. But the idea of being married to... well, not specifically Felix but a man like him—one who carries me down a trail when I stumble and then feeds me—makes me feel a little dizzy, and I sink into the chair before my knees give out.

It's the exact opposite of the relationship I had with my ass-hat ex-fiancé. A twatwaffle who seemed to believe that because I was younger and not a doctor, I owed him just for picking me. Turns out, that kind of selfish love does not do great things to a person's self-esteem. And even though I've seen my sister and book club friends taken care of by the men who love them, I convinced myself I'm better on my own. Safer.

Felix is dangerous on a lot of levels.

He plates the food—some kind of chicken dish with roasted vegetables that I'm definitely not eating—then cuts thick slices of the still-warm bread. I take a bite of the bread first and swallow back a moan. After making a fool of myself over his focaccia, I'm committed to keeping it together, but it's tough with so much deliciousness exploding on my tongue.

"I seriously hate you," I say around a mouthful, "for ruining store-bought bread for me forever."

He shrugs like this is also no biggie as he slides into the chair next to me, but I catch the pleased expression that flashes across his face. "It's just bread."

"It's not *just* bread. It's carb art."

He grins. "No one has ever called me an artist. Well, other than analysts talking about my signature creative style in running routes."

"Bake them some sourdough." I pop another morsel into my mouth with a sigh. "You're more than football, Felix."

I know the simple compliment shocks him, because he's just taken a bite and starts coughing like crazy.

"You okay?" I thump on his back as he downs his water in one gulp then gets up and heads to the sink for a refill. Felix has had me discombobulated for days, so it's more than a little bit gratifying to return the favor.

"'M fine," he mutters after taking another long drink. "Chicken went down the wrong pipe."

"It happens."

He swipes under each watering eye with his sleeve. "For the record, I don't need to be more than football. Football made me what I am, and I'm fucking grateful for it. It's all I need."

"Okay," I answer, even though we both know he's lying.

"You want wine?" he asks suddenly, grabbing a bottle he must have brought up from the small cellar in the basement. "I meant to uncork it earlier. I can pour you—"

"I can't—" I catch myself, clearing my throat. "I mean, I shouldn't. Since you're not drinking because of training, I'm not going to either."

He sets the bottle down, a small smile playing around his lips. "You're a solidarity gal, Hart?"

"Something like that."

"Ronnie used to love my dry spells," he says, slicing more bread and pushing the cutting board toward me. "It meant she had a designated driver."

My eyes roll to the ceiling. "Your ex was a real treat."

"We have that in common."

His eyes meet mine, and his gaze goes dark. There's a lot we haven't said about Bradley and Veronica. About choices and mistakes and the invisible scars we carry from all of it.

"Tell me more about your secret bread obsession," I say as I study the piece in my hand. "Are you in a baking club?"

He lets out a long exhale and then takes a seat next to me again. "No sourdough clubhouse," he says as he polishes off the last of his dinner and shakes his head when I push my plate toward him. "Eat your veggies."

"Carb loading is way more fun." I nudge my knee against his. "Besides, I see you eyeing my food. Don't act like you don't want it."

His low laugh sends shivers skating up my spine. "I wouldn't dare."

"Back to the bread." Oh, crap. Why does my voice suddenly sound husky?

"I get a lot of tips from the forums."

I blink and try to force myself back to the conversation for real. "Felix Barlowe hangs out in sourdough forums?"

"I don't go by Receiver Paws Felix or anything," he says like, duh.

"Color me fermentation bubble intrigued." I point my last bite at him. "What do you go by?"

He leans closer. "You planning to online stalk me?"

"I don't need to go online," I answer. "I can stalk you in real life."

"Kind of creepy," he murmurs, but his eyes are dancing.

My heart does that annoying topsy-turvy thing again. If I were a puppy, this would be the point where I'd flop on my back and offer up my belly. "Spill it, Felix. You know you want to."

He grunts—or maybe it's supposed to be a scoff—and after finishing off my veggies in two bites, takes both of our clean plates to the sink. I collect the water glasses and follow him over, resigned to the fact that he's not going to spill a thing. Why does it even matter? His bread forum username is none of my business, and I'm clearly not the person he would share it with. I don't want to be that person for Felix, I remind myself.

Who's lying now?

"Filsbury Dough Boy."

The words are spoken so softly I almost miss them. "Come again."

"That's my handle. Filsbury Dough Boy. No one is going to trace it back to me. But if you tell anyone, I'll deny it." He finishes rinsing the plates and silverware, bends down to put it all in the dishwasher, then straightens and reaches for the glasses. "Then I'll kill you."

"It's fucking brilliant," I whisper, and I mean it. It's original and fun and unexpected—just like Felix. Almost as unexpected as how much I like being with him.

"For the record, I didn't go out tonight," he says quietly, "because I wanted to be here with you, Piper. Just the two of us." He glances over to the monitor sitting on the island. "Well, the three of us, but you know what I mean."

I know exactly what he means, and my heart is suddenly hammering against my ribs. "That's...Felix...you know we can't..."

"I know all the reasons we *shouldn't*." He steps close enough that I can feel the heat radiating from his skin. "I know you're my brother's sister-in-law and we don't even like each other most of the time. I know this whole situation is temporary and complicated."

He has no idea *how* complicated, but I don't step away. "So why are you standing so close to me?"

"Because Tyler was right." That massive chest rises and falls with an unsteady breath. "I *am* wound too tight. But it's not because I need to let off steam in a bar." His hand comes up to cup my face, his thumb brushing across my cheekbone. "It's because I can't stop thinking about you and me. How wrong and right it feels at the exact same time."

I should leave now. Retreat upstairs and stay in my room until tomorrow, when the morning light can burn off this irresistible connection holding us both in its sway.

But I don't.

Instead, I lean into his touch and whisper, "I'm a sucker for bad ideas."

10

PIPER

"SAME." That one word is a low rumble that seems to vibrate through Felix's chest and into mine.

"We're going to regret this."

"Probably."

"Felix—"

His name hangs in the air as he cuts me off with a kiss that's nothing like yesterday's tentative exploration. This is a full-on claiming that says *mine* and *now* and *fuck the consequences*.

And I agree completely.

His mouth is hot and demanding, and his tongue slides against mine in a slow glide that tastes both sweet and spicy, a dichotomy I'm getting used to when it comes to Felix.

When my knees threaten to buckle, one strong arm bands around my waist while the other hand tangles in my hair. He angles my head exactly where he wants it, and I answer with the same reckless heat, fingers spearing through his hair to yank him closer. Until there's no space left between us, and the only thing I can feel is the heat rolling off him in waves, the scrape of his stubble, and the dark sound he makes when I bite his lower lip and soothe it with my tongue.

That soft moan shoots straight to my core, lighting me up like the scoreboard after an overtime touchdown. The way Felix Barlowe kisses me gives new meaning to the phrase "the crowd goes wild."

His hands drop to my waist, fingers slipping under the hem of my shirt to find bare skin. The calloused pads of his thumbs sweep over my ribs and trace the curve of my waist. I arch into him without thinking, needing more of what he has to give me. All of it.

My shirt rides higher, and his palms flatten against my back to pull me flush against him so I can feel every hard inch of him through our clothes. His hips roll once, and the promise of his thick length makes me gasp into his mouth. The friction is at once too much and not nearly enough.

"Bedroom," I manage when we break apart. "Now."

"As you wish," he says and scoops me up like I weigh nothing.

Even with need and desire muddying my mind, I breathe out a soft laugh. "Felix Barlowe, did you just quote *The Princess Bride* to me?"

He takes the stairs two at a time. "Fuck yeah, Buttercup," he whispers, which might be the hottest thing I've ever heard.

Somehow, he's able to walk at the same time he scrapes his teeth across a spot just below my ear that makes me shiver. "And I plan to make you scream my name," he murmurs against my skin. "Until you forget every reason this is a bad idea, and the only thing you can think about is how good I feel inside you. How wet you've been since the second I touched you."

Drenched, but I'm not admitting that quite yet.

He lays me down on his big bed, and I yank him down with me. The solid, heavy weight of him settling between my thighs feels far too right. His hips roll again, and my nails dig into his shoulders, urging him closer. He braces himself on one forearm, the other hand sliding up my side to cup my breast through my shirt, and his thumb brushes over my nipple until it's a tight peak. The fabric is in the way, and I want it gone. Now.

"You can tell me to stop." His lips smooth a trail along my jaw, and I gasp when he sucks my earlobe into his hot mouth. "Tell me all the reasons this is the worst fucking idea in the world."

"Can't think of a single one." I fist his shirt, rip it over his head...and hello, muscles. My hands trace the sharp planes of his chest and the ridges of his abs. I lean up and drag my tongue across the faint scar on his collarbone, tasting salt and skin and Felix. He shudders, hips jerking against mine. "Zero fucks to give about bad ideas, Felix. Zero."

He growls, which I love, and then his hands are everywhere. In my hair, on my skin, mapping me like he's been waiting for this moment forever. My shirt's gone in a blink, and my bra quickly follows, flung across the room with a flick of his wrist. His eyes go dark, almost black, as he drinks me in, cataloging every inch.

He presses open-mouthed kisses along my throat, down the slope of one breast, until his mouth closes over my nipple. I bow off the bed with a broken moan, fingers tangling in his hair to hold him there. But he doesn't seem in any hurry to move on. He sucks hard, then uses his tongue to soothe me with slow, wet circles. The sensation makes my head spin, and my hips arch up to meet his in a silent plea.

"Felix—"

"Fucking perfect," he whispers, switching sides to give the other breast the same treatment. His fingers roll the abandoned nipple between them until I'm writhing. "The way you say my name, like you're begging and bossing me around all at once."

His hand slides down my belly, and his fingers dip beneath my waistband to tease the edge of my panties. He traces the lace, then slips beneath it, finding me slick and ready. One finger slides through my folds, and I jolt with a sharp cry of pleasure. "Christ, you're soaked. This started downstairs, right?"

The intensity of his gaze is both shocking and somehow

freeing because I can tell how much he likes it. And I don't even have it in me to be embarrassed. "Since the moment you touched me," I admit, voice shaky.

"Say it again."

I draw in a slow breath. "Make me."

His smile remains boyish, but his laugh is pure sin. "Challenge accepted, sweetheart."

He draws my leggings and panties down my legs, then tosses them aside and spreads me wide. His broad shoulders force my thighs apart, and he just looks. And looks some more. It's like he's starving, and I'm the buffet. I squirm under his scrutiny, hands fluttering to cover myself.

"Don't you dare." He catches my wrists with one hand while his other trails down my body, fingers skimming over my breasts and stomach and the curve of my hip. "Don't ever hide from me," he murmurs, pressing a kiss to the inside of one thigh. "Every damn inch of you is beautiful."

Then—oh, God—his mouth is on me. His tongue drags up my slit in one long, filthy lick. A low moan escapes my lips, and my fingers grip the sheets. He hums out his approval, the vibration making my clit throb.

"Fuck, you taste better than I remembered," he mutters, voice muffled against me.

His hands grip my thighs, holding me open as he explores with broad strokes, then focused flicks, then suction that makes my vision go hazy at the edges. Two thick fingers slide inside, curling to reach a spot that turns my spine to liquid. He adds a third, stretching me open, and I whimper at the fullness, hips bucking to meet his hand.

"Felix, please."

"That's right," he practically purrs as his fingers pump faster, that talented tongue brushing my clit in tight, perfect circles. "I need to feel you come on my tongue, Piper. I want you dripping down my chin."

His wicked words add to the pleasure swirling through me like a windstorm. Pressure builds and coils in my belly, and when he sucks my clit into his mouth and crooks his fingers in the exact right way, I shatter.

I come hard, and I can't stop my thighs from clamping around his head. My back arches off the bed as a million sparkles shimmer behind my eyes. He continues licking, sucking, and finger-fucking me through the aftershocks. I'm a trembling mess, and I gasp his name like it's the only word I've ever heard. The orgasm rolls into a second one before he finally pulls back, pressing one last kiss to my inner thigh.

When he crawls back up my body, lips shiny with me, his smug cat-got-the-cream grin is infuriatingly hot. Or maybe the orgasms have blown away all my good sense. Either way, he kisses me deep, letting me taste myself on his tongue, and it's so earthy and raw, I could come again just from that.

"Still think this is a bad idea?" he asks, voice supremely self-satisfied.

"The worst." I smile against his lips, reaching into his shorts and boxers to wrap my hand around his cock. He's so hard, the head of his cock slick with precum, and the way he thrusts into my fist makes my insides clench with need all over again. I slowly stroke him, my thumb circling the tip, spreading the wetness. "Now get naked."

"So bossy." He stands and shoves his shorts off the rest of the way. And sweet baby Jesus. He's even bigger than my hazy tequila memory, long and thick as he fists himself, eyes locked on mine.

"See something you like?"

I lick my lips. "Come back here and find out."

He settles between my thighs again, nudging my entrance with the blunt head of his cock, then freezes. "Shit. No condom."

My heart stutters, and I know I should tell him now, but the words jam in my throat. Instead, I whisper, "We're okay."

His eyes search mine, and he lets out a slow breath. "You sure?"

I nod because my throat is tight with both guilt and desire. He kisses me with a reverence that makes the back of my eyes sting, then pushes in, stretching me open inch by inch. I gasp at the momentary burn that morphs into pleasure as he fills me, and his answering groan sounds like it's been ripped from somewhere deep inside him.

"Breathe, sweetheart," he murmurs, forehead pressed to mine. "I've got you."

I exhale shakily and wrap my legs around his waist, heels digging into his ass. "I've got you right back, Barlowe."

"For as long as you want me," he agrees, then starts to move—long, deep strokes that feel like some kind of carnal promise. The angle shifts, and suddenly he hits a spot that makes stars burst behind my eyelids. He keeps changing the pace—slow and deep, then fast and shallow, then slow again—pushing me to the edge, but never letting me fall.

"Look at me," he whispers. His gaze is fierce but also filled with tenderness. "I want to watch you come undone on my cock and feel you milk every drop out of me."

His words are all I need to tumble over the edge of oblivion. I come again, raking my nails down his back hard enough to leave marks. He follows with a guttural curse, hips bucking wildly as he spills inside me, pulse after pulse, my name a ragged chant on his lips.

His weight is a delicious anchor as he collapses on top of me, then rolls us so I'm draped over his chest. One giant palm splays almost possessively over the curve of my ass, while his other hand finds mine, lacing our fingers together over his heart.

"Piper?" he murmurs into my hair.

"Mmm?"

"This doesn't have to change anything."

The words slice clean through the afterglow, and what a damn fool I am to think otherwise. I swallow hard, nodding against his chest even as my heart cracks open. "Of course not. I still hate you."

He chuckles at the lie, then tightens his arm around me like he's afraid I'll slip away. A moment later, his breathing evens out, and I know he's fast asleep.

I stare at the ceiling and try not to notice his hand resting innocently on my still-flat stomach, but the secret I'm keeping settles over me like a blanket.

Tomorrow. I'll tell him tomorrow.

Tonight, I'm going to pretend Felix Barlowe's arms are big enough to hold all my secrets and still want me anyway.

11

FELIX

WHEN I WAKE up the next morning, the bed beside me is empty, the sheets cool to the touch. Morning light filters through the edge of the curtain, pale gold banding across the dresser on the other side of the room. Except for the soft hum of the baby monitor, my room is quiet. Too quiet.

I barely have time to register Piper's absence before a sound from down the hall makes my stomach tense. That's definitely retching.

I'm out of bed before my brain fully processes what's happening, grabbing shorts from the floor and yanking them on as I move. The noise is coming from Piper's room, the one she didn't sleep in last night but apparently retreated to at some point while I was dead to the world.

The bedroom door is cracked open, and I can hear her being violently sick in the adjoining bathroom.

"Piper?" I push the door open and find her hunched over the toilet, one hand braced on the seat, the other clutching the edge of the vanity.

She's wearing one of my new Grizzlies T-shirts, her long legs curled under her. For a moment, my body—and heart, if I'm being honest—has a visceral reaction to seeing her in my shirt. *Mine*, the internal choir chants, like she belongs to me.

I tell the stupid chanters to shut the fuck up. Because it isn't true, and this isn't the time to go full-on caveman. Not when it's clear she's suffering, her normally creamy skin clammy and tinged green.

"Go away," she manages weakly.

No fucking chance.

I cross the room and drop to my knees behind her. Smoothing away the strands of hair that have escaped her messy bun, I rest my other hand on her back.

"I've got you, Hart."

"Felix, I'm serious. Leave." Another wave hits her, and she curls forward with a miserable groan.

It makes my chest ache, and I stay right where I am, rubbing small circles on her back the way I do when Ellie's upset, murmuring nonsense that I hope is soothing. When the wave finally passes, she flushes the toilet and slumps back against the wall with her eyes closed. I grab a washcloth from the rack, run it under cool water, and press it to her forehead.

"I hate this."

And I hate hearing her sound so defeated. "I know." The words feel inadequate, but I don't know what else to say. "Let me help."

"You can help by leaving. I look disgusting, I feel disgusting, and I don't need an audience right now."

"Think of me as a super fan." I keep the washcloth on her forehead, using my free hand to stroke her bare thigh. "For the record, you could never look disgusting."

She cracks one eye open to glare at me. "I just threw up everything I've eaten in the past day. There's nothing attractive about that."

"Agree to disagree."

"You're insane."

"Not the first time I've heard that. Is it safe to move away from the porcelain throne?"

"For now," she whispers.

I help her to her feet, keeping one arm around her waist because she's swaying slightly. She seems too fragile, and something protective flares in my chest. "Come on. Let's get you to bed."

"You're missing it." She gestures weakly to the perfectly made bed in her room as I steer her toward the door.

"My bed is more comfortable."

I don't give her a chance to protest, just scoop her up as carefully as I can and carry her down the hall to my room. She doesn't argue, which tells me how awful she feels. The Piper Hart I know—and like more than is smart for either of us—would rather gargle shards of glass than let me take care of her. But this is becoming a habit I don't mind at all. I pull back the covers with one hand and lay her down, tucking the sheet and comforter around her. She immediately curls on her side, and I grab another pillow to prop behind her back.

"When's the last time you kept food down?"

She shrugs, not meeting my eyes. "I don't know. Yesterday morning? The focaccia didn't bother my stomach, so I thought I'd turned a corner. Not much else has agreed with me the past couple of weeks."

Weeks? Jesus Christ.

"That's it. We're going to urgent care."

"No, we're not." She shifts against the pillows, pulling the covers higher. "I'm fine, Felix. It's just—"

"Don't tell me food poisoning, because you've been sick the entire time we've been here. That's not normal." I pace to the window and back. "You fainted on the trail. You barely eat. You're exhausted all the time. Something's wrong, and we're getting it checked out."

"Felix—"

"I mean it, Piper. I'll get Ellie up and then we're going." I rake a hand through my hair. "I'm going to call ahead and arrange for us to enter through a back door so—"

"I know what's wrong." The words hang between us, the panic in her eyes making my stomach drop.

"Okay." I try to keep my voice calm, even though my heart is suddenly trying to punch its way out of my chest. I take a step closer. "What is it?"

She takes a breath, closes her eyes, and says, "I'm pregnant."

My world tilts sideways like I'm on one of those carnival rides designed to make you hurl the hot dogs, soda, and cotton candy you spent hours shoving in your face. I understand the words individually. She's pregnant. But my brain can't seem to take them on board in a way that makes sense.

"You're..." I shake my head, trying to clear it. "Pregnant."

"About twelve weeks," she confirms quietly.

Twelve weeks. The math clicks into place with all the subtlety of a freight train.

"That would mean April," I say. "Denver?"

She nods. Her eyes are open now, but she's staring down at the striped pattern of the comforter like it can give both of us the answers we need.

One night in Denver, celebrating my signing with the Grizzlies. The same night Piper was at her college friend's bachelorette party. Drinks. Dancing. Shots. The hotel room and a night we both agreed was a mistake and swore we'd never mention again.

"Holy shit." I run both hands through my hair, my mind racing almost as fast as my heartbeat. "It's my baby."

"Yes."

Turns out that freight train was carrying a shit-ton of emotions, dumping them on me until it feels like I'm buried alive. I move toward the bed and crouch down so Piper and I are at eye level, not even trying to hide the frustration I can feel radiating from every cell of my being.

"When the fuck were you going to tell me?"

12

FELIX

THE QUESTION COMES OUT HARSH, like my vocal chords were just scraped across gravel, but I can't help it. Piper's known for a while, definitely the whole time I've been here, and hasn't bothered to share the information? What the fuck.

Her eyes lock on mine, and there's fire in them now, which is strangely comforting. Turbulent Piper is way more familiar than the fragile version, puking her guts out into the toilet. "I've been trying to figure out how."

I rise to my full height and place my hands on hips, glaring at her. "How about 'Hey Felix, remember that night we're pretending didn't happen? Well, surprise, I'm having your baby.' That seems pretty straightforward."

"Oh, really?" Her voice rises. "Should I have mentioned it that first night when you showed up exhausted and frustrated with Ellie? Or maybe when you told me you weren't keeping her because you don't want to be a father?"

Her words hit like a full-body tackle. "I never said that."

"You did. Multiple times. Loudly and on repeat." She wraps her arms around herself, looking smaller than I've ever seen her. Fuck, now I want to punch myself in the gut. "So yeah, I was trying to decide when and how to tell you without it seeming like I was trapping you or expecting something you've made very clear you don't want to give."

"Piper—"

"I thought if I stayed here to help with Ellie, maybe I'd get to see what kind of father you could be. If you'd…" She trails off, shaking her head. "I don't know what I thought. Maybe that you'd magically change your mind about kids, which would make what's coming way easier on both of us."

The vulnerability in her voice wrecks me. Especially when I realize she's not angry, she's scared of my reaction. And probably of doing this alone. She thinks I'm going to be another guy who lets her down.

"You offered to nanny for me because this is some kind of covert audition?" I ask, still trying to understand. To put aside the maelstrom of emotions pounding through me and think about this from Piper's point of view. "Like if I did good with Ellie, you'd tell me?"

"No. I…" She hesitates just long enough that I'm pretty confident my guess might be at least partially true. "I wanted to figure out what's best for the baby. And for me."

"What about what's best for me? For *us*?" I sound like a little bitch, but I can't help it.

Her eyes go wide. "Us? There's no us. We had amazing sex. Twice now. But most of the time, we barely tolerate each other. We're not together. We're two people who made a mistake."

"Don't call it that," I snap, then clear my throat and say in a quieter voice, "Don't call our baby a mistake."

"I wasn't—" She shakes her head, pressing two fingers to each temple. "I meant the situation."

"Are you keeping the baby?" The question is out before I can stop it, and I hold my breath waiting for her answer.

"Yes. A thousand times yes." She sounds almost offended, and the relief that floods my veins nearly knocks me off my feet. "I know it's complicated and the timing is terrible and you don't want kids, but this is my baby and I'm—"

"Our baby," I interrupt.

"You don't want kids," she repeats.

Fuck. Why does she keep reminding me of that? It's not like I can deny it, but she doesn't understand. Hell, I barely understand. I never believed I could be the kind of dad a kid deserves, but I was willing to try. Right up until Ronnie's betrayal. Then, something broke inside me. If I wasn't worth a woman sticking around, I sure as hell wouldn't be good enough to be someone's dad.

I didn't have a great role model in my own father. My brother is a fantastic dad now, but it took him a hot minute to get it together for Riva. And Ian is better than me in every way, which means it could take me decades—hell, a lifetime. My dad always said the Barlowe men were cursed in love, and with a trail of failed relationships in my wake, I'm living up to his prediction.

It sucks to grow up with parents who hated each other, and I'd never want to put that on a child. But Piper's doubt cuts deeper than any knife could. "Do you really think I'm going to let you do this alone?"

"I don't know, Felix." Her voice cracks. "All I know is that I'm pregnant and puking on the regular and sue me for not saying anything. I thought I could figure this out by myself. I want to be able to stand on my own two feet without needing somebody to rescue me. This baby needs a mom who can take care of herself."

The fear in her eyes guts me. She's been carrying this all by herself because she didn't think she could count on me. But, even worse, she doesn't believe she can count on herself.

I own my part in this. Those offhand comments about not wanting kids. The interviews where I've said football is my only priority. She believed all that. And the truth is, I meant it at the time.

But this changes everything.

"We had sex last night." The sudden realization feels like being dunked in an ice bath.

"We did," she agrees, like *no shit, Sherlock*.

"What if I hurt the baby?"

She blinks. "Um...how?"

I throw my hands up. "You know."

"I don't."

I thrust my hips forward a couple of times. "You *know*."

Her lips twitch and she coughs to try to cover her laugh, which is such a big improvement over sad Piper that I don't even care that she's laughing at me. "You didn't hurt the baby with your giant elephant trunk of a—"

"I'm being serious, Piper."

"So am I." Now she's grinning outright, which is possibly the most baffling thing that's happened in this already confusing morning. "The baby is fine, Felix. Perfectly cushioned and protected. You can't hurt it by...you know."

"You're sure?" I know she's a nurse and all, but still...

"I'm sure."

I massage a hand along the back of my neck and draw in a long breath, still trying to process everything.

"I'm going to be a dad."

"Yep."

"You're having my baby."

"We've established that, Barlowe."

"When are you due?" My brain can't do that math right now.

"Around the third week of January."

Seven months away. And smack in the middle of playoff season —not that I'm going to mention that not-so-small detail right now. I thought being traded to Denver was a big change, but this is...

I sink down onto the edge of the bed, head spinning and knees weak, like I'm the one who needs attention. She's still got the covers pulled up nearly to her chin, watching me with those soft hazel eyes, and I can see the doubt start to resurface.

Shit. My intention isn't to add to Piper's already overflowing plate of worry, yet I can't seem to figure out how to ease her fears when mine are coming at me like a defensive lineman.

I run both hands through my hair, gripping hard enough that it almost hurts. "I need a minute. This is—" I gesture helplessly. "I don't know what to say next." Let alone what to do.

"I get it." Her voice is gentle now, and somehow that makes it worse. "It's a lot to process."

"Yeah." My brain cells seem to be whirring around in a blender. "I just need—"

"Fee! Fee!" Ellie's cry cuts through the monitor on my dresser, getting louder with each shout. "Pi! Up!"

Piper and I freeze, staring at each other, and the king-size guest bed might as well be an ocean between us.

"I need to..."

"Go get her."

I head for the door, then turn back. "Piper—"

"Go," she says softly. "We can talk more later. After you've had time to *process*."

I nod, even though I have no idea what I'm going to say when "later" comes. My entire world just shifted on its axis, and I'm not sure which way is up anymore.

I grab a T-shirt from the dresser on my way out the door and head down the hall to Ellie's room. She's standing in her crib, holding onto the rail, her face red and tear-streaked.

"Fee!" She reaches for me with those cute, chubby hands.

"I've got you, munchkin." I lift her out and settle her against my chest. She immediately burrows in, her tears soaking into my shirt.

"Bad dweam," she mumbles into my neck.

"It's okay, Bean." For now, anyway. I carry her downstairs as I grasp at answers to help me figure out what the hell I'm supposed to do now.

I'm going to be a father, a role I never expected to play. But now that it's happening, I can't stop thinking about what it means. I'm not just going to be a toddler's temporary guardian, but an actual dad to a tiny baby who's half me and half Piper. The thought terrifies me.

But there's also something else underneath the panic. It feels almost like...hope.

I'm in the kitchen, Ellie on my hip as I put together breakfast with shaking hands, when Piper appears. She's still wearing my Grizzlies T-shirt with pajama pants covering those gorgeous legs. Her hair is down around her shoulders, and she looks pale. Exhausted. And more beautiful than any woman I've ever seen. My chest does something complicated that I don't bother to try to understand. All I know is Piper Hart has changed everything.

"Hey," I say.

"Hey." She moves toward the fridge. "Want me to make eggs?"

"Are you going to eat them?"

She rolls her eyes. "Not when there's leftover focaccia."

"Hart, come on. You need to—"

The sound of a car door slamming cuts me off, followed by voices out the open window above the sink. Familiar voices.

Oh, hell no.

The front door opens, and my brother's voice booms through the cabin. "Wakey-wakey, sis-in-law."

"You're going to piss her off if you wake her," Sadie chides, but there's laughter in her tone.

Piper's eyes go wide as saucers. "This can't be happening."

"Pip loves me," Ian answers with his usual confidence.

"Fuck," I mutter, then quickly amend at Ellie's curious stare, "Fudge. Fudge fudge fudge."

Sadie and Ian round the corner into the kitchen and stop dead in their tracks. The two of them glance from Ellie in my arms to

Piper in my T-shirt, and I can only imagine the rumpled, morning-after scene we must present.

Sadie's eyes go wide. "Oh, my God."

"It's not what it looks like," Piper says, which might be the worst thing she could say, because it's exactly what it looks like.

Ian's eyebrows climb toward his hairline as he looks from me to Piper and back again. "Then what is it?"

My mouth opens and closes. For possibly the first time in my life, I'm completely speechless. Piper looks like she might pass out or throw up again. Maybe both. And this is about to be a very different conversation than the one we were supposed to finish.

13

PIPER

FORTY-FIVE MINUTES and copious amounts of sibling side-eye later, my sister and I are taking a short hike on the trail behind the cabin. This much-needed (by me, at least) nature break is quiet except for our footsteps crunching on pine needles and the sounds of birds and squirrels doing their woodland creature thing in the trees overhead.

Beast—Sadie and Ian's so-ugly-he's-cute rescue mutt—leads the way, and watching him prance down the trail like he's the king of the forest makes me miss Max and his furry version of unconditional love. We're walking at an easy pace after my previous issue hiking. Following Sadie feels steady and familiar, and as some of the stress I've been carrying this morning eases, I'm grateful she suggested we get out of the house.

Give the boys time to talk, she'd said. Which really means give Felix and Ian space to have whatever conversation brothers need to have when one of them drops a bomb about suddenly becoming a guardian to a toddler.

There was a crap ton of tension in the kitchen this morning after that revelation, with Felix defensive and Ian obviously pissed at not being told about Ellie. Then another round of morning sickness hit, which upset both Sadie and Felix, but I had to hide it because Ellie isn't the only thing Ian doesn't know about yet. And the sweet girl picked up on the strain and somehow decided all of it was Ian's fault. She burst into tears when his deep voice rose, and it took both Felix and me to calm her down.

"Do you think they're okay?" I glance back toward the cabin even though we can't see it through the trees.

Sadie adjusts her ponytail, her blonde hair shining in the late morning sunlight filtering through the forest. "They'll be fine. I think he's most upset that Felix didn't tell him."

I kick at a rock on the trail. "Felix is trying to find someone from Julie's family to take Ellie permanently, someone more equipped to raise a child than he is."

"Yeah." Sadie's voice goes soft. "That sounds like Felix."

"What do you mean?"

She pauses and reaches out to press her palm against the trunk of a pine tree, as if the rough bark can answer that question. "Things weren't easy for Ian and Felix growing up. You know some of it. But their parents..." She shakes her head. "There were a lot of lies and secrets. Their mom and dad hated each other, and the boys ended up as collateral damage in the divorce. It affected both of them, more than either wants to admit."

I rub two fingers against my suddenly aching chest. "That's awful." Though it explains some of Felix's doubts about raising Ellie.

"They don't talk about it much." Beast gives a little bark like *keep it moving*, and Sadie starts walking again. "But Ian's shared some of what happened. Their parents didn't fight over custody. They fought over who got a *break* from custody, as if the boys were a burden to be passed back and forth instead of children to be loved."

"Jesus."

"And then Felix..." She looks over her shoulder at me, her expression troubled. "Under all those muscles and tattoos beats the heart of a golden retriever who keeps getting dumped on the side of the road by someone he thought was his person. He's been left three times, Piper. And Ronnie cheated on him with Russ, who was supposed to be his friend as well as his teammate." Sadie shakes her head. "It really did a number on him. Ian says Felix doesn't believe he's capable of being enough for anyone long-term. He's decided women break up with him because they know he'll eventually let them down the way their dad always did."

I swallow hard, remembering the vulnerable look on Felix's face this morning when I told him about the baby. It was more than shock, and different than anger that I'd kept it from him. Now I wonder if I was seeing a glimpse of that golden retriever scared of being hurt again.

"But he has so much to give," I say quietly. "If he could just see that."

"I know." Sadie brushes a strand of hair out of her face. "And I think deep down, he does too. He just doesn't trust himself not to screw it up. Being left—first by their parents, who made it crystal clear neither of them wanted the responsibility, then by three women he loved—it messed him up. Ian says some guys can't adjust to real life once their career ends. They've spent so long being defined by football that they don't know who they are without it. And Felix..." She sighs. "Felix is scared that when football ends, there won't be anything left worth keeping."

"That's not true."

"We know that. But Felix doesn't. Not yet, anyway."

We walk in silence for a while, the trail winding through the forest. The nausea hasn't returned, and even though my legs are already tired, I need to keep moving. Moving is helping me process everything that's happened in the past few hours.

"I hope he changes his mind," I say finally. "About Ellie."

"Me too." Sadie squeezes my arm. "He just needs time to get out of his own way."

"What if he doesn't? What if he really believes someone else would be better for her?"

"Then that's his choice to make." Sadie's voice is gentle but firm. "You can't force someone to see their own worth, Pip. They have to figure it out themselves."

I think about how Felix has been with Ellie since that first night at the cabin. The way he reads to her and makes her smile. Stays up late researching toddler development. He's already a good father. He just doesn't know it yet.

"Can I ask you something?" Sadie's voice breaks into my thoughts.

"Sure."

"Why did you agree to nanny for Felix?"

The question catches me off guard. "What do you mean?"

"I mean…" She gives me a sideways look. "You don't even like him. Or at least, I thought you didn't. Why didn't you come home when he got here?"

I don't answer right away. The truth is complicated and messy, and I'm not sure I can explain it in a way that makes sense.

"Piper. What's going on?" Sadie's studying me more closely now. "If that scene in the kitchen this morning was any indication—"

My face flames. "It's not…we're not…the baby is Felix's."

Sadie stops dead in her tracks, staring at me with wide eyes. I suddenly remember being thirteen years old and getting caught egging the math teacher's house with my friends. I seriously considered running away and joining the circus instead of having to face my sister, and the urge now is just as strong. Except I have no talents that would be applicable in the circus ring.

"That can't be true," Sadie says, sounding even more stunned than she looks, if that's possible.

"The baby is Felix's," I repeat, and now that I've said it, I can't stop. "We ran into each other in Denver in April. I was at a bachelorette party, he was celebrating signing with the Grizzlies, and we..." I gesture helplessly. "We were drunk. We slept together. And I got pregnant."

Sadie's mouth opens and closes several times. "But you said... When you called the book club meeting to tell us, you said it was a one-night stand with someone you'd never see again."

"I know, and I lied." I wrap my arms around myself, suddenly cold despite the warm morning. "I'm sorry, Sadie. I couldn't tell you the truth. Not then."

"Why?"

"Because I'm a terrible sister!" The words burst out of me. "You gave up everything to take care of me when Mom died, and I didn't appreciate it. I was embarrassed by your dog training business. I was a brat, and then I got engaged to Bradley—the guy you had a crush on—and I just assumed you'd be fine with it and I ignored the fact that he's a complete asshat and now—"

"Piper, stop."

Only I can't. The dam is broken, and the words just keep on flowing. "I'm pregnant by Ian's brother, and I know you guys are trying to get pregnant and it's not... You shouldn't have to support me through one more thing, Sads. You've done too much already, and you should hate me for—"

She grabs my shoulders, her grip firm. "Stop talking and listen to me."

I snap my mouth shut, blinking back tears. Beast trots over and headbutts my shin.

"You were twelve when Mom died," she says, her voice gentle. "We both lost her."

"But you had to raise me—"

"And I wouldn't change that for anything." Her eyes are fierce now. "Yes, it was hard. Yes, I gave up some things. But I never resented you, Piper. Not once. You were—you are—my sister. My family. Taking care of you wasn't a sacrifice. It was a privilege."

The tears spill over, and I don't bother to wipe them away. "I wasn't any better once I grew up. I'm still selfish. Bradley—"

"Is a dick," Sadie cuts in. "Yeah, I had a crush on him in high school. A crush, Pip. But he did us both a favor by showing his true colors before you married him. I would have figured it out eventually, too, if we'd dated. He's not a good person."

"What about the baby?" My voice cracks. "You and Ian are trying, and here I am, knocked up from a one-night stand."

"First of all," Sadie says, "I'm going to be an aunt. Do you have any idea how excited I am?"

"But you're not—"

"Ian and I will add to our family when the time is right. Sure, sometimes it's frustrating." She swipes at her own eyes. "But that has nothing to do with you or your baby. We aren't keeping score. I'm not going to sit around being bitter because you got pregnant and we haven't yet. That's not how love works."

"I just..." I shake my head, trying to find the words. "I feel like everything I touch turns into a mess. First, I was engaged to a guy you liked, then I got myself pregnant by Ian's brother—"

"You're not a mess." She pulls me into a hug. "And even if you were, I'd love you anyway."

"You can't deny that I was a brat."

"So are most kids, and they don't have to deal with losing their only parent. You need to stop carrying this guilt around like it's a badge of honor. You were allowed to be a mess. You're still allowed to make mistakes without thinking you owe me some kind of debt."

"But I do owe you—"

"You don't." Her voice is firm. "Stop being so damn hard on yourself and start living your life. Make choices for you, not because you're worried about what I think or how it affects me."

We stand on the trail, her arms wrapped around my shoulders, for a long moment. And I realize she's right. I need to figure out my own life.

If only I knew how to do that.

"What am I going to do?" I whisper as I return her embrace. "About Felix and the baby."

"What do you want to do?"

"I don't know." That's the truth. "I stayed here because I wanted to see what kind of father he'd be with Ellie. To understand if..."

"If he could be a good father to your baby?"

"Sort of." I wipe the back of my hand under my dripping nose. "But it's more complicated than that. And it got even more complicated last night. We slept together again, and then this morning I told him about the baby."

Sadie's eyebrows shoot up. "*After* you slept with him?"

"Not the best choice," I admit with a watery laugh. "I guess I thought things were changing for him, but he's still talking about finding Ellie a different family. And I can't—" My voice breaks. "I don't want to be with someone who's looking for the exit before he's even walked through the door."

"Did you tell him that?"

I pull back. "Not yet. This morning was a lot. Even before you and Ian showed up."

"Then that's where you start." Sadie links her arm through mine again, and we turn back toward the cabin. "Tell him what you need and give him a chance to show you who he is instead of assuming you already know."

Can I do that? Do I even know what I need? "What if I tell him and he can't give it to me?"

"At least you'll know." Her voice is gentle. "Then you figure it out from there. You're stronger than you think, Pip."

"I don't feel strong."

"The best things in life are usually hard," Sadie says. "But they're almost always worth it in the end."

"Do you ever get sick of being so annoyingly perfect?" I ask, elbowing her gently.

She pretends to consider the question. "Not really."

We walk in silence after that, and by the time we reach the cabin, I'm exhausted but also oddly clearer about what comes next. Maybe talking to Felix won't be quite as terrifying as I thought.

Or maybe it'll be worse. I guess I'm about to find out.

14

PIPER

FELIX AND IAN are in a standoff when we walk back into the kitchen—there's no other word for it. Two football gods going toe-to-toe, all that strength and gridiron power vibrating between them. The testosterone in the room could choke a donkey.

Ellie's nowhere to be seen, which means Felix managed to get her down for her nap despite how agitated she was for most of the morning. Small miracles and all that.

Ian is obviously pissed. His shoulders are about as relaxed as granite, and the way his jaw is clenched so tight, I'm surprised his teeth don't crack. Felix looks just as irritated, probably because he thinks Ian is acting like a know-it-all pain in the ass, which could be the purview of older siblings everywhere.

This is some gladiator-coded shit, and I kind of hate that I find it hot.

"I have something to say." My voice cuts through whatever silent battle they're waging.

Felix's deep blue gaze flicks to me, and he starts to take a step closer. "You don't have to—"

"I do." I hold up a hand. "I'm done with secrets."

Sadie moves to Ian's side, placing a hand on his arm. "You need to listen without reacting."

Ian's eyes narrow, but he nods. Then he looks at me with his big-brother smile, the one that's gotten me through more hard moments than I can count in the past year. "You can tell me anything, Pip."

The words stick in my throat for a second, but I take a breath and let them out. "I'm pregnant." My voice sounds steadier than I expected. "And Felix is the father."

All three of us watch Ian, whose face goes through about seventeen emotions in three seconds. Shock. Confusion. A glare at Felix. Understanding. More shock. And then, finally, something that looks almost like acceptance.

He glances at Sadie, who confirms it with a nod. Then he walks to me and pulls me into a hug.

"Congratulations, Piper," he says into my hair, his voice calm and steady. "You're going to be an amazing mom. Anything you need, I'm here for you."

"Thank you," I whisper, emotion clogging my throat. Even more than Sadie, Ian's support makes me feel like I'm not alone in all of this. I'm also impressed that he's taking it so well. Maybe even a little suspicious about how well.

He releases me, walks directly to Felix, and punches him in the face.

Felix staggers back, hand flying to his cheek. "The fuck, Ian?"

I gasp and take a step forward, but Sadie grabs my wrist. "Let them figure it out," she says quietly enough that only I can hear. Not that either Barlowe brother is paying a lick of attention to us at the moment.

"That's for messing with my sister-in-law." Ian shakes out his hand, wincing. "Jesus, your face is like concrete."

"I hope you broke your jackass knuckles." Felix massages his jaw as if testing whether it still works. "For the record, she's *your* sister-in-law, not mine. And I didn't mess with her. We—"

"I know what you did." Ian flexes his fingers. "And now she's pregnant."

"I'm aware."

"After telling everyone at Christmas you never wanted kids." Then, Ian's lips twitch. "Fucking concrete."

Felix touches his jaw again. "Serves you right. Feel better?'

"Much." Ian claps him on the shoulder, the gesture somehow both affectionate and threatening. "But if you hurt her—"

"I won't."

"You'd better take care of her."

"I will," Felix promises, his eyes flashing as they meet mine.

"I can take care of myself," I mutter, pretty sure I'm convincing no one.

My sister moves to her husband's side. "Is your hand okay?"

"Better than Felix's face."

Felix snorts. "My face is fine."

"It's swelling," Sadie tells him.

"Your husband has a decent right hook for a guy who used to throw a football on occasion."

"Quarterbacks have strong hands," Ian says mildly. "It's kind of our thing."

As I watch this insane exchange between two overgrown children in adult bodies, something bubbles up in my chest that might be laughter. Or maybe it's hysteria. Either way, it spills out before I can swallow it back.

Three pairs of eyes land on me. "Did you seriously just punch your brother for getting me pregnant?" I ask Ian.

"Yes," he answers. "I'll do it again if you want."

"Hey," Felix protests.

"No," I say at the same time. "How does that help the situation?"

"It doesn't, but it made me feel better." Ian grins, apparently satisfied with his unnecessary defense of my honor. "And it put him on notice in case he hurts—"

"I'm not going to hurt her," Felix grumbles.

"Then we're good." Ian wraps an arm around Sadie's shoulder. "We should go."

"You guys can stay," Felix says quickly. "It's your house."

"Right," I agree. "Felix and I can—"

"We just came up to check on Piper," Sadie interrupts, giving me a meaningful look. "You've been weird in your texts. Not answering calls."

"Now we know why," Ian adds with a smirk that earns him an elbow from Sadie.

"We'll get out of your hair," Sadie continues. "I'm guessing you two have some things to talk through."

The thought makes my lungs feel like they're being squeezed in giant NFL player hands. "It's an hour and a half back home," I protest weakly. "You should stay."

"We're fine." Sadie walks forward and pulls me in for another hug. "Call me later." She lowers her voice and says against my ear, "Remember, you're stronger than you think."

I don't feel strong at the moment. I feel weak and overwhelmed. And like I just want to sit on the couch and eat my weight in sourdough.

Ian gives Felix one more warning look—the kind only an older brother can pull off—before scooping up Beast and following Sadie to the door.

Then they're gone, and it's just me and Felix in the kitchen, the silence so loud that it almost hurts my ears.

There's a red mark blooming across his cheek. "That's going to bruise. You need some ice or a pack of frozen peas."

One corner of his mouth lifts. "I'll survive."

"You didn't deserve it."

"Oh, I definitely deserved it." He meets my eyes. "We should talk."

"Yeah." My arms wrap around myself automatically. "We should."

But neither of us moves, and the space between us feels like endless miles I don't know how to cross. Not when I'm afraid anything I say could heighten the awkwardness between us.

"This morning was...um..." Felix runs a hand through his perpetually tousled hair. "A lot."

I choke out a small laugh. "That's one way to put it."

"Especially since neither of us got much sleep." His eyes darken slightly, and I feel heat creep up my neck.

I don't answer. I'm not sure I can without revealing what last night meant to me. And I'm sure as hell not ready for that. What would I even say? 'Yeah, last night was amazing. And by the way, I'm already halfway in love with you and terrified that our baby is going to be born into a situation where their father is looking for an exit strategy?'

Felix frowns at my silence, then tilts his head. "I think I heard Ellie."

I glance at the monitor on the counter, which is not making a sound. "I don't hear anything."

"I definitely heard her." He's already moving toward the stairs. "I should check. She had a rough morning, too."

"I can do that," I say, moving to follow him. "I'm the nanny, remember?"

He stops moving, back to me and shoulders rigid. When he turns around, his expression is neutral in a way I'm coming to recognize—one that means he's pissed. "Despite what some people think, I'm capable of handling my responsibilities."

"I never said you can't."

"Can't or won't? Which one is worse, Hart?"

I take a step back, cowed by the ferocity in his tone. "Felix—"

"But I will, and I am. I'm taking care of Ellie because she's my responsibility. At least for now."

He turns and heads upstairs, leaving me alone in the kitchen with the echo of "for now" ringing in my ears.

I sink onto one of the barstools, my hand automatically going to my stomach.

For now.

That's what terrifies me most, isn't it? That we—my baby and I—will fall into the same category as Ellie. A temporary responsibility he's managing until he can find a way out or pass us off.

My sister had no relationship with her father after he made it clear his new wife and kids were his priority. She was still only a kid when he pushed her out of his life. I saw the damage that kind of inconsistency caused and figured I was better off never knowing my dad. I also swore I'd never put a child of mine through the hell of being with someone who saw parenthood as an obligation rather than a gift.

But here I am, pregnant by a man who's made it crystal clear he doesn't want to be a father and is actively searching for a way to rehome the little girl upstairs—the one he's so sweet and tender with and who clearly adores him. If he can walk away from sweet Ellie, who lights up when her Uncle "Fee" enters a room, what makes me think he won't eventually walk away from our baby, too?

From me?

I press my palms against my eyes, fighting back tears I refuse to shed. I have to be smarter than this. It's time to protect myself and my baby from the inevitable hurt that's coming. Felix Barlowe wants me, that's a given. Hell, he might even care about me.

But wanting someone and choosing them and the life they come with are two very different things.

And I'm terrified he's never going to choose us.

15

FELIX

I'm elbow-deep in flour at five in the morning, only to realize I'm taking my frustrations out on a ball of dough that never did a damn thing to me.

The rest of the house is dark, which fits my mood. Outside the kitchen window, there's nothing but the faint outline of mountains against the pre-dawn sky. Inside, it's just me, my thoughts, and the pummeled dough.

I force myself to ease up. Bread responds to careful handling, not unjustified aggression. Kind of like relationships, I guess. Not that I'm an expert on those.

Yesterday was a clusterfuck of epic proportions, from my brother finding out about Ellie to me finding out about the baby. Then getting punched in the face—which, fair. And the cherry on top of the shit show sundae? Piper going upstairs for a nap only to return two hours later, sleep-rumpled and looking at me as if the father of her child is a problem she needs to solve.

Our child.

The thought hasn't stopped making my heart do funny things.

I start kneading with a gentler hand, folding the dough over itself in the rhythmic pattern I perfected during months of late-night baking sessions. Push, fold, turn. Over and over. It's meditative in a way nothing else is. Sourdough takes control and patience, which I'm not exactly known for in other areas of my life.

The worst part of yesterday wasn't Ian's right hook, although it's been years since I was clocked that hard. But that punch didn't land as hard as the look on Piper's face when I said Ellie was my responsibility "for now." Apparently, I confirmed every fear she's carrying about me and proved I'm exactly the kind of man she thought. One who makes an exit strategy before the game even starts.

Maybe she's right. But who can blame me with my track record? Three serious relationships and three times getting my heart stomped on. My parents hated each other, and made damn sure Ian and I knew raising us was a major inconvenience. Why would anyone think I'll be any different as a father?

I want to be different for Piper and the baby. Hell, maybe even for Ellie, who's totally oblivious to all of this. Well, not totally. She definitely caught onto the tension yesterday. And I have to admit, it was hilarious watching my golden-god older brother try to win over a pint-sized female who was having none of his patented charm.

Damn if I didn't love that. The sweet girl is impossible to resist, and I'm already in love with her. But love isn't enough.

I shape the dough into a ball and place it in the proofing bowl, covering it with a damp towel. Now comes the hard part—having the patience to let the magic happen without interference.

"I guess I'm not the only one who can't sleep."

I nearly jump out of my skin. Piper stands at the edge of the kitchen wearing one of my T-shirts, this one from Cincinnati, which means she went into my room and took it—baller fucking move—and sleep shorts that showcase her long legs in a way that makes me need to adjust my own. Her hair is loose and tangled, and once again it's confirmed: she's the most beautiful woman I've ever seen. I can't imagine a world where that ever changes.

My heart starts doing that stupid hammering thing it does whenever she's close. Jesus, I've got it bad.

"Not sleeping, so..." I wipe my hands on the towel and try to look like I'm not freaking the fuck out about all of this. "Thought I'd make some bread."

"At five in the morning?"

"No distractions." Except now she's here, and she's the only thing I can think about. "You feeling okay? How's the morning sickness?"

"I'm fine so far." She moves closer, shimmying her hips. "So the Filsbury Dough Boy rides at dawn?"

It takes me a second to realize she's trying to make a joke because...Christ, those hips. It's about the bread and catching me stress-baking at dawn like some kind of certifiable housewife. But I'm too raw for jokes right now, and too scared of saying the wrong thing and making everything worse.

"I want to be a father," I tell her quietly, forcing out the words before I'm too chicken shit to say them. "There's a good chance I might suck at it, but I want to try. Even if the only support you want from me is financial, you've got it. You don't ever have to work again."

The temperature in the room drops about twenty degrees.

Piper's eyes go from soft to icy so fast I get whiplash. "Excuse me?"

That part about how I was afraid I'd say something stupid? Nailed it.

"I just mean—"

"Do you think I'm looking for a sugar daddy, Felix?" Her voice could cut glass. "Is that what this is? You throw money at me and I go away?"

"That's not what I meant—"

"Or do you think I got pregnant on purpose?" She takes a step toward me, and even though I dwarf her in size, I feel like I'm being backed into a corner. "That I was trying to trap you?"

"Jesus, Piper, no." I run both hands through my hair, making it stand up in directions that probably match my stress level. "Of course, I don't think that."

"Then what are you saying?"

"I'm saying I want to take care of you. Both of you. Fucking sue me, but I thought that's what men were supposed to do when they get someone pregnant, right? Take care of the—"

"If you say problem," she seethes through gritted teeth, "I'm going to make Ian's punch feel like a love tap."

"I wasn't going to say problem."

"I don't need you to be my personal ATM."

"When you put it like that—"

"How else should I put it, Felix?" She crosses her arms, and I try very hard not to notice how the movement showcases those gorgeous tits.

"I don't know, but this isn't like..." I take a breath, trying to find the right words. "Come on, Hart. You know I'm not angling to be your sugar daddy. Christ, if we were in that kind of relationship, you'd be a lot more accommodating—"

She swats my arm then growls low in her throat, kind of like a feral cat. And I'm shocked to find feral cat kink might be my thing, which is not helpful right now.

"This is not going the way I thought it would." I hold up both hands in surrender. "But I fucking promise that I don't think you were trying to trap me. I don't feel trapped. I feel shocked still, yeah, but I'm going to figure it out."

"Sooner than later, I hope," she murmurs and takes a step away.

She doesn't sound like she believes in me, and honestly, I don't blame her. How the hell am I supposed to be a father when I can barely get my thoughts out in any sort of coherent manner?

"While you figure it out, or process or whatever you need to do, I've made a decision." She opens the fridge and pulls out the orange juice and the container of leftover focaccia. "About what I'm doing next."

Relief floods through me. "Thank God."

She arches a brow, and I have a feeling I'm not going to like what's coming. "I'm going home."

The words hit me harder than my brother's right hook. "You can't."

"I have things to figure out," she says as she slices a thick piece of bread and slides it onto a plate. "Not just with you and me, but for myself."

I want to argue, to tell her she can figure things out here with me, but something in her expression stops me.

"When I graduated college," she continues, pouring a glass of juice and then taking a seat at the island, "I moved to Kansas City because a friend from nursing school invited me to live with her and got me a job at the hospital. I didn't have to take care of anything. Then I started dating Bradley because I knew him, and it was easy. When my friend decided to become a traveling nurse, it was easy to move into Bradley's house." She pauses, worrying her bottom lip as she gazes at a place beyond my shoulder. "When the wedding didn't work out, I moved back to Skylark, and Sadie transferred the deed of our childhood home to me."

"Piper—"

"And when I found out I was pregnant and saw Bradley right after that, I ran away to this cabin." She finally looks at me, and the determination in her eyes makes my chest ache. "Do you see a theme here, Barlowe? I let other people make things easy for me."

"That's not a bad thing—"

"I'm twenty-three, and I want to stand on my own."

"Jesus fucking Christ." The words slip out before I can stop them. "I forgot how young you are."

"I'm not a baby." Her eyes flash. "Even though I let people treat me like one."

"I'm nearly a decade older than you." That age gap suddenly feels massive, another reason I'm all wrong for her.

"So is my sister."

"Yeah, well, she didn't get you pregnant."

"Can your premature midlife crisis take a backseat for a minute?" She rolls those gorgeous eyes, and despite everything, I feel my lips twitch.

"What about the baby?"

"He or she is tucked away for seven more months. We have plenty of time to work out an arrangement."

An arrangement? I hate how sterile and detached that word sounds. "What about Ellie? I mean, I know you don't owe her anything or—"

"I was thinking I could take her with me."

My jaw actually drops. "She's my responsibility."

"Yes, I know. I'm not trying to take your place." Piper's voice softens. "But I need to go back today. The book club is meeting, and I want to see my friends. I want to sleep in my own bed, even if it's in a house that doesn't truly feel like it belongs to me. This is La La Land up here."

"Not exactly La La Land."

"Maybe not for you. You're training every day, working toward something. You have a purpose." She wraps her arms around herself. "I need to figure out who I am outside of being someone's sister or someone's ex-fiancée or someone's nanny and baby mama."

Everything she's saying makes sense, but I hate the idea of her leaving. Hate that I'm part of the pattern she's trying to break.

"I'll pay you," I blurt out. "Double your nursing salary to stay."

"Stop trying to buy me off." Her voice goes sharp again. "It makes me feel cheap."

I nearly laugh at that. Piper Hart has no idea what she's costing me, and I don't mean financially. But I'm smart enough not to say it.

"I'll go with you," I offer instead.

She scoffs. "You've got your whole setup here. You've got Tyler."

"Tyler will go wherever I am. And Ellie's staying with me, but she likes you, and I trust you. You can keep being her nanny while we both figure our shit out."

She studies me for a while, and I expect her to say no. "Would you stay with Ian and Sadie?" she asks softly, and it feels so much like a victory that I nearly break out my end zone dance.

"Hell, no." I shake my head. "I love my brother, but I don't need him up my ass on the daily."

By this point, the first rays of morning light are starting to creep through the window, turning the sky from gray to shades of deep purple and pink.

"I'll rent a house," I continue. "One for me and Ellie, one for Tyler. We'll find a gym to use."

"Felix." Her smile is sweet, almost hesitant, and my heart starts to gallop in response. "My mom's house—my house," she corrects herself, "has three bedrooms. You've been there when it was Sadie's. It's not fancy or full of expensive gym equipment, but being together in one place would make the logistics one less thing either of us has to deal with."

"Now who's taking care of who?" I ask, but there's no heat in it.

The space between us is suddenly charged with all the things we have to figure out—together and on our own.

Then we both blurt: "We can't have sex again."

"Exactly," I say.

"Too complicated," she agrees.

I reach across the island to shake on it. Our palms press together, and I can't help but think about pulling her closer. Except, nope. *Way* too complicated. I force myself to release her and pretend to adjust the towel covering the proofing bowl. "You just want me for my bread."

She rolls her eyes but laughs at the joke. "You might be right."

I'll fucking bake like it's my full-time job if that's what she needs.

"I should start packing," she says as she stands. "I need to head down this morning to make the meeting."

"Sure." I grab her empty plate and juice glass. "Ellie and I will follow."

What I want to say is, now that our baby's involved, I'll follow her anywhere. Skylark. Vail. Timbuktu. Doesn't matter, as long as we're together.

But that sounds stalkerish and desperate. And I learned my lesson—three times over—about being too needy.

She starts to leave, then turns back. "For what it's worth, I think your face looks better with a little character."

I press two fingers to the impressive bruise Ian left on my jaw. "Thanks, Hart."

"Anytime, Barlowe."

I watch her head upstairs and wonder if just maybe we're going to figure this out after all. Or if we're just going to keep finding new and creative ways to make this harder than it needs to be.

With Piper and me, it could go either way.

I fill the dishwasher, then start a pot of coffee, the scent of the roasted beans oddly comforting. The dough sits in its bowl, slowly rising in the warmth of the kitchen as dawn breaks through the cabin's windows. The beans and the bread aren't stressed about what comes next. They're just waiting for time to do its work so they can become something better than they started out as.

Maybe there's a lesson in that for me.

16

PIPER

I'VE BEEN SITTING in my Jeep in the parking lot behind Cover to Cover Bookstore for twenty minutes, trying to psych myself up to go in and face my friends.

Well, really, they're Sadie's friends. Although the longer I'm back in Skylark, the more this group—the five other women who make up the book club, along with Sadie—feel like my friends, too. There's Iris Dixon, who, after a short-lived stint as Skylark's mayor, began working for her fiancé's family foundation; local librarian Taylor Maxwell; sassy and brassy marketing expert Avah Harris; single mom and flower farmer Molly McAllister; and Sloane Winslow, Cover to Cover's owner and the one who brought the book club members together in the first place.

Out of all the women, I feel closest to Molly. She's close to my age and also had a habit of letting people take care of her and not making her own decisions. Until recently, when she agreed to volunteer for Sloane's bucket list challenge.

I'm not sure how Sloane knew this group of women would click when she invited them to join the Cool Girls Book Club. But shortly after they started meeting last spring, she was diagnosed with cancer—acute lymphocytic leukemia. She still doesn't like to talk much about it. And although she seems to be doing well now, her prognosis last spring was questionable.

She got the idea for the bucket list challenge after the group read a part self-improvement, part-memoir book called *The Year of Losing It*. Sloane is determined to have the author visit the group as a guest, but Kristen Quinn hasn't responded to any of the messages members of the group have sent her. And since I started following her online, I've noticed that her more recent feed seems to be recycled posts or faceless quotes.

Either way, her book about spending a year doing things that scared her in order to embrace life and lose fear resonated deeply with Sloane.

The bucket list is what initially brought my sister and Ian together. She decided she wanted a fake boyfriend to bring to my wedding to Bradley. And, unbeknownst to me, Sadie also had a mission to lose her V-card.

Yep, in addition to robbing my sister of her dream of going to vet school, our mother's death and having to come home and raise me also threw a huge wrench in her dating life. So huge that it wasn't until Ian Barlowe that she popped the old cherry. But it worked out in the end.

In fact, things have worked out for every member of the group who's taken the challenge. And I'm so grateful they added me to their cool-girl fold when I moved back.

Oh, sure, I have high school friends still in town. In fact, I'm attending the wedding of my former bestie in a couple of weeks. But somehow, I don't fit with who I used to be.

And I'm not sure of who I want to become.

My phone dings with an incoming text. It's from Avah.

Avah: We think you're being held captive.

Avah and I both have strong opinions, and we aren't afraid to share them. I think we also both use humor and sarcasm as defense mechanisms, but neither of us is likely to admit that out loud.

> Avah: Sloane refuses to begin discussing the book until every one of us is present.

> Me: Not sure I'm going to make it. Traffic coming down Floyd Hill. And I didn't finish the book.

My phone rings a minute later—Avah again.

"It's not a big deal."

"Of course not. Also, you'd make a terrible criminal. The window in the bookstore's meeting room looks out to the parking lot."

I glance up and see Sadie and Molly waving at me. Avah, cell phone pressed to her ear, gives me the finger.

"Okay, I'm coming," I tell her with a sigh. Clearly I'm distracted if I didn't realize they could see me sitting here.

I disconnect and slap a smile on my face as I grab the container of brownies I bought at a bakery on my way out of Vail. These ladies already know about the baby. I called an emergency book club meeting when I couldn't stop freaking out after I found out.

I still haven't told any of my high school or college friends, which says something I prefer not to examine about the state of those relationships.

The familiar bookstore smell greets me as the bells above the door chime. It's a mix of paper, coffee, and whatever candle Sloane has burning today. Lavender, I think.

I wave to the woman at the register and head toward the back, Molly immediately bouncing up to hug me as I enter the meeting room. "You're here. How was the cabin?"

"Eventful," I murmur.

Sadie breathes out a soft laugh. "That's one way to put it."

I shoot her a look and place the brownies on the table that's already covered with snacks.

"Tell me these are from Sweet Surrender," Iris says, immediately reaching for one.

"Only the best for the cool girls." I manage to hold my smile in place and sink into the empty chair, trying to calm my nerves.

"Now that we're all here," Sloane says, settling into her usual spot and pulling out the book we're supposed to have read, "let's talk about this month's selection. Overall impressions?"

"I loved it," Taylor says. "The way the author wove the true crime elements with the fictional narrative was masterful."

"I thought the ending was predictable," Avah counters. "I knew who the killer was by chapter three."

"Not everyone did," Molly says mildly. "I was genuinely surprised."

"That's because you were too busy hoping the detective and the witness would get together," Avah points out.

Molly grins. "There was undeniable chemistry."

"Barely," Avah scoffs. "Like two sentences of chemistry."

"Sometimes that's enough to start," Iris says with a grin, and everyone laughs.

I try to focus on the conversation, but my mind keeps drifting to Felix and Ellie, who are arriving later this afternoon. He texted an hour ago that they were almost packed up. My house—my empty, too-quiet-without-Max house—is about to become a lot less empty.

I don't know if I'm ready for that. Or any of this, if I'm being totally honest.

"Piper?" Sloane's voice breaks through my thoughts. "You with us?"

"Sorry. What?"

"It's okay that you didn't get through the whole thing," she says gently, as if she can sense my emotional upheaval. If only it involved something as simple as an unfinished book.

"I meant to," I admit. "I got about halfway before everything kind of exploded."

"Exploded how?" Iris asks, leaning forward with interest.

"You aren't talking about your newly returned ex, right?" Avah eyes me over the rim of her coffee mug. "You can't give a douche canoe that kind of power over you."

This is it. The moment I've been dreading and needing in equal measure.

"No." I shake my head as Sadie reaches out from her seat next to me to squeeze my arm. "This isn't about Bradley. But before we get into that..." I take a deep breath. "I want to volunteer for the bucket list challenge."

"Yaasss, queen." Sloane applauds, then glances at Avah. "Your turn is coming."

Avah scrunches up her nose. "Maybe I'm in line behind you."

"You can't rush the cancer patient," Sloane says sweetly.

"Well played," Avah says with a smirk. "Again."

"Thank you." Sloane's grin is unapologetic. "Back to our newest member and latest bucket list volunteer."

"Victim," Avah mutters under a fake cough, making some of the tension inside me ease.

Molly pops a bite of brownie into her mouth. "What do you want to do, Pip?"

"I want to learn to stand on my own two feet." The words come out steadier than I expected. "I want to stop relying on other people to take care of me, or to make things easy for me. I want to figure out who I am when I'm not a little sister or an ex-fiancée or someone's..." I trail off, doing my damndest to avoid eye contact.

"Someone's what?" Taylor asks gently.

I glance at Sadie, who gives me an encouraging nod. I need her support right now.

"Someone's baby mama," I finish. It feels like my throat is coated in sawdust, but I force myself to continue. "Which you already know. What you don't know...is who the father is."

The room goes completely quiet for a few long seconds.

"You said it was a one-night stand," Avah says slowly. "Some random dude from a bar."

"I might have left out some key details. Like the fact that I do know his name and–"

"Who is the father of your baby?" Iris asks slowly.

"Felix Barlowe."

The silence that follows is even louder than before.

"Somebody say something," I insist, squeezing the arms of my chair so hard it's almost painful.

"Ian's brother?" Taylor's voice comes out as almost a squeak.

Avah elbows her. "Do we know any other Felix Barlowes?"

Taylor shakes her head. "But I thought you hated Felix."

"I don't exactly *hate* him," I protest.

"You called him an insufferable meathead when he was here at Christmas," Molly reminds me.

"He was," I agree weakly. "We've always been like oil and water. We don't mix."

"Except you apparently mixed just fine," Iris points out. "One time."

"Twice, actually," I admit before I can stop myself.

The room erupts.

"Twice?"

"When was the second time?"

"Oh my God!"

"Can we please rewind the past thirty seconds?" I plead, covering my face with my hands.

"Not a chance." Molly leans back in her chair with a small smile. "This is way better than a book discussion. Does Felix know about the baby?"

"As of yesterday morning, yes." I release the chair and reach for a brownie, needing something to do. "He's been at the cabin with me, which was a coincidence."

"Wink, wink," Avah says.

"It's true."

Sloane holds up a hand. "Let's stay focused. Felix wants to be involved?"

I nod but don't look at Sadie again. There's no point in explaining that I'm not sure *how* he wants to be involved until he and I work out that part.

"That's good, right?" Taylor asks carefully.

"I think so. I hope so." I swallow the bite of brownie, grateful when my stomach doesn't immediately rebel. "But he also offered me money to keep being his nanny, and it felt like—"

"Whoa, there." Molly holds up a hand. "His nanny? Why does Felix need a nanny?"

"He's helping some friends out," Sadie offers.

I nod. "Taking care of their two-year-old daughter until...well...while his help is needed."

Avah barks out a laugh. "What kind of parents would ask Felix Barlowe to watch their kid?" she asks skeptically. "He's an immature showboat, and one of the league's biggest players."

"He's not a showboat," I snap, surprising myself with how defensive I sound. "He's actually really good with her. Patient and gentle and..."

"Oh wow," Molly murmurs. "You don't hate him. You like him."

"I don't *not* like him," I hedge.

"Which isn't a ringing endorsement for the father of your child," Iris points out.

I set down the brownie. "I don't know what I feel. But he makes me laugh. I know he's thoughtful." Warmth spreads through my chest. "He researched high-altitude nutrition and ordered special meals because I was barely eating. I know he stress-bakes sourdough at five in the morning. He looks at the little girl he's caring for like she hung the moon, even though he's convinced he's going to fail her." I offer a weak smile. "And I know that when he touches me, I forget every reason this is a bad idea."

"Oh," Molly breathes.

"He's also not a player," Sadie adds. "Felix is complicated. But he's not the guy the world thinks he is."

The room is quiet for a moment. Avah taps one manicured finger on the table. "You know how I always say hate sex is the hottest kind?"

"Um...yeah?" I ask, wondering where she's going with this.

"I'm rethinking that." She takes a sip of her drink. "Hate sex isn't all it's cracked up to be, so if this is—"

"It's not hate sex," I insist. "Like I said, we don't hate each other. We're just...we're like fire and gasoline. Sparks fly."

"That's one way to describe it," Sadie murmurs.

"What's the plan for standing on your own two feet?" Taylor asks, getting us back on track. "What does that look like for you?"

"I need a new job," I say firmly, and my sister gives me a nod of encouragement.

"Would you go back to the hospital?" Iris asks.

"Maybe." I cringe slightly. "If I didn't totally burn that bridge. But I don't think I want to go back to the NICU." The admission feels like a weight lifting. "I loved it, but I need something different. Something that doesn't remind me of...before."

"There are always families looking for private nurses," Molly suggests. "That would give you some flexibility in your schedule."

"I'm sure a local private practice would love to have you," Taylor adds.

"Nurses are in high demand," Iris assures me. "We can all ask around. Discreetly until you decide exactly what you want."

"That would be amazing," I say, feeling tears prick at my eyes. Damn hormones. "Thank you."

"That's what friends are for," Sloane says gently. Then she studies me more closely. "How's the morning sickness?"

"It's been better today, actually. I think the altitude was making it worse." I take another bite of brownie. "Carbs help the most. Something about Felix's sourdough settles my stomach in a way nothing else does."

Molly sighs. "A man who looks like Felix Barlowe *and* bakes bread? No wonder you don't hate him."

"It's his stress relief." That warm feeling in my chest spreads through the rest of my body as I think about Felix in the kitchen. "He's really good at it."

"Okay, you're definitely in love," Avah says with a laugh.

"I'm definitely no—" I start, then stop. Am I in love with him? Oh, crap. I might be. Maybe I have been since that night in Denver. Or since he carried me down the mountain. Or since I watched him read the same story to Ellie for the third time because she wanted "mo bunny."

"Oh, Pip," Sadie whispers, reading my mind as always.

"That's why I need this challenge." I dash a hand across my cheeks. "I can't keep letting people make decisions for me. It's tempting to accept whatever Felix is willing to give me. But I need to know I can stand on my own."

"So the challenge is getting a job?" Iris asks, studying me intently.

"Partly," I admit. "But a job that means something to me. One that I can keep doing once the baby comes." I take a breath. "I need to prove to myself that I can do this. That I'm not just jumping from one person taking care of me to another."

"We'll help however we can," Sloane promises, and everyone nods in agreement.

Which I appreciate, even though it would also mean letting them take care of me, which kind of defeats the purpose of my bucket list goal.

"Enough about me," I say, looking at Sloane. "How are you doing? Are you officially finished with treatments?"

Something flickers across her face—a mix of relief and exhaustion—but she smiles. "Yeah, mostly. It's all good."

"Of course it is," Taylor says, and everyone chimes in with our support.

"Fuck cancer," Sloane agrees. "Now can we talk more about the book? I have a rep to protect as a bookstore owner."

We circle back to discuss the thriller more thoroughly. Sadie loved the true-crime media commentary, Avah thought the pacing was off, Molly appreciated the complex female protagonist, and Taylor wished there was more romance. Iris defends her book choice, while I mostly stay quiet, still processing everything.

By the time the meeting winds down, it's after six. We help clean up, packing leftover snacks for Molly to bring home to her twins and Chase. As we head to the parking lot, Avah falls into step beside me.

"Hey," she says quietly. "Can I give you some advice?"

"Sure."

"I meant it when I said hate sex isn't all it's cracked up to be. Or even bordering on angry sex." She pauses, her expression unusually serious. "Neither is being with someone who could hurt you."

"I'm not going to let him break my—"

"I'm not talking about your heart," she interrupts. "Though that too. I'm just...be careful, okay? Make sure you're not just seeing what you want to see."

I stop walking, studying her face in the golden hour parking lot light. "Avah, is everything okay with you and Jonathan?"

Her expression shutters immediately, and the bright smile returns. "Everything's peachy keen. We're still planning to elope in August and then go on the most epic beach honeymoon."

I don't believe her. There's something in her eyes—not exactly fear, but I can't quite identify the emotion. I do know it doesn't match her words.

"If you ever need—"

"This isn't about me, Pip. Really." She pulls me into a quick hug. "Focus on yourself and that baby. And then Felix. Figure out what you want, not what you think you should want."

Before I can press further, she's gone, heading to her car with a wave.

I stand there for a moment, confused and concerned. But then my sister appears beside me, linking her arm through mine.

"You okay?" she asks.

"Yeah," I say, even though I'm not entirely sure. "Just processing."

"Ian's smoking ribs. Want to come over?"

I shake my head. "Thanks, but I need to get home. Felix texted. He and Ellie are at the house."

Sadie squeezes my arm. "Call me if you need anything. I mean it."

"I know. Thank you."

I hug her tight, then make my way to my Jeep. The drive home takes less than ten minutes. My house sits on a quiet street, and I pull into the driveway and sit for a moment.

Max's absence hits me all over again—the way he'd bark when I pulled up and meet me at the door with his whole body wiggling.

The house has felt so empty without him. It's empty and sad and like a place I'm just passing through.

But tonight, it isn't empty. Tonight, Felix Barlowe and little Ellie are here. I don't know what happens next, or if Felix and I can figure out how to be parents together. Heck, I don't know if I can really stand on my own while letting him help me, or if I'm setting myself up for heartbreak.

But I do know one thing. I'm glad I won't be alone tonight. More importantly, I'm glad I'll be with Felix.

17

——————

FELIX

THE PAST THREE days in Skylark have been remarkably perfect, and I'm starting to understand why my brother settled here. It's a hidden gem of a town but not so small that you can't have a decent private life, even as a celebrity.

Tyler's staying in the guest house on Ian and Sadie's property, which allows us to keep to our training schedule at a local gym. No frills, but it gets the job done and has been blessedly clear of rabid autograph seekers.

The neighbors have been chill about having an NFL player in residence once more. Ian's been around enough that they're used to it. Although it's a little different since I'm going to be wearing the orange and blue uniform of the hometown team. Ian never played for Denver and arrived after he retired. Most people in Colorado are convinced God made sunsets orange because He's a Grizzlies fan.

The eighty-year-old lady at the end of the block stopped me on my run yesterday to tell me she expects the Grizzlies to make the playoffs next season. "My grandson plays receiver for his high school team," she'd informed me, hands on her hips. "He watches your highlight reels. Don't let him down."

It was sweet, and a good reminder that what I have to prove on the field this season is as much for the fans as it is for me.

It's Wednesday morning, and I'm sitting at Piper's kitchen table watching her make coffee while Ellie colors at my feet. The house is way smaller than either the cabin or my Denver McMansion, but there's something about it that makes my chest feel less tight than it has in months.

Maybe it's the worn hardwood floors that creak under my weight, or the way the rooms feel comfortably lived in, like it's a place to build a life and welcome you home. I'm guessing that last part is just the fact that Piper's here, moving around the space with an ease that makes me crave things I have no business wanting.

The house itself is kind of a time capsule. Most of the furniture looks like it could have been purchased when her mom was alive. There's an overstuffed plaid couch that's seen better days, a scuffed coffee table and a worn recliner in the corner. Family photos line the walls, most of the sisters as kids. There are a few touches that are obviously Sadie's, like dog-training certificates and a wedding photo, but nothing in the common living area screams Piper.

The lack of personality reminds me uncomfortably of my childhood home. Not that our house was welcoming. Quite the opposite, actually. We lived in a run-down duplex where nobody gave enough of a shit to fix the leaky faucets or patch the drywall. After the divorce, Dad moved to a bachelor condo, filling it with fake-leather furniture and a fridge perpetually empty except for beer, olives and mustard.

Once we were old enough, Ian and I tried to fix things at Mom's place. I mowed the lawn, and he updated what he could. But you can't fix everything with elbow grease and embarrassment.

Our fingers brush as Piper hands me a mug. You'd think I'd get used to the jolt of electricity every time we touch, but a bit of coffee sloshes over the side of the cup before I manage to hide my reaction.

"Thanks," I grunt, and she gives me a funny look.

"Fee, wook!" Ellie holds up a drawing that's mostly purple scribbles.

"I'm looking, munchkin." I bend down to study it. "Is that a dinosaur?"

Her feathery brows draw together. "It doggy!"

"Oh, yeah. Obviously a doggy, and so purple. I can see that now."

"Pi, wook at Ellie doggy."

Piper smiles as she slips into the seat across from me. "That is an excellent doggy, Ellie Bean."

I take a sip of coffee, trying not to think about how perfect this feels. How I can imagine Piper smiling down at our baby in a few months.

"I have a meeting in Denver today," I blurt.

Her head tilts as she shifts her gaze to me. "Thanks for sharing?"

"It's at my new house. With the interior designer."

"Okay." Something that could be disappointment flickers across her face. I guess I'm not the only one enjoying our pretend life together. "Ellie and I will be great here."

"Actually, I was hoping you'd come with me." The words come out before I've fully thought them through. "I'd like your opinion on some things. And after, we could take Ellie to the zoo. Make a day of it."

She blinks, clearly surprised. "You want my opinion on your house?"

"Why do you sound so shocked?"

"Because it's *your* house. My opinion doesn't matter."

A whole bunch of wrongs tied up in that response, but I decide to let it slide. "It matters to me. Plus, the interior designer is kind of terrifying. I need backup."

The truth is, I want to show her the house and have her see where I'll be living. Where our baby might visit. I'm curious to know if she can picture herself in it, even though there is zero indication that will ever happen.

"Okay," she says after an interminably long pause. "But we need to get a polar bear stuffed animal at the zoo gift shop. Ellie needs one for her collection."

"Ellie needs one, huh?"

Her cheeks flush. "Fine. They're my favorite animals at the zoo. Sue me."

God, she's adorable when she's flustered.

The morning goes by in a flash, and at around twelve-thirty, we pull up to the house in a newer gated community near the Cherry Hills neighborhood. I watch Piper's face as she takes it in. The house is definitely impressive—all stone and glass and perfectly manicured landscaping.

"Wow," she says. "This is...big."

"My agent insisted," I admit. "He went on and on about 'establishing my brand in Denver.'"

"It's very nice," Piper says carefully.

"You hate it."

"I didn't say that."

"You didn't have to. Your face said everything I needed to know."

She laughs. "Okay, fine. The modern mausoleum vibe is not what I expected from you. But I'm sure the inside is cozier."

I run a hand along the back of my neck and sigh. It's not, but I don't tell her that. She'll find out soon enough.

Leslie Cummings climbs out of her Mercedes sedan, looking like she walked off the set of *Selling Sunset* with her sleek black hair, designer heels, and a smile that looks like it's waging war against whatever toxins and fillers she's injected. She was my agent's pick, too. I was so overwhelmed with taking care of Ellie, I let Brandon make the decisions for me.

"Felix." She air-kisses near my cheek like we're old friends, even though we've only met in person one other time. "So glad we could finally get together. And you brought—"

"Ellie," I supply as the toddler nestles against my chest, suddenly shy. "And Piper. A friend I enlisted for decision-making assistance."

Leslie's smile tightens slightly as she gives Piper, who is throwing some major side eye, a full once-over. "The more the merrier."

"It's going to be *so* merry," Piper agrees with a smirk as she takes Ellie from my arms.

Leslie's kohl-rimmed eyes widen. "Right. Shall we?"

The designer, who has a key, unlocks the front door and ushers us through the vaulted-ceiling foyer to what will soon be my updated kitchen. She has samples and paint swatches ready for my approval, although to me they all look like variations of "rich asshole gray."

"And for the backsplash," she says, her manicured nails clicking against her tablet, "I'm thinking a geometric marble in Calacatta gold. Very high-end and statement-making."

The statement her choices seem to make is that I'm an uptight prick, but I nod anyway, because what the hell do I know about interior design?

"Looks great."

"Which paint color?" Leslie asks, and I realize I've been staring at the doorway to the kitchen because Piper hasn't followed us in. Did she get lost? Did she make a break for it?

Leslie clears her throat, and I turn my attention back to her.

"Uh..." I gesture vaguely. "That one?"

"Dove Wing or Revere Pewter?"

They look identical to me, but before I can randomly choose one, another voice cuts in.

"Neither."

I turn to find Piper finally entering the kitchen, and my heart does that stupid skip thing. Ellie is pressed tight against her, as if she finds this house, or maybe just the woman facing me, scary as shit. Can't say I blame her.

"Excuse me?" Leslie's tone could freeze molten lava.

"Your color palette is too cold." Piper rubs her palm in slow circles on Ellie's back. I might be jealous. "Felix needs warmth. He wants a house that feels like a home, not a museum."

"Piper, right?" Leslie raises one delicately arched brow. "Do you have a background in interior design?"

"I know Felix," Piper says smoothly, and you couldn't pay me enough to argue with her. "May I?"

She shuffles through the samples as we watch. I, for one, am fascinated. Also slightly enamored, but that's becoming par for the course with Piper. "Here." She holds up two swatches from the bottom of the pile. "These are warm but not overwhelming. They'll make the space feel inviting."

"Those are far too traditional," Leslie protests stiffly. "Felix needs a modern aesthetic, something that screams success and—"

"Felix wants to feel like *he* belongs in his own house," Piper interrupts. "He doesn't care if it looks like a magazine spread with a bunch of furniture he's afraid to sit on."

"True statement," I agree, grateful beyond belief that my temporary nanny agreed to have my back today. Because what Piper described is exactly how I've felt looking at Leslie's inspiration boards. They're impressive but also stuffy and sterile. Definitely not me.

"As far as the backsplash," Piper continues, "forget the geometric marble. What about subway tile in a muted blue? Classic, timeless, and a nice nod to his new team." She turns to me. "You're putting in a deck oven for bread baking, right?"

I nod, surprised she remembered that detail.

"Then you want the space to highlight that, not overshadow it." She looks back at Leslie. "He's a talented baker, so the oven becomes a focal point. Everything else supports it."

"Do you have an opinion on the countertops?" Leslie asks, a challenge in her voice.

"Quartz," Piper says without hesitation. "It has most of the good properties of natural stone and none of the bad. It will also stay cool to the touch for working with dough."

She's not wrong. I've been researching countertops late at night, and quartz kept coming up on the sourdough forums. But I know Leslie wanted a solid black marble because it would be masculine and dramatic. It would also show flour dust like nobody's business.

Other than feeling like I'd be showing my lack of taste if I disagreed with the professional, I'm not sure why I'm such a wimp when it comes to voicing my opinion. But Piper could not apparently give a rat's ass about Leslie's expertise. She's advocating for me, and it's hitting me square in the feels.

"Fine," Leslie agrees with obvious reluctance. "I'll put together some new concept boards with these choices. Now, as far as the living room, I have some spectacular sculptural lighting—"

"That's going to make him feel like he's perpetually on display," Piper interrupts. "He needs comfortable furniture. Extra deep, plush couches. Or possibly an oversized sectional. A comfy seating arrangement where he can actually relax."

Leslie turns to me. "Felix, perhaps we should discuss *your* vision."

"Piper nailed it," I hear myself say, trying not to sound as dumbfounded as I feel. "I appreciate all of your time and effort, Leslie. Everything you've shown me is beautiful, but it's not me. It's what you and my agent think I should want, or what will look good in a photo shoot. But Piper knows me. She gets what I need."

The truth settles in my chest like a weighted blanket, wrapping me in a kind of safety and security I didn't even realize I needed. Piper Hart understands me better than anyone. Better than my exes, better than my agent, even better than my own brother sometimes.

Piper sees the real me, and she doesn't seem to expect me to be someone different. She's good with a guy who bakes bread at five in the morning and wants a home that feels lived-in and loved.

And fuck me, it might be the hottest thing I've ever experienced.

"Okay, well…" Piper looks as shocked by my statement as I feel. "Now that that's settled, I'll let you two finish your meeting."

"Yes," the designer agrees. "That's for the bes—"

"To be clear, we're going with Piper's suggestions," I say before she can make her escape. "All of them."

I hear Piper's soft gasp, but she doesn't stop walking. "Ellie and I will wait for you out front," she calls over her shoulder. "Take your time."

As far as I'm concerned, this meeting is done, and it couldn't have gone any better.

I glance at the swatches and samples then back at Leslie. "Is there anything else?"

"We need to discuss a plan for the bedrooms and your office."

"Send me options that fit with the vibe Piper described." I look around the space, confident that, thanks to my temporary nanny, this is going to be a home I want to live in. "We'll get back to you. Oh, and one of the upstairs bedrooms is going to be a nursery."

"For a baby?"

Leslie's cheeks color when I throw her a stony look, not bothering to answer the question. "It should have a gender-neutral color scheme. Maybe a zoo theme." I pause then add, "Make sure there are polar bears. Elephants, too."

"Polar bears and elephants?"

I cross my arms over my chest. I don't want to be an asshole, but my patience is running thin. "Should you be taking notes?"

Leslie shakes her head. "I'll email you a revised design plan," she tells me, and she might be grinding her molars to dust.

We walk out together, and she slams her car door shut with way more force than is necessary. Piper straps Ellie into her car seat as I approach the SUV, and I wait until I'm pulling out of the driveway to speak.

"That was—"

"I'm sorry," she blurts. "I shouldn't have just taken over. It's your house and she's the professional and—"

"It was amazing. *You* were amazing," I add quietly. "How did you know about what I'd want as far as the countertops and colors?"

She shrugs. "You talked about that oven the way most guys talk about sports cars. And I know you like to be comfortable. Plus, you clearly hated your place in Cincinnati because it didn't feel like yours." She offers me a tentative smile. "It wasn't that hard to figure out."

But no one else has figured it out. Or at least cared enough to try.

"Thank you," I tell her. "Really."

Our eyes lock when I stop at a red light, and the air suddenly feels charged. I'm acutely aware of how close she is. How easy it would be to lean over and kiss her. We agreed not to do that again, but I'm seriously reconsidering the decision.

"Fee!" Ellie shouts. "Zoo! El'phants!"

"That's right, munchkin. We're going to see the elephants." I do my best trumpet, and the toddler squeals in delight.

We spend the rest of the drive discussing the list of animals we're going to visit. Ellie is practically vibrating with excitement by the time I pull into the parking lot. The Denver Zoo on a Wednesday is blissfully uncrowded, but I still pull my Buffaloes cap low and slip on sunglasses.

"Is that supposed to disguise you?" Piper asks with a laugh.

"At least let me fly under the radar a little." I wink at her. "Celebrities use the ol' ball cap disguise all the time."

"Most celebrities aren't six-three and built like a brick wall."

"I'm six-four."

She rolls her eyes. "I guess that extra inch makes all the difference."

"You know it does," I deadpan, and she laughs.

God, I love making her laugh.

We start with the elephants since Ellie is obsessed. Watching her face light up makes me think about Troy and Julie. How they'll never again have any of these tiny, perfect moments. The enormity of the responsibility they left me lodges between my ribs, and I'm not sure how to trust myself to live up to their expectations.

"You're thinking too hard," Piper murmurs even as she keeps her gaze on Ellie, who stands at the fence bordering the elephant enclosure, gesturing to the two massive animals as she holds a conversation with them that only she can understand.

I laugh softly. "How can you tell?"

"The crease between your eyebrows gives it away." She turns toward me, reaching up like she's going to smooth it away, before dropping her hand. "I know you're scared of messing this up. But Felix, you have to believe in yourself."

The words hit somewhere deep, in a place I've been protecting since my parents' divorce. Since Veronica. Since every relationship that confirmed I'm fundamentally not enough.

"I can play football and bake bread, Piper. It's a limited skill set and not one that equips me to take care of an orphaned child." I hate myself for disappointing her, but the truth is what it is. "You know the plan."

"I know the plan," she says tightly. She points toward the primate house. "Let's go see some other animals. Maybe you'll get some ideas on how to be part of a family unit."

Ouch.

Before I can respond, Ellie runs over and grabs hold of my pant leg. "Monkeys!"

"Monkeys for the munchkin," I say as I swing her into my arms.

At the lions, a dad recognizes me. "Holy cow, you're Felix Barlowe."

He asks for a quick photo, telling me his kid watches every game. We chat for a minute about route running, and he thanks me three times before leaving.

"That wasn't so bad." Piper is standing a few feet away with Ellie, her tiny hands pressed to the plexiglass as she watches a baby gorilla climb all over its mother.

"Most people are cool. It's the ones who aren't that make it complicated."

On the way to the giraffes, two teenagers ask for selfies. Then a mom at the penguins wants me to record a video message for her son's birthday. Each time, Piper steps back with Ellie, giving me space. Each time, I wish she'd stay closer.

I'm screwing this up, but I can't seem to stop it. Ellie falls asleep against my shoulder on the way out, and Piper and I walk in silence toward my vehicle.

"I'm sorry," I say finally.

"For what?" She won't look at me as she transfers Ellie to her car seat.

I rub a hand along the back of my neck. "For not knowing what the hell I'm doing."

"Figure it out." Her voice cracks. "Because I can't keep watching you be perfect with Ellie, imagining what you could be with our baby, only to remember that you're counting down the days until you can hand her off to someone else."

"Piper—"

"Let's just go home, okay?" She's already moving to the passenger side. "It's been a long morning."

The drive back is quiet except for Ellie's tiny toddler snores. I'm not sure what to say or how to manage the emotions tumbling through my head and heart like my skivvies on the spin cycle.

"I'm going to head over to Sadie's," Piper says as we pull into the driveway. "Give you some space."

"You don't have to—"

"I want to." She's already pulling her keys from her purse. "I need to talk to my sister anyway."

I watch her get into her Jeep before I open the back door of the SUV to retrieve Ellie. I'm missing something important. Something I should have said in that parking lot.

The older woman from down the block walks by, offering a 'Go Grizzlies' greeting, and I lift a hand in return. At least someone thinks I'm capable of not screwing up.

Too bad she's wrong.

18

PIPER

THE HOUSE IS dark except for the glow from the muted television. Olivia Benson is giving some perp hell on SVU, but I'm not really watching. It's nearly midnight, and I'm curled on the couch, clutching the most pathetic but precious-to-me baby doll ever. There's a piece of peanut butter and jelly toast on the coffee table that I made ten minutes ago and haven't touched.

I'm also crying. Not pretty, delicate tears. Full-on ugly sobbing.

"Piper?" Felix's concerned voice drifts down the stairs.

Oh, hell, no.

"Go away!" I whisper-yell, not wanting to wake Ellie as I wipe my cheeks with the edge of the doll's ratty dress. The last thing I need is for him to see me puffy-eyed and snotty, clutching this decrepit toy.

But his footsteps move closer instead of retreating. Because of course they do. I should know Felix Barlowe doesn't take direction well.

"I mean it, Felix. I want to be alone."

"Not happening."

I make a frustrated sound and hurl the doll at him as he rounds the corner to the family room. He snatches it out of the air one-handed, barely even looking.

"First a shoe and now..." He cringes as he examines the doll. "Whatever this thing is. You could've been a quarterback with an arm like that, Hart."

Despite everything, a watery laugh bubbles up inside me. I reach over and flick on the side-table lamp, flooding the room with warm light, then shake my head and wipe my eyes again. Not that I'm fooling either of us into thinking I'm okay.

"I don't want an audience for my meltdown."

Felix moves around the coffee table and sits on the couch without touching me. He's giving me space even as he refuses to leave me alone.

"Too late." His voice is soft. "Talk to me, Piper."

I stare at the uneaten toast, throat tight.

"Is it the nausea?" he asks.

"It's the doll," I murmur.

He looks down at the toy dangling from his hand, then back at me. One eyebrow climbs toward his hairline. "I get that. This thing is creepy as fuck, but it's no reason to cry." He turns it to examine the faded painted eye. "I'm mostly sure those possessed-doll movies are fake anyway."

I laugh again. "No, I mean—" I take a shaky breath. "That was a Christmas present from my mom, and one of my first memories. I wasn't much older than Ellie."

The teasing light in his blue eyes drains away.

"Now I'm having a baby, and Mom will never meet him or her. She won't—" My voice cracks. "It's not fair."

"No," Felix says quietly. "It's not."

He moves closer, his thigh pressing against mine, and takes my hand. His palm is warm and rough and solid and makes the vise in my chest loosen slightly.

"But you're not alone. You know that, right? You've got Sadie and Ian. Your friends. Riva." He squeezes my fingers. "Me if you want."

I look up into those impossibly blue eyes that got me into this mess in the first place. "You've done enough processing?"

"You have to know that was all bullshit. I'd never walk away from my child."

"I didn't..." I swallow hard. "You know that Sadie and I both grew up without fathers?"

He nods. "Ya, but not the details."

"Sadie's dad left when she was a baby and started a new family in Nebraska. He only called when he needed a summer babysitter for his do-over kids." The old bitterness creeps into my voice. "My dad was apparently great with Sadie when he started dating our mom but left before I was born." I move to pull away, but he holds fast to my hand, his thumb tracing circles on my knuckles.

"So I'd rather you not be involved at all." I hate myself for pushing, but need him to understand. "Than to have you bail later. I can't do that to my baby."

"I won't bail."

"But what if—"

"Piper." He shifts to face me more fully. "I spoke to my attorney yesterday. That relative he was trying to track down—the great-aunt who was supposed to be Ellie's chance to stay with family? She hasn't replied to his messages." He pauses. "Maybe that's a sign that Troy and Julie were right." He clears his throat. "Maybe Ellie belongs with me."

My heart thuds hard against my ribs, because this isn't the same situation exactly, but his words also feel like a sign. The fact that Felix is choosing to stay, to commit to the sweet girl who adores him, gives me hope I hadn't known I needed.

He holds up the doll. "We might need an upgrade on this thing, but I bet Ellie would love playing dolls with her future sibling."

"What if it's a boy?"

"Wow, Piper." He lets out a low whistle. "Way to be sexist. Boys can play with dolls, too."

I roll my eyes, but I'm smiling despite the tears still drying on my cheeks. "You know what I meant."

His eyes go wide. "Wait. Do you know? Is it a boy?"

I shake my head. "No, they won't be able to tell for a while. But I have an ultrasound appointment tomorrow." I pick at a loose thread on my pajama pants. "I wanted to ask you to come, but I didn't want you to feel pressured."

"What time?"

"Two-thirty."

"I'll be there."

"Felix, really, you don't have to—"

"I want to." He studies the doll before his gaze flicks back to me. "Are Baby Chucky and the appointment related?"

I take the toy and place it on the cushion behind me, fighting a smile. "I've been a little nervous, and when I couldn't fall asleep tonight, I dug the doll out from the bottom of my closet." I shrug helplessly. "Kind of a hormonal version of *If You Give a Moose a Muffin*. One thought spiral led to another."

Felix reaches out, cupping my face with one large hand. His thumb brushes away a tear still clinging to my lower lashes. Then he leans in and kisses one cheek, then the other, his touch featherlight.

"No more secrets," he murmurs against my skin. "I want to be involved in whatever way you'll let me. Appointments, late-night crying sessions, peanut butter sourdough toast at midnight." He pulls back just enough to meet my eyes. "Let me in, Hart."

I press my mouth to his.

Felix makes a surprised sound, but kisses me back for a heartbeat—or three—before pulling away.

"We agreed this was a bad idea."

"I remember." I slide my hand to the back of his neck, fingers tangling in his hair. "But I need our version of a bad idea. Please."

He freezes, every muscle tense, before heat and want and tenderness crowd his gaze.

"Yeah," he breathes. "Me, too."

His hands move to my waist, dragging me closer, and I go willingly. He claims my mouth again, and it's different this time. Deep and needy. My hands explore the broad expanse of his shoulders, then down the corded muscles of his arms, memorizing the geography of his body.

"Upstairs," I manage between kisses.

Felix is already standing, pulling me with him. His hand finds mine as we climb the stairs, both of us trying to be quiet even as we pause to kiss, first on the landing and then against the wall of the hallway.

When we make it to my room, Felix kicks the door closed behind us and pushes me against it, his mouth finding that spot beneath my ear that makes everything go fuzzy.

"You sure about this?" he asks, as his hands slip under my pajama top, palms warm against my skin.

"One-hundred percent." I tug the Ole Miss shirt up and over his head. "Unless you're not—"

He silences me with another kiss, this one almost bruising, and it makes heat and wetness pool between my legs. "I want you morning, noon, and night, Hart." His laugh is rough against my skin. "I'm trying to be a gentleman."

"Right now, I don't need a gentleman."

"Yeah?" Something fierce and dangerous flashes across his face. "What do you need?"

"You," I say simply. "Just you."

Felix groans and lifts me, my legs wrapping around his waist as he carries me to the bed. He lays me down carefully, like I'm precious to him. For a moment, he just looks at me. I know my hair is spread across the pillow, top rucked up to show the slight swell of my belly. My chest rises and falls under his scrutiny.

"You have no idea how beautiful you are," he says.

I reach for him. "Show me."

He settles between my legs, his weight grounding me in the most delicious way. When he pushes my top up further and kisses my stomach, right where our baby grows, tears prick my eyes again. The good kind this time.

"Hey," Felix says, looking up at me. "You okay?"

"Yeah." I smile and pull him back up to me. "I'm perfect."

His hands slide to my hips, thumbs hooking in the waistband of my pajama pants. "These need to go."

"Yours first."

He grins and makes quick work of his athletic shorts and boxer briefs. Then I'm staring at those defined muscles, the light dusting of hair across his chest, the obvious evidence of exactly how much he wants this. I reach out and wrap my fingers around him, stroking him slowly.

He hisses, hips jerking forward. "Careful," he warns, his voice nearly a growl. "Or this'll be over before it starts."

"I have faith in you," I tease as he helps me shimmy out of my own panties.

When we're both naked, skin to skin, he kisses me again. It's slower this time, a savoring. "Tell me if anything doesn't feel right."

"I will, Felix. But I need—"

He cuts me off with a wicked grin. "I know what you need." He slides down my body and settles between my thighs. His hands spread me open, and then his mouth is on me—hot, wet, perfect. His tongue circles my clit with devastating precision, and I cry out, fingers threading through his hair.

"Felix—oh god—"

He hums against me, the vibration sending sparks up my spine, as he slides two fingers inside me. I'm already teetering on the edge, embarrassingly fast, and he doesn't let up, just licks and sucks and strokes until I'm writhing with pleasure. My hips buck, chasing the release I know is so close.

"Come on, Piper," he murmurs, breath hot against my skin. "I want to feel you come all over my face."

That does it. The most exquisite wave crashes over me, and my body clenches around his fingers as I come with a broken moan. I'm trembling and nearly boneless, but he doesn't stop until he pulls every ounce of pleasure from my oversensitive body.

His grin is adorably self-satisfied as he finally meets my gaze.

"Your turn," I pant, pushing at his shoulders until he's on his back. I straddle his thighs, taking him in my hand again. He's thick and hot, pulsing against my palm. I lean down, licking a stripe up the underside, swirling my tongue around the tip.

He groans, hips lifting. "Piper—fuck—"

I take him deeper and hollow my cheeks, loving the way he fills my mouth. His hands fist in the sheets, then in my hair, brushing it away from my face. I bob slowly at first, then faster as I savor his salty taste and the way his thighs tense under my palms.

"Stop," he gasps suddenly, and pulls me off with gentle but firm hands. "Not like this. I want to be inside you when I come."

I crawl back up his body, kissing him so he can taste himself on my tongue. "Then take me."

He flips us in one smooth motion, settling between my legs again. The head of his cock nudges my entrance, slick and ready. He pushes in inch by inch, eyes locked on mine. I'm so full with him I can barely breathe.

"Christ, you feel—" He breaks off with a groan as his hips go flush against mine. "Perfect."

We move together, and I relish every slow thrust. His fingers interlace with mine above my head, and the other hand cups my breast, his thumb teasing my nipple until I arch into him.

"More," I whisper, and he obliges, plunging deeper and faster. The old bed creaks beneath us, and the headboard taps the wall in a rhythm that would be funny if it didn't feel so damn good.

"I'm ordering you a new bed tomorrow," he pants against my neck.

I laugh, then go breathless as he angles his hips to hit the spot inside that makes me see stars. His hand slips between us, thumb circling my clit in time with his thrusts.

"Come again for me, Piper."

I'm surprised at my willingness to follow his command, but another orgasm tears through me, sharper this time. It leaves me shaking, and Felix follows seconds later, burying himself deep with a guttural groan.

For a long moment, we stay tangled together. I can feel his heart racing as fast as mine, both of us slicked with sweat. Then he rolls to the side, pulling me with him so I'm tucked against his chest.

"Hi," he says, pressing a kiss to my forehead.

"Hi yourself." I trace soft patterns on his chest, feeling boneless and satisfied and maybe just a little bit hopeful.

"For the record," Felix says, "I'm definitely staying, Hart. Doctor appointments, midnight crying sessions, teaching our kid to throw a proper spiral." He tilts my chin up to meet his eyes. "Girl or boy. You're stuck with me now."

"Is that a threat or a promise?"

"Both." He grins. "One hundred percent both."

I snuggle closer and let my eyes drift closed. We still need to figure out the complicated parts—logistics, fears, and the thousand questions neither of us has answers for yet. But tonight, enveloped in his heat with our baby safe between us, I'm happy to feel not quite so alone.

"Felix?"

"Yeah?"

"I'm glad you caught the doll I threw at your head."

His chest rumbles with quiet laughter. "Me, too, sweetheart."

I fall asleep with his heartbeat steady beneath my ear and his arms solid around me, Olivia Benson probably still kicking ass on the TV downstairs.

19

FELIX

I'M LURKING in the parking lot of Skylark Women's Health like some kind of stalker, which is not exactly how I pictured spending a Friday afternoon.

The plan is for me to wait out here until Piper texts me that it's safe to sneak in through the back. She doesn't want anyone at the clinic to see the Grizzlies' high-profile new team member entering an OB/GYN office and start doing the math.

Smart, I guess. But it's also making me feel like I'm some kind of liability when all I want to do is see my kid for the first time.

I've checked the phone sitting on my thigh approximately four hundred times in the last ten minutes. Sadie came over to watch Ellie, accompanied by Ian, who clapped me on the shoulder on my way out the door with "Good luck, bro. Don't screw it up."

Not exactly reassuring.

I drum my fingers on the steering wheel and try not to think about all the ways I could mess this up. What if I say something stupid during the ultrasound? Or what if I don't say enough? What if the baby looks weird on the screen and I make a face and Piper thinks I'm not excited? What if—

My phone buzzes.

Piper: Back door. Now.

I'm out of the SUV before I can overthink things anymore. I jog across the parking lot toward the rear of the building, and the door opens just as I reach it. A nurse who looks about twelve years old ushers me inside with a finger pressed to her lips.

"This way," she whispers, like we're in a spy movie.

I follow her down a hallway that smells like antiseptic, past exam rooms with closed doors. The whole thing reminds me of being snuck through the back entrance of clubs in Vegas when I was still riding high on college football fame.

Except this is nothing like that.

This is about Piper and our baby, and that thought makes my chest squeeze in a way that's sharp and soft all at once.

The nurse stops at a door, knocks twice, then pushes it open. "Your plus-one is here," she says cheerfully before disappearing.

I step into the dim room, and it takes my eyes a second to adjust before I see her.

Piper's lying on the exam table, thin paper crinkling under her as she shifts. The overhead lights are off, but there's a soft glow from the monitor beside her.

"Hey," I say, incapable of anything more eloquent.

"Hey." She sounds as anxious as I feel. "Sorry about the cloak-and-dagger routine."

"Are you kidding? I feel like James Bond." I take in the rest of the room as I move closer. There's a chair up against the wall, a rolling stool, a sink, and what I assume is the ultrasound machine with its wand thing sitting in some kind of holster. "Although Bond probably doesn't pit out from nerves."

She grins, and some of the tension in her shoulders eases. "You're nervous?"

"Terrified." I scoot the chair closer to her head and take a seat. "My nose on a newborn? That should come with a warning label."

"Your nose is fine."

"It's been broken three times."

"Still fine." She reaches out and takes my hand, her fingers cold against mine. "Thank you for being here."

"Where else would I be?"

Before she can answer, the door opens again, and a woman in navy scrubs walks in. She's in her mid-forties, with a friendly smile and the efficient energy of someone who's done this a thousand times.

"Hi, Piper. I'm Suzie, your ultrasound tech." She extends her hand to me. "And you must be Dad."

Dad.

I'm glad I'm sitting down, because the word steals my breath. I'm going to be a dad. Not a guardian or a temporary fill-in, but an actual father to a tiny human who's half me and half Piper and fully themselves.

"Felix," I manage, giving a little wave. "Felix Barlowe."

"Nice to meet you, Felix." If she recognizes my name, she doesn't show it. She turns to wash her hands at the sink, then rolls the stool over to the ultrasound machine. "Let's take a look at this baby, Mom and Dad." She offers Piper a smile. "This is going to be a little cold."

She squirts gel onto Piper's stomach, which only shows signs of a tiny swell, and Piper gasps then gives a nervous laugh. "More like Arctic tundra freezing."

"Sorry." Suzie doesn't sound sorry at all as she picks up the wand. "You'll warm up in a second."

I'm still holding Piper's hand, but I can't take my eyes off the monitor. It's just gray static as Suzie moves the wand across Piper's belly, also focusing on the screen.

"Here we go," she murmurs.

Then I see it.

It's a shadowy blob until Suzie angles the probe and the image snaps into a recognizable shape.

"Say hi to your baby," she murmurs.

Our baby.

Holy hell.

Piper leans in. "Is that the head?"

"Exactly." Suzie traces along the rounded shape. "That bright line right there is the spine." She taps a few keys. "Baby's measuring right on track for fourteen weeks."

More tapping, and numbers that don't mean a thing to me pop up on the monitor. "The crown-rump length is good."

"Crown-rump," I repeat. "Sounds like something I'd order at a fancy steakhouse."

Suzie laughs. "Well, this one's much cuter."

I'm not sure about that because, honestly, I can't discern much. Then Suzie adjusts the wand, and the baby's profile appears. There's a tiny nose, a rounded forehead, and hands with actual fingers near their face. I see a real person. *Our* person.

Piper's breath catches. "Can we hear the heartbeat?" she asks.

"Of course." Suzie clicks a button to switch modes but frowns when there's just static.

My heart feels like it stops as Piper squeezes my fingers.

Then we hear it.

Whoosh-whoosh. Whoosh-whoosh. Whoosh-whoosh.

A strong and steady heartbeat.

Suzie smiles. "There we go. Sometimes they wiggle out of the way for a second. Heart rate is perfect at one-fifty-eight."

Piper's tears start immediately.

"Our baby's heartbeat," she whispers and glances up at me. The emotion in her wide eyes steals my breath. Or maybe that's my own reaction to this miraculous moment.

"Our baby," I murmur. I haven't cried since my parents sat us down about the divorce, but that steady sound and Piper's reaction cracks me open, clean down the middle.

The baby suddenly shifts on the screen, one tiny kick followed by another.

"Is it moving?" I ask.

"A he or she and yes," Suzie answers with a laugh, then adjusts the angle of the wand again. "The baby is active. You won't feel it for a few more weeks, Piper, but the baby's having their own dance party in there."

I could watch this all damn day. "The dance skills come from me," I tell Piper, automatically lifting her hand to my lips and pressing a gentle kiss to her knuckles. "Can we get a picture? Or a dozen? I'm happy to pay for extra."

Suzie snorts. "Lucky for you, pictures are included in the prenatal package. It's a little early, but do you want me to take a guess on the sex?"

"Do you want to know?" Piper asks me, and it feels as though the question in her eyes is about more than just finding out if we're having a boy or a girl. It's about all the other things we haven't discussed. Like what comes next. And whether we're doing this together or separately.

I squeeze her hand. "Your choice."

"I asked you," she says softly.

"I'm all good either way." As soon as I say the words, I know they're true. "As long as the baby's healthy, that's all that matters."

Piper's smile trembles a little on either side. "Let's be surprised."

"Love it." Suzie finishes up, wiping the gel off Piper's stomach and handing us four grainy images of our baby from different angles. "Congratulations, you two. Everything looks great."

"Thank you," Piper says, her voice thick with emotion.

Suzie pats her shoulder. "You're doing wonderful, Mom. We'll see you at your next appointment."

She leaves, and I help Piper sit up. She adjusts the hem of her shirt, holding the photos gingerly, like they're made of glass. Her expression is dazed, and I'm pretty sure the same look is mirrored on my own face.

"That was..." I trail off, not sure how to finish.

"Yeah," she agrees.

We're silent as we leave through the back door, because what is there to say? We heard our baby's heartbeat. Nothing else matters at the moment.

The drive back to her house is just as quiet. Not in an uncomfortable way. We're both processing what we just experienced. I park in her driveway, and we sit here for a minute, neither of us making a move to get out.

"That was...um...real," Piper says finally.

"Very real."

She laughs, then looks down at the strip of ultrasound photos in her hands, running her thumb over the grainy images. "I keep thinking about my mom, and she won't get to meet..." Her voice cracks.

I reach over and cover her hand with mine. "Hey, Hart?" She looks up at me, tears gathering in her eyes. "Our kid is going to know they're wanted and loved," I say. "You're going to make your mom proud."

A tear spills over, and she swipes at it with her free hand. "You can't say shit like that, Felix."

"Why not?"

"Because it makes me want—" She stops herself, shaking her head. "Never mind."

But I can guess what she was going to say, and I feel it too. I want to give in to this pull between us that has nothing to do with the baby and everything to do with moments like these. Moments when we see each other so clearly.

"Come on," she says, opening her door. "Let's go show Sadie and Ian before I completely lose it."

I follow her toward the house, my eyes on her trembling fingers holding the ultrasound photos, and realize something with sudden clarity.

I don't just want to be this baby's father.

I want to be the person Piper turns to full stop.

20

—————

FELIX

WE FIND Sadie and Ian in the living room watching Ellie on the floor with Beast. After trotting over to greet us, the mutt races back to Ellie, who's holding a braided rope with knots. As she lifts the rope toy in the air, Beast's tail wags so hard his whole back end starts to shake.

"Ellie dog!" the toddler shrieks, throwing the toy. It goes approximately two feet. Beast retrieves it anyway, bringing it back to drop at her feet. "Ellie dog!"

That's pretty much what she exclusively calls him, apparently unable to reconcile the fact that Beast is *a* dog but not *her* dog.

Sadie takes one look at our faces and smiles. "How'd it go?"

"Really good." Piper holds up the strip of photos, and my heart trips over itself all over again. Even with photographic proof, I still can't believe this is happening. "We have pictures."

"Let's have a look," Ian says.

Piper hands them over, and both Sadie and Ian lean in closer. I'm shocked by the pride that swells in my chest, as if I've done anything other than contribute sperm to make this perfect baby. But watching them coo over the tiny features only strengthens my resolve to do more—both for the baby and Piper.

"Oh, Pip," Sadie says, her smile widening. "Look at that little kiwi fruit."

"Right?" Piper sits on the couch next to her sister, leaning her head on Sadie's shoulder. "I'm having a baby."

"A perfect wee nugget," Ian says, studying the grainy images. Then he looks up at me with a grin. "I hope the baby looks like Piper."

"Same, bro. Same."

"That's rude." Sadie swats his shoulder.

"Just being honest." His expression shifts to something more serious. "Congrats, though. I mean it."

"Thanks." I should say more, but I don't know what, or if I could even get any other words out around the ball of emotion lodged in my throat.

Ellie abandons Beast and climbs into Piper's lap, reaching for the photos. "What dat?"

"Just some pictures, sweetie." Piper redirects her attention to Beast, who's wagging his tail hopefully. "Beast is ready for more fetch."

"Ellie dog!" She scrambles down and grabs the rope toy.

Piper watches her for a moment, then glances at Sadie. "I'm glad you brought him over. It's nice having canine energy in the house again. Even if it's from Beast, the chicken dog."

"When you're ready," Sadie says, her voice gentle, "I'll help you find a new four-legged friend. Not to replace Maxie, of course, but so you don't feel alone."

Am I chopped fucking liver? I'm sure Sadie doesn't mean it like that. And I ignore her words because I haven't officially stepped up. Maybe that needs to change.

Piper shakes her head. "I've got enough on my plate right now. First, I need to figure out the job situation."

"About that." I take a step forward. "You don't have to rush into anything."

She looks confused, like she's not in any way picking up what

I'm laying down. "I'm not going to desert you and Ellie, if that's what you're thinking." My heart starts to beat like crazy in my chest. Because what in the world am I trying to say?

"Is that what *you're* thinking, Felix?" Sadie asks slowly.

"No...not exactly...I mean..." I'm fumbling here, my mind racing as fast as my heart.

Ian visibly cringes, then makes a slashing motion across his throat with one finger, like he knows I'm about to step in it.

But I can't stop now, even though I still have no idea where I'm going with this. I focus on Piper, grounding myself in her clear gaze and those ultrasound pictures she's still holding. "I mean, you don't need to worry about money or finding a new job right away. You've got me."

Her eyes widen a fraction, and her gaze cuts to Sadie for a moment before returning to me. "We've talked about this, Felix." Her voice is measured. "I can't just—"

"We should get married."

The words are out before I can stop them, hanging in the air like a bomb that just detonated in the cozy living room. Ellie keeps playing with Beast, completely oblivious to the fallout about to land on me. But Piper, Sadie, and Ian go completely still.

"Excuse me?" Piper whispers.

"A wedding. You and me." Now that I've said it, I'm doubling down. It makes a strange sort of sense, at least in my heart. "Your job can be as my wife. I'll take care of you, the baby, and Ellie if I end up keeping her. We'll be a family."

Yeah, I like the sound of that. A family of my own.

Except Piper's staring at me like I suggested we join a cult. "Have you lost your mind?"

"As proposals go," Ian says slowly, "that was stupendously bad."

Sadie elbows him, but she's not looking much more supportive. "Felix, maybe you should—"

"I'm serious." I drop onto the sofa–fucking weak knees–but

keep my focus on Piper, whose hazel eyes are filled with an emotion I can't read. I don't think it's excitement, though, which...okay, I get that. But it's a legit idea. "I'll get you a ring with a diamond you can see from outer space."

Ian snorts, and I resist the urge to flip him the bird. Where's the brotherly love when a guy needs it? "Come on, Hart. We're good together. This could work."

"'Your job can be as my wife?'" Piper repeats, her voice climbing. "Did you seriously just say that?"

"I meant—"

"I know what you meant, Felix. I should give up on having my own life, my own career, my own identity, and become Mrs. Felix Barlowe, my entire existence revolving around you and showing off the giant diamond you're going to put on my finger."

Oh, shit. When she puts it like that, stupendously bad doesn't even cover it. "Piper, I didn't mean—"

"Just like Bradley wanted. Just like everyone thinks I *need*. Poor little Piper, so lost and helpless. She obviously needs a big, strong man to take care of her."

"That's not what I'm saying at all."

"Then what are you saying?" Her eyes are blazing now, and... fuck, this is going so very wrong. "Because it sounds like you're trying to turn me into some kind of trad wife fantasy."

She stands and heads for the stairs, not waiting for an answer.

I also get up like I'm going to follow her. "Piper wait—"

Only, she's gone. A moment later, the sound of her bedroom door slamming echoes through the house, cutting off whatever pathetic excuse I was about to make.

Ellie continues to happily babble to Beast as he follows her around the main floor of the house. At least someone survived my stupidity unscathed.

"Well," Ian says with a grimace, "that went well."

I drop my head into my hands as I sit down again. "Shut up."

"As proposals go—"

"I know, bro. Giant fumble."

Sadie is staring at me with an expression I've never seen on her face before. Sadie is usually the sweet, mild-mannered one. But right now, she clearly wants to go full mama grizzly on my ass.

"You need to understand something, Felix." Her voice is quiet but has an edge to it that makes my shoulders go ramrod straight. "My sister might be young, but she can handle her own life without someone trying to fake rescue her."

"That isn't what I was—"

"It's time for her to stand on her own two feet without being rescued or running away," Sadie cuts me off. "It's part of her book club bucket list challenge. You need to respect that."

"I do." If I've learned one thing from hanging out with my brother's wife, it's that you don't mess with the book club.

Ian laughs like he can read my mind. "Oh shit, you're going to incur the wrath of the book club. Those ladies will shank someone who tries to take down one of their own."

"I'm not trying to take down anyone," I protest. "Especially not Piper."

Sadie stands, poking me hard in the shoulder, and I'm reminded that she trains dogs for a living. She's a woman who knows how to establish dominance. "Then do better."

She picks up Ellie, who protests leaving Beast, and heads upstairs. I hear her knock softly on Piper's door, murmured voices, and then the door closing.

I close my eyes and lean my head back on the couch cushions. Something furry climbs into my lap. Beast gets comfy on my thighs, his weird little chicken-dog mug inches from mine, and starts licking my chin like he's a therapy dog who knows I need comfort.

"At least someone likes you," Ian observes.

I open one eye to glare at my brother. "Fuck off."

"For a guy known for his charm and flash, you really are in over your head here." Ian's grin is wide and completely unsympathetic. "As your older brother, I love it."

"Fuck. Off."

"Already established that." He leans forward and points that big brother finger in my direction, clearly enjoying this. "But seriously, Felix. That was epically awful."

"Already established that." I repeat his words back to him as I scratch behind Beast's ears. "I just wanted to fix things and—"

"You can't fix Piper. She's not broken." Ian's voice loses some of its teasing edge. "She needs to figure out who she is without feeling like people are trying to manage her life."

"I know."

"Do you, though?" Ian raises an eyebrow. "Because it sounded like you were trying to turn her into one of your responsibilities. Something to be checked off a list."

The words sting, because they're true. It's exactly what I was doing. It's what I do.

"I'm in way over my head," I admit.

"Yeah, you are." Ian grins again. "Stick with the dog."

As if on cue, the animal shifts his position, his back end facing me, and lets out a long, rumbling fart directly onto my lap.

The smell hits me like a defensive lineman smackdown.

"Hell, no." I try to push the dog off, but he's surprisingly solid for something that looks like it was assembled from spare parts. "What the hell do you feed this thing?"

Ian is laughing so hard he can barely breathe. "That's pure karma, brother."

Beast, completely unbothered, settles into my lap and closes his eyes.

"I hate this dog," I mutter.

"No, you don't," Ian wheezes. "He's your only fan in this house at the moment."

He's not wrong. If Ellie was old enough to understand the way

I'd just stepped in it with her "Pi", I'm sure she'd be as disgusted with me as Sadie is.

From upstairs, I can hear the muted sound of voices. I hope to God Sadie's able to talk Piper down from rightfully wanting to murder me. Ellie's giggle filters through, and I think about how happy Piper makes her. Both of us, if I'm being honest.

Beast farts again.

"Seriously?" I glare down at him, but he just looks up at me with his weird little bug eyes.

"Get used to it, Felix," Ian says, still grinning. "This is your life now."

He's right.

My life is a woman upstairs who hates me, a toddler who isn't mine even though she feels like she is, a brother who's enjoying my suffering way too much, plus a flatulent chicken-dog using my lap as his personal throne.

And somewhere in all this chaos, there's a baby. Mine and Piper's.

I hope I can figure out how to be the man they both need before I screw this up beyond repair.

Beast shifts again.

"Don't you dare," I warn him as I brace myself.

He dares.

"That's it." I place him on the floor, and he trots over to Ian, who immediately scoops him up.

"Come here, buddy. Daddy doesn't mind your gas." Ian scratches the dog's head. "Some people can't appreciate a good fart."

"There's nothing good about that." I wave a hand in front of my face. "That dog needs an exorcist."

"That dog..." Sadie's voice comes from the stairs. "Can hear you."

My sister-in-law doesn't look quite as murder-y as before as she approaches, which I'm taking as a good sign.

"Is Piper okay?" I ask.

"She will be." Sadie's expression softens slightly. "She just needs some time."

"I screwed up."

"Yes, you did." She moves to collect Beast from Ian. "You can also fix it."

"What do I do?"

"Give her a little space. She needs to figure out her situation without anyone trying to rescue her."

"Space is also what we're going to give you," Ian adds as he stands and follows Sadie toward the door. I kind of want to beg them to stay, but that makes me seem like a huge wimp. "Good luck, man."

"I'm sorry, Sadie," I call to my sister-in-law.

She turns and gives me a sympathetic smile, which I also consider a good sign. "I'm not the one you need to apologize to. But, pro tip, Felix. Next time you want to propose to someone, maybe don't lead with 'your job can be as my wife.'"

"Noted," I say weakly.

"You'll be fine," Ian assures me, but I'm not certain either of us believes it. "But when you're ready to try again, run the proposal by me first."

"So you can tell me how badly I'm about to screw up?"

His grin is all annoying big brother. "Exactly."

They close the door behind them, leaving me in a living room that smells faintly of dog farts and my own failure. Upstairs, I hear Piper moving around. I want to go up there, apologize, and try to explain what I meant versus what I said.

But for once in my life, I'm going to listen to advice and give her space.

Even if it kills me.

Because I get now that the best way to help Piper isn't to fix things for her. It's to step back and let her fix them herself.

I just hope I haven't already blown my chance to be part of her life once she does.

21

FELIX

Later that night, I pull up to the address Ian texted me.

"Tell me you have money without telling me you have money," I mutter under my breath as I look at the house. It's set in the trees, and while we're not far out of town, it feels like I could be back in Vail or Aspen or some other fancy high-altitude enclave. Which tracks, I guess.

When Ian texted me the invitation to join him and some of his local Skylark buddies at a poker game, he told me Jake Byrne was the one hosting it. I know from comments Ian has made that Jake comes from money. His family's community foundation funds projects both in Colorado and Texas, where his grandfather's business started.

The whole reason Ian connected me with Jake in the first place was that my fledgling charity, Felix's Flyers—which raises money for youth sports—was looking to expand. Ian thought I could partner with the Byrne Family Foundation now that I'm going to be a Colorado resident, and have them manage my grant-making process. I've let it flounder since the breakup with Ronnie last summer because she was supposed to be running things.

Mostly, she wanted to wrangle invitations to fancy charity

functions and buy the designer clothes she said were necessary for an executive director. Fool that I was, I believed her. Up to a point anyway.

If I'd offered Ronnie the option of becoming Mrs. Felix Barlowe so that she wouldn't have to work, she would have grabbed onto the opportunity with both hands. Not act like I kicked her identity into the dirt the way Piper had.

I run a hand through my hair and climb out of the car. It was a shitty proposal, but my intentions were good. She's going to realize that. And of course I'm fine if she works. She can do whatever the hell she wants with her time. I wanted to make it easier. Instead, I made it a lot fucking harder.

I tried to talk to her when she came downstairs this afternoon, but she told me she needed time to "process." Oh yeah, she used air quotes for that word. And for Ellie's sake, she didn't want tension between us, but she wasn't going to talk about it anymore.

So I let it go. Because I'm not that big of a fucking fool.

She also told me that she was doing a girls' night out at her friend Molly's house, because Molly's hosting some big wedding this weekend at her flower farm, and the book club ladies were going over to help put the centerpieces together. She kind of lost me at 'textural elements' and 'natural movement', but I nodded along like I knew exactly what she meant.

She also asked if she could take Ellie with her because her friends wanted to meet the little girl, and Molly's twins were excited to play with her. She didn't mention anything about her friends wanting to meet her baby daddy, but I figure that will come in good time.

I get out of the car and start toward the house. Ian also let me know that Jake isn't just a trust-fund baby. He's also a successful mystery author under the pen name Spencer Charles. I don't read a lot other than playbooks, but I've seen the books in airport bookstores.

I approach the house, feeling eight kinds of awkward. Don't

ask me why. I haven't felt out of place in a social setting since my breakout freshman year football season in college. There was no place on campus where a member of a national runner-up team wasn't welcome. Hell, people would have paid to get me at their events.

The same thing was true once I got to the NFL—especially after I won my first Super Bowl ring. Most cities that have pro teams turn the players into royalty, and Cincinnati was no exception.

I never knew if people wanted me around because they liked me or because they wanted a selfie with their team's star wide receiver. Even my teammates were more work friends than anything else. I thought Russ was a real friend, and we all know where that got me.

There also weren't a lot of guys, other than Troy, who I kept in touch with after college. I can shake hands and slap backs and give a good "hey, bro" when the moment calls for it. But I don't let a lot of people in to see the real me. Hell, I barely let myself see the real me.

Ian was much the same way. Or, so I thought. So it surprised the shit out of me when he said he's gotten to know some of the guys who are partnered up with Sadie's friends, and they hang out even when the women aren't involved.

I considered texting Tyler to tell him I was finally taking his advice, but then thought better of it. Because if he asked what prompted my change of heart—he'd also think my foot-in-my-mouth moment with Piper was a damn laugh riot. Besides, my trainer is in Vail for the weekend. We did a pre-dawn run and workout so he could head out to see Mindy, the meal-prep lady.

They basically met a minute ago, and he's already calling her his girlfriend, like it's so simple.

Not for me.

The door opens after one knock, and the guy who answers—

tall, although not quite my height, with brown hair and hazel eyes—grins at me.

"Hey, Felix, come on in. I'm Jake Byrne. Welcome. Glad you could make it."

"Thanks for having me," I say. Except why do I sound angry about it?

I shove the case of beer I picked up at a liquor store on my way over toward him. Maybe a little too hard, judging by the soft "oof" he lets out.

"The guys are in the kitchen. This way."

He leads me down the hall, and I take in the house. The style is mountain modern, tasteful. Obviously high-end, but without that weird showy feel I'm afraid my place in Denver is going to have. Or at least would have had if it wasn't for Piper intervening on my behalf. Add it to the list of ways I owe her.

"There's Baby Barlowe," Ian says as we enter the kitchen.

"Don't make me bench-press you," I shoot back, earning a round of laughs from the two other guys in attendance.

"That's Eric Anderson," Jake says, hitching a thumb toward the giant, dark-haired man leaning a hip against the counter. He lifts his beer in greeting.

"He goes with Taylor," Ian explains.

The librarian, I think to myself. I've heard both Piper and Sadie talking about the book club.

"I go with Molly," the other man offers with the barest hint of a smile. His words are slow and measured, like he might have to pay extra if he speaks too many of them at one time. "Chase Calhoun."

"Molly's the flower farmer," I say, nodding.

"Chase is flower farming with her," Eric says.

"Beats getting the shit kicked out of me by a bull every weekend," Chase replies.

Right. I think back to some of my conversations with Ian. He's mentioned both Chase, a Skylark native and retired bull rider, and

Eric Anderson, who used to play professional hockey in Germany before getting together with Taylor and moving to Skylark.

"You want a beer?" Jake asks.

"No, I'm dry until the end of the season."

"Do a lot of guys do that?" Eric asks, sounding genuinely curious. "I don't think that's a thing in hockey."

"Wasn't a thing when I was in my twenties," I answer. "But it's for the best now."

"Baby Barlowe isn't a baby anymore," Ian says, and damn if I don't feel my face color at the approval in his voice.

Will I ever outgrow wanting my big brother to be proud of me?

"I hear congratulations are in order," Jake says as he hands me a can of sparkling water. "You're going to be a dad."

I feel my nostrils flare, and my hand tightens on the can, the aluminum giving slightly under my grip. I flick an irritated glance toward Ian.

"Don't worry." He shakes his head, reading me as easily as ever. "We're in the book club trust tree here."

I nod because my brother might be annoying, but he wouldn't let me spill my guts to a bunch of assholes. "Thanks," I tell Jake. "Piper's doing all heavy lifting at this point, but I'm..." I can't quite make my lips move the way I want them to. "... Scared shitless," I answer instead of "excited," which is what I meant to say.

"Here's to being scared shitless and showing up anyway," Chase says, lifting his beer in my direction.

Ian claps me on the shoulder, loosening something in my chest. Maybe this won't be so bad after all.

"Help yourself," Jake says, gesturing toward the kitchen island where an impressive spread is laid out. "We've got wings, nachos, and some kind of fancy dip Iris made before she escaped to Molly's."

I load up a plate with wings and nachos, suddenly starving

despite the protein shake I downed before leaving. The wings are baked, not fried—I notice these things now—and there's a respectable array of vegetables on the platter that I'm pretty sure is just for show.

"Were the veggies your idea?" I ask Jake.

He grins. "Iris made me promise. But I'm betting they'll still be here when she gets back."

"Fair enough." I grab a few carrot sticks anyway. Tyler would be proud.

Eric reaches for the nachos. "Do you think they're talking about us?"

"We should be so lucky." Chase snorts. "But also, of course they are."

"Probably planning our lives for the next ten years," Jake adds. "They know what they're doing."

"Piper took Ellie because the twins wanted to meet her," I say, surprising myself by volunteering the information. "She's two. My best friend and his wife named me as guardian in their will, and they..."

I break off, wondering how to stop this embarrassing case of diarrhea of the mouth. It's awkward but also comforting to talk about how the toddler came to be with me. Instead of the looks of shock I expect from the guys, they seem to take my revelation in stride. There's a good chance either Ian or the book club ladies prepped them, but I still appreciate it.

"Luke and Laurel are the best," Chase says, unmistakable affection in his voice. "They'll take good care of her." His thick brows draw together. "Their dad died a few years ago. We were best friends growing up, and I certainly didn't expect to be raising his kids, but it's a fucking honor, you know?"

The tight ball of emotion in my chest loosens ever so slightly. "Yeah," I agree. "I know."

"I came back from Germany to take care of my nephew when my sister was having some issues," Eric says quietly. "Talk about shit not on a bingo card. Raising a teenager. But we do what we have to when the people we love need us."

"Right." I nod, and damn if that ball hasn't shifted higher, making the backs of my eyes sting. This is about to get epically bad if I don't pull my shit together. "The book club vibe," I say, needing a subject change. "Are they really as close as they seem?"

Ian nods. "Sadie says the book club is the best thing that's happened to her. Well, second best." His smug-ass smile should be annoying, but it just makes me think about how lucky the bastard is.

"They're tight," Eric confirms. "Piper's new to the group, but she's one of them now. Which means, by extension, you're one of us."

The idea of that settles over me like a soft blanket. Piper's life is becoming tangled with mine in ways that have nothing to do with the baby or our temporary nanny arrangement and everything to do with this town, these people, and the strange new normal I'm stumbling into.

"You doing okay with the whole instant dad thing?" Jake asks.

I take a long drink of my sparkling water, trying to decide how to answer that. I figure the truth is the way to go. "I have no fucking clue what I'm doing most days. But Piper's great with Ellie. I don't know what I'd do without her."

"That's a common theme around here," Chase says with a laugh.

"You just show up and do your best," Eric tells me.

I'm not sure I've got that part down, but damn I want to.

The conversation shifts to safer territory. Chase's truck breaking down, the new brewery opening in town, and whether the Rockies have a shot at the playoffs this year (they don't). It's oddly normal, and I find myself relaxing into it.

"So," Eric says after we've demolished most of the food, "you want to weigh in on the upcoming season? The Grizzlies' chances and all that?"

I glance around the kitchen. They're all watching me with varying degrees of interest. Eric is avidly curious, Chase politely attentive, Jake somewhere in between. Ian's trying not to look too invested, which means he's absolutely invested.

"For the record," Jake adds, "We didn't invite you here to grill you about football."

"We invited you to take your money at cards," Chase adds, deadpan.

"Good luck with that." I'm grinning now, feeling the last of my tension drain away. "But I think we have a hell of a chance at going all the way, and I'm going to work my ass off to make sure the fans have something to cheer about."

"Fuck yeah," Eric says with a fist pump. "Now let's play some poker."

"The table's already set up in the basement." Jake grabs his beer and the remaining wings.

The guys file out of the kitchen, and I'm about to follow when Ian catches my arm.

"You good?" he asks quietly.

I look hard at my brother—at the contentment in his face, the peace that's settled into the lines around his eyes. He found a life beyond the noise of the pundits and the constant pressure to perform. He repaired his relationship with Riva and found Sadie and this town in the process. Now he has friends who actually give a shit about him, not just the quarterback he used to be.

"Is normal as awesome as it seems?" I ask, my voice rough.

Ian's laugh reminds me of when we were kids. "Normal's underrated, Felix. It took me a long time to figure that out, but it's pretty fucking awesome once you do."

"I can see that," I say, thinking about Piper and Ellie. Feeding my sourdough starter and being on sandbox duty and the way my heart squeezes when Ellie snuggles into me. The best part of normal is coming home to people who know the real me, not just the wide receiver who makes highlight reels.

"You'll get there." Ian squeezes my shoulder. "You're already closer than you think."

From downstairs, Eric yells for us to hurry up before they start without us.

"Coming," Ian calls back, then studies me for a few seconds. "You ready?"

I consider the question. Am I ready for poker with these guys who don't expect anything from me except my company? Or am I ready for this new life that's taking shape around me, whether I planned it or not? Maybe I'm ready to believe I could have something like what Ian's found.

"Yeah," I say. "I'm ready."

We head downstairs, where the others are already settled around a professional-grade poker table. Cards are shuffled, chips distributed, and trash talk initiated. A night like this is exactly what I didn't know I needed.

I love football and always will. I get off on the adrenaline of game day, the precision of a perfect route, and the roar of the crowd when I make an impossible catch in the end zone. The game is in my blood.

But I could also get used to normal.

Hell, I think I already am.

"Felix, you in or you gonna sit there daydreaming about Piper all night?" Ian asks, grinning like the asshole he is.

"Fuck off," I say, tossing a chip into the pot. "And I'm all in."

Eric raises an eyebrow. "Bold move for the first hand."

"That's how I play."

And just maybe, it's how I'm going to win.

22

PIPER

THE SKYLARK COMMUNITY HOSPITAL parking lot looks the same as it did three weeks ago when I stormed out of here with my dignity in tatters. The pothole near the employee entrance is still there and the scraggly ornamental grasses lining the walkway are still struggling against Colorado's unpredictable weather.

Some things never change.

Except me, apparently. Three weeks ago, I was Piper Hart, the pediatric nurse who couldn't keep her shit together long enough to make it through a single shift after seeing her ex-fiancé's smug face in the hallway. Now I'm Piper Hart, the secretly pregnant pediatric nurse who's shacking up with an NFL wide receiver and playing house with his adorable ward. Either way, I'm still trying to figure out if any of this is real, or if I'm going to wake up and discover it was all some bizarre fever dream brought on by excessive morning sickness.

I pull into a spot three rows back from the entrance and cut the Jeep's engine. My hands shake slightly on the steering wheel, which is ridiculous because I'm simply here to talk to Casey Plummer, my old nurse manager. Casey is kind and understanding and definitely didn't deserve the way I bailed on her and the entire peds unit without so much as a two-week notice.

My phone buzzes with a text from Felix.

Felix: Good luck, Hart. You've got this.

Felix: Also Go Pi from Ellie, so she believes in you, too.

I smile despite the nerves twisting my stomach.

Me: Thx, Barlowe. Needed that kick in the ass.

It's followed by a photo of Ellie, with what looks like an entire container of yogurt smeared across her face, grinning like she's over the moon for the man snapping her pic.

Can't blame her, given that I feel the same. After I got home from Molly's Friday night, where the book club ladies grilled me about Felix as if they were casually curious and not totally obsessed with my love life, Felix tried again to apologize for the proposal disaster.

"I know you're capable of taking care of yourself," he'd told me, running a hand through his hair in that way he does when he's frustrated. "I didn't mean to make it sound like—"

"It's fine," I'd interrupted because I couldn't handle the sincerity in his blue eyes or the way my heart was doing a little dance in my chest. "Let's just move on. Please."

And we did move on. We went hiking on Saturday, with Felix carrying Ellie in the backpack carrier and pretending not to notice that I had to stop every ten minutes to catch my breath, followed by a picnic with sandwiches from the deli in town. Yesterday was lazy and domestic, my favorite kind of day. Felix made a loaf of honey and oat sourdough while I read approximately four thousand books to Ellie, then dined on the plastic food meal she made in the play kitchen Felix had delivered to my house, one that's a more manageable size than the one at the cabin. Ellie seems to love it just as much as the gourmet version.

The weekend was easy and comfortable, like we'd been doing it for years instead of weeks.

Which is exactly the problem. Comfortable is dangerous. Comfortable makes you forget that Felix Barlowe announced that he never wanted kids. It makes you overlook the fact that his marriage proposal came from obligation rather than affection. And it makes you want to believe that just maybe this could be your life.

But I learned a long time ago that comfortable doesn't last. My mom was comfortable until the car wreck that ended her life. My relationship with Sadie was comfortable until I started dating her secret crush, not realizing I was twisting a knife in her back. My engagement to Bradley was comfortable right up until the moment I realized comfortable was just another word for "settling for someone who treats you like a pretty accessory instead of a human being."

But now I'm doing the bucket list challenge, and there are things I need to accomplish to prove I can stand on my own two feet. Number one: Get my career back on track. Number two: Stop relying on other people to define my worth.

Except this weekend made it hard to remember what's so wrong with leaning on Felix's very broad, very sturdy shoulders instead.

Which is why the visit to Casey and a potential return to my job are so important. I need to prove to myself that I can do this— be a mother, have a career, build a life—without becoming so dependent on anyone that I forget I'm capable of it all by myself.

I check my reflection in the rearview mirror. My blonde hair is pulled back in a neat ponytail, and I'm wearing my favorite navy dress. I look like someone who has her life together, even though I'm growing a tiny human inside me who enjoys making me vomit at the most inconvenient times.

"Fake it till you make it," I mutter, then grab my purse and head toward the entrance.

The automatic doors slide open, and I'm hit with the distinctive antiseptic hospital smell. My stomach does a little roll in response, but then blessedly settles again. I'm giving credit to the toast I had for breakfast. I might want to stand on my own two feet, but I've got no problem letting sourdough prop me up.

The volunteer at the front desk, Ed Masterson, looks up with a bland smile that turns into something real when he sees me. "Piper Hart, I've missed you. Tell me you're back."

"Only for a visit," I answer with a smile that feels only slightly strained. "I have a meeting with Casey."

"That's a start." Ed nods his approval. "You know the way."

Yep. Past the gift shop with its shiny balloons and overpriced stuffed animals, up the elevator to the third floor, then through the double doors with the cheerful rainbow mural that some local artist painted years ago.

Casey Plummer is standing at the nurses' station, which appears to be the same organized chaos of charts and computers it was three weeks ago. I hear the faint sound of a child crying somewhere down the hall.

Casey's dark hair is in its usual no-nonsense bun, and she's wearing scrubs with cartoon dinosaurs all over them. She's in her early forties with three kids of her own, and has the kind of calm presence that makes her perfect for managing a unit where emotions run high. Her face breaks into a genuine grin as I approach, and my guilt over how I left intensifies about ten thousand percent.

"Piper, it's so good to see you." She comes around the desk and pulls me into a quick hug as a nurse I don't recognize looks on. "Let's go to my office. Janie, you good here?"

Janie nods. "Got it covered."

"Thanks," I say automatically to the young woman, then follow Casey down the hall. Her office is about the size of a storage closet, but it has a door that closes, which is the important part as far as I'm concerned. She gestures for me to sit and settles into her own chair with a sigh.

"Long day already?" I ask.

"Long month. We've been short-staffed since…" She pauses, clearly rethinking whether to finish that sentence.

"Since I bailed without notice?" I supply with a wince. "Casey, I'm so sorry. I know I left you in a terrible position. Seeing Bradley and Marie here was just—"

"I get it." My former boss leans forward, her expression kind. "Breakups are hard enough. Ones where your ex shows up at your workplace with his new wife might be their own special circle of hell. You don't owe anyone an apology for protecting your mental health."

The relief that washes over me is so intense I nearly tear up, which is probably hormones mixed with a healthy dose of gratitude for this woman's basic human decency.

"I might like to come back," I tell her. "If that's possible. I know I probably burned some bridges, but I love working here. I was thinking maybe I could try something different than peds."

"You're one of the best nurses I've seen," Casey agrees without hesitation. "Any unit in this hospital would be lucky to have you, but I need to be honest about something."

That vaguely ominous statement causes my stomach to churn once again. "What is it?"

"Dr. Carlson's wife started here two weeks ago, and she's been picking up a lot of shifts. If you come back, there's a good chance you'll be working with her."

Talk about a special circle of hell. Of course Bradley's wife would be working here. I'm guessing she's perfect and docile and everything I was unwilling to be. Hell, she probably gets along with his mother, who chose to serve a dish I'm allergic to at our rehearsal dinner. More power to her with that insufferable cow.

"I'm sure I can handle it," I say, trying to sound more

confident than I feel. "Bradley and I aren't exactly enemies." Although we sure as hell aren't friends. "I don't even know Marie. It might be a lot given my—"

I stop myself just in time, but Casey's sharp enough to catch the near slip.

"Given your what?" she asks gently.

I take a breath. Casey has been nothing but kind to me, so if I'm coming back to the hospital, she deserves to know what she's dealing with.

"My condition," I say quietly. "I'm fourteen weeks pregnant. No doubt the hormones are at least part of why I had such a strong reaction to seeing Bradley and his wife. Everything feels about a gazillion times more intense."

Casey's eyes widen slightly, but her expression stays kind. "Congratulations. That's wonderful news. If you don't mind me asking, are you and the father together?"

I let out a laugh that's only slightly hysterical. "Not exactly? It's complicated, but we're figuring it out. I have a great support system in town with Sadie and my friends. And the father is..." How do I even begin to explain Felix? "He's supportive." Also infuriating and charming and a puzzle and far too easy to fall for. But I don't mention any of those things, of course.

"That's important." Casey taps her pen against her desk. "Look, Piper, I want you back. But you need to be sure this is what you want. We're a community hospital. You could be working with Marie, and you're bound to see Dr. Carlson in the halls or the cafeteria. Dealing with the stress of this job and the long hours while pregnant is no joke. You know that."

"I also need to stand on my own two feet," I tell her, echoing the phrase that's been running through my head like a mantra. "For myself and my baby. I can't rely on other people to take care of me."

Casey's expression turns thoughtful as she studies me. "I have no doubt you're going to be a good mother, but being independent doesn't mean doing everything alone. The best thing you can do for your child is build a strong community around both of you. You have options, Piper, and accepting help doesn't translate to weakness. You know that, right?"

Her words land in the vicinity of my heart, lodging there like a splinter I can't remove, because I don't know anything of the sort.

"I appreciate you reminding me," I say finally. "Can I think about things and let you know by the end of the week?"

"Of course. There's always a place for you here. Whatever you decide, I'm rooting for you."

I thank her and leave the office before the tears stinging the backs of my eyes can make an appearance. I'm halfway down the hall when I see him.

Bradley Carlson is handsome in a polished, bland way that photographs well but makes him look like a generic toothpaste commercial model in real life. In his white doctor's coat, tablet tucked under one arm, there's that familiar look of mild superiority on his face. I used to mistake it for confidence, fool that I was. Fool that I am, thinking I'd be safe from running into him, given my short visit to the hospital today. What the hell is an orthopedic surgeon doing in the peds unit anyway? Oh, right. His wife works here.

He's alone—praise the Lord—but spots me before I can duck into a stairwell. "Hey there, Piper. I heard you might be coming back."

"News travels fast," I say, keeping my voice neutral.

He studies me in the way that always made me feel like I was being graded but could never earn an A. "Running away didn't work out so great, huh?"

The comment stings, as I'm sure it was meant to, but I refuse to give him the satisfaction of knowing it. "I needed a break. But Skylark is my home, and I'm a kick-ass nurse."

"Right." His smile doesn't reach his eyes. "If you decide to come back, you'll have plenty of chances to get to know Marie. Everyone loves her. My mother certainly does."

"Lucky Marie," I mutter. I don't need the reminder of Mrs. Carlson's thinly veiled disdain for me, or to know that Marie fits into Bradley's family in a way I never did. My life might be more questions than answers at the moment, but I know for sure I dodged a bullet when my future mother-in-law put that shrimp-laced sauce on the rehearsal dinner menu. I might have gone through with marrying the douche canoe standing in front of me if it hadn't been for that.

"Oh, and you'll see us both at Christy's wedding next weekend," Bradley continues, like he's doing me a favor by sharing his social calendar. "Marie and Christy go to the same yoga studio in town. They've gotten really close."

"You've been back less than a month."

He shrugs. "Marie has that effect on people. You wouldn't understand. Are you bringing a date?"

The question catches me off guard, and I answer without thinking. "No."

"I'm surprised." Bradley's laugh is laced with a layer of judgment that lands like a calculated cut. Just as he intended. "I thought you would have found someone else to take care of you by now. I guess Sadie's still stuck in that role."

Right. Because I'm the helpless little sister who can't manage her own life, incapable of standing on my own.

The worst part is that a piece of me believes he's right.

My stomach lurches suddenly, and I'm not sure if it's morning sickness or just an innate physical reaction to Bradley and the mistake I almost made. The nausea builds into the uncomfortable roll I've been dealing with for weeks now.

"I need to go," I manage and walk away as quickly as I can without actually running. No need to give the asshat more ammunition about my inability to handle things like an adult.

I make it to a bathroom near the stairwell and lock myself in a stall, breathing through the nausea and trying very hard not to think about how much that conversation encapsulated all my worst fears. I'm not capable. I need constant rescuing. I'm going to spend my entire life being taken care of because I can't manage it on my own.

By the time the nausea passes, my eyes are burning with unshed tears, and I'm pressing my palms hard to the metal on either side of the stall like it's closing in on me. I cannot be the girl who falls apart in a hospital bathroom because her douchebag ex-fiancé makes a snide comment. I'm carrying a little life inside me. I'm going to be responsible for an entire tiny human who deserves a mother who has her shit together.

I need to prove I can do this alone.

The drive back to my house—not "our house," not "the house where Felix is staying," MY house—takes fifteen minutes, and I spend the entire time alternating between anger at Bradley and disappointment in myself for letting him get under my skin. Again.

My phone buzzes as I pull into the driveway.

> Felix: Did you kill it? We're at Ian's. Riva's back
> from her mom's and was dying to meet Ellie.
> Come over when you're done.

I can picture Felix and Ian in the living room while Ellie and Riva play, probably with Beast and whatever other dogs my sister's watching as part of the mix. Sadie will be prepping snacks and generally being the perfect hostess. The whole thing will feel welcoming and easy, the way things with my sister always are.

And that's exactly why I can't go.

> Me: Have fun and tell Riva I said hi. I'm actually
> pretty tired. Going to rest for a bit.

I hit send before I can second-guess myself, then drop the phone in my purse like it might bite me if I look at it too long.

The house is quiet when I let myself in, which shouldn't feel wrong because this is how it was before Felix showed up at the cabin with Ellie. I lived here with only Max as company for months, and I liked having the space to myself without having to account for anyone else's needs.

But now, instead of peaceful, the silence feels heavy. The living room looks empty with Ellie's toys all tucked away. And the kitchen feels too big without Felix taking up space at the counter, kneading bread dough with those massive hands.

I sink onto the couch and pull my knees up to my chest, wrapping my arms around them in a gesture that's more a defense mechanism than a comfort stance. Max's old dog bed is still in the corner, even though he's been gone for over a month now. I should get rid of it, along with a lot of things that don't serve any purpose except to make me feel anchored to a past that wasn't that great to begin with.

Maybe what I need is a fresh start that doesn't involve depending on anyone else to make me feel whole.

My phone buzzes again in my purse, but I ignore it. This is what standing on my own two feet means, right? I need to get comfortable with being alone.

I don't need Felix and Ellie to make my house feel like a home.

So why does it feel like I'm punishing myself instead of proving something?

As I sit in the too-quiet living room of my childhood home, one hand drifts to rest on my stomach, and I try very hard to convince myself that this is what independence looks like.

I'm not afraid of accepting help like Casey suggested. But I'm terrified of depending on someone who might leave the moment things get hard. My father did exactly that before I was even born, and Bradley couldn't handle it when I finally stood up for myself. So what will Felix do when he realizes that obligatory proposals and playing house in a mountain cabin are very different from the actual work of building a life together?

The quiet house doesn't seem to have any more answers than I do, so I close my eyes and try to figure out if what I'm doing is strength, or just the fear wearing a different mask.

23

FELIX

I ADJUST my grip on the steering wheel and glance toward Tyler, who's riding shotgun Friday morning as I head to the Grizzlies' training facility for a mandatory meeting with the team and interviews with a few members of the press. He's scrolling through his phone, probably texting Mindy. I should have argued harder when Piper said she and Ellie weren't coming with me.

"Are we going to hide on the floor of your giant SUV?" she'd asked with a laugh when I issued the invitation this morning. She'd been standing in the kitchen with Ellie on her hip looking every inch a goddess–domestic and otherwise. "Or are you ready to explain either of us to your new teammates or to curious reporters?"

Of course she was right, but that didn't stop the knot in my chest from tightening when I walked out the door without them. I'm not sure why things feel different today, but it's like I don't want to step back into my regular life without them, terrified of reality truly setting in.

"You're doing it again," Tyler says without looking up from his phone.

"Doing what?"

"Thinking so loud I can practically hear it." He finally glances over at me. "You wanted them to come."

"Piper didn't think it was a good call." I signal to change lanes. "She's way smarter than me, as usual."

"You don't like leaving them."

I don't answer. What's the point? Tyler knows me too well. He knows that I've developed this annoying protective instinct that makes me want to bundle them both in bubble wrap.

"It's weird," I say finally.

"What is?"

"The feeling of needing to know where they are all the time. To make sure they're okay." I shake my head. "It's fucking unhinged."

Tyler laughs. "It's called caring about people, dumbass."

"I care about lots of people. It's not the same."

"Because lots of people aren't Ellie and Piper."

"Speaking of which," I say, because I've been putting this off long enough. "I need to tell you something."

Tyler straightens in his seat, and I can feel his eyes on me. "This doesn't sound good."

"Piper's pregnant."

A beat of silence and then, "Holy shit."

I glance over to see him staring at me, slack-jawed. "That about sums it up." I still can't quite wrap my head around the fact that I'm going to be a father when the new year rolls around. Again. Or for real this time, since Ellie technically isn't mine—even if she does have me wrapped around her chubby little finger.

"How far along?"

"About fourteen weeks now. She's due in January."

He claps a hand on my arm several times. "Dude, that's awesome. You're going to be a fa—"

"There's more." I grip the steering wheel tighter. "The attorney called yesterday. He finally tracked down Julie's aunt."

"Ellie's relative?"

"Yeah. The aunt—her name's Nancy—and Julie's mother were estranged, but she's interested in meeting Ellie."

The words hang between us.

"So you're going to dump one kid before you have another?" Tyler's voice has lost all its warmth.

Heat flashes through me, but I'm not sure whether it comes from anger or self-recrimination. "What the hell, Ty? You know the plan has always been to find a family for Ellie. People who can take care of her."

"But not you?"

"She needs someone who actually knows what they're doing."

"You're figuring it out." It's not a question.

I open my mouth to argue, then close it again. I hate that he's right. I *am* figuring it out. And I want to keep going. I want to hear Ellie call me Fee every morning. Read her favorite books, most of which I already have memorized. I want to teach her how to throw a football and protect her from every bad thing in the world. But I'm terrified the thing she needs to be protected from the most might be me.

"This isn't about me," I say finally. "It's about what's best for Ellie."

"You're still convinced that's not you?"

"Tyler—"

"What does Piper think?"

I don't answer. I haven't told her about the call from the attorney. I've been too busy trying not to think about what it means.

"Jesus, Felix." Tyler shakes his head. "You have to tell her."

"I will. It's just that I don't know where things stand with us so—"

"Where things stand is you knocked her up."

"Fuck off, Tyler. It's more complicated than that. I also asked her to marry me. Badly."

"Are you joking?" Tyler shifts to face me fully.

"Do I look like I'm joking? I asked her to marry me, and she said no."

"So instead of talking to her like an adult about Ellie's aunt, you're going to pretend like it didn't happen?" He shakes his head. "You're a giant idiot."

"Thanks, man," I answer through gritted teeth. "Super helpful."

He lets out a low whistle. "You like her."

"Of course I like her. She's—" I stop myself before I can list all the things that are awesome about Piper. The way she calls me on my bullshit. How she makes me laugh even when I'm trying to be mad. The softness in her eyes when she looks at Ellie. The way she fits against me when we—

"Maybe more than like," Tyler amends.

"We both know where that's gotten me in the past." The bitterness in my voice surprises even me. "High school, college, Ronnie. Every time I give a woman my heart, she finds a creative way to destroy it."

"Piper's different."

"Yeah. She tells me to my face when I'm being a twatwaffle."

"Exactly." Tyler's laugh is almost diabolical. "And she doesn't want you for your money or your status."

I'm not going to lie. It's refreshing to have someone look at me and see Felix instead of the NFL star. At first, I was annoyed that she clearly wasn't impressed by my hype, but it's made me work harder to be a man she can admire.

"How do I know if she wants me long-term?" The question pops out of my mouth before I can stop it, my deepest fear spoken out loud. If Piper doesn't care about my money or status, is just being me going to be enough? I certainly have no track record in that area.

"We'll figure it out," Tyler assures me, and damn, I want to believe him. "But first, what are you going to do about Ellie?"

My heart clenches, because the truth is, I don't want to let her go. But I also don't want to mess her up the way my dad messed up Ian and me with his constant criticism and impossible standards. He made everything about football and nothing about actually being a father. I've seen Ian do better, but even my perfect brother struggled to connect with his daughter at the height of his career. And if Ian couldn't manage football and fatherhood, how do I stand a chance?

"I don't know," I admit. "She deserves better than my lifestyle, better than—"

"Better than a guy who stays up late researching toddler development and reads her the same damn books over and over because they make her happy?" Tyler's voice is gentle now. "Felix, you're already being the dad she needs. You just don't see it."

I don't know what to say to that, so I focus on the road. We're getting close to Denver now, the city skyline appearing in the distance.

My phone buzzes, and I grab it from the cupholder to glance briefly at the screen while keeping one eye on the road. It's a picture of Ellie with what looks like syrup in her hair.

Piper: oops. pancakes are messy business

I find myself smiling despite everything I'm struggling to figure out.

"You've seriously got it bad." I can hear the smirk in Tyler's voice.

"Shut up," I tell him and turn on the radio.

THE GRIZZLIES' training facility is on the south end of the city. It's state-of-the-art, massive, and hums with an energy that I recognize at a soul-deep level. As soon as we walk through the doors, I'm swept up in it.

"Barlowe!" Someone claps me on the shoulder. It's Jameson Davis, the team's best defensive back. "It's about time you showed your face."

My hand is dwarfed by his giant paw as we shake, which is saying something. "Glad to finally be here."

"You've been incognito as hell, man. Hiding out in the mountains?"

Yes, actually. "Just settling in."

More guys appear to welcome me to the team, and some of my worries melt away. The camaraderie is familiar in a way I didn't notice I missed. This is my world. What I know how to do.

The press conference is exactly what I expected, too. There are the usual questions about my move from Cincinnati and what I'm looking forward to with the Grizzlies.

"I'm excited to make a home in Colorado," I say into the microphone, and the words feel strange in my mouth.

A home. What does that even mean to me?

It's not the sterile McMansion I bought or my condo in Cincinnati. Home has become a cozy house in a small foothills town with two females who make me want things I never thought I could have.

When the press conference ends, I do more handshaking and small talk making.

"Felix Barlowe," someone says from behind me. The voice is deep and authoritative. I turn to find Tom Matheson, the Grizzlies' franchise quarterback, leaning against a nearby doorframe. He's shorter than me by a few inches, with the kind of steady presence that clearly communicates he's the team leader.

"Tom. Nice to see you again. I'm—"

"Walk with me." It's not a question.

We head down a hallway away from the crowds, and it feels like I'm being called into the principal's office.

"I heard about what happened in Cincinnati with Russ," he says once we're alone in a small conference room.

My jaw clenches. I didn't think anyone outside of Cincinnati knew about that. About finding Ronnie and Russ together. The spectacular implosion of both my relationship and my friendship, not to mention the effect it had on the field.

"That wasn't—"

"You don't have to explain." Tom crosses his long arms over his chest, studying me. "I'm going to say this once: some of the guys on this team are partiers. Young guys, mostly. You know how it goes. They like to hit the clubs, get wild, live that baller lifestyle."

I do know, even if that lifestyle doesn't hold a lick of interest for me anymore. But I stay quiet, curious to see where this is going.

"If that's what you want, more power to you. You're not a young gun anymore, but we both know you've got a lot of football left if you play it right." He pauses. "We're going to prove something together this season, and that's a hell of a lot easier when you've got something solid off the field too."

"Like what you've got," I murmur, thinking of how Tom's reputation off the field is as steady as his arm on a third down and long. Everyone knows he's a family man through and through. He never cared for the spotlight, the headlines, or the brand deals. He plays his heart out and then goes home to the only thing that really matters to him.

"Exactly like what I've got. Football's a huge part of my life, but it's not the whole of it. My wife and three kids are what's most important. When I have a shit game, they remind me I'm more than the stats. When we win, they celebrate with me. But they also expect me to take out the trash and help with homework. My career doesn't give me a pass on showing up for what really matters, and that's made a huge difference."

"I don't have a wife or three kids," I tell him. But where a few months ago I couldn't have imagined myself with either, now I know what he means. I understand what it's like to value the people I love over the game.

Love. Oh, fuck.

I wait for the panic to roll through me, but instead, my heart seems to settle. Like it's been waiting for me to figure it out. I love Ellie, and I'm in love with Piper. Head over fucking heels.

"Figure out what matters to you." Tom studies me like he's seeing more than I want him to. "Because having something waiting for you at home makes every part of the job even better."

He claps me on the shoulder and walks away, leaving me alone with my spinning thoughts.

Can I be the guy who has it all—the career, the family, the home that actually means something?

An image pops into my head of Ellie, Piper, and our baby. The four of us are in a house that's more than a stale showpiece. There are toys scattered around and laughter filling the rooms.

And I want all of it, which scares the living crap out of me because wanting something like that means opening myself up to the possibility of losing it. Of having my heart shattered all over again.

But maybe that's the point. Maybe the things worth having are supposed to scare you.

My phone buzzes with another picture from Piper. This time, she and Ellie are making faces at the camera.

Piper: the bean says hi

I stare at the photo for a long moment, memorizing the way Piper's eyes crinkle when she smiles, and how Ellie's downy curls look like angel wings on the side of her head. My heart is flinging itself against my ribs because it knows these two amazing women belong to me.

One of the assistant coaches appears at the end of the hallway, waving me toward him, and I head back to the locker room. I spend another hour talking with my teammates and getting the lay of the Grizzlies' land.

Eventually, I make my way toward the front of the building. Tyler is waiting for me in the lobby. "How'd it go?"

"Good. Really good." I follow him out into the bright afternoon sunlight. "Hey, Ty?"

"Yeah?"

"I'm not giving Ellie up."

He stops walking and turns to look at me, a slow grin spreading across his face. "About damn time you pulled your head out of your ass on that one."

"I still have no idea what I'm doing."

"The way my sisters talk, that's the whole point of parenting. You figure it out as you go."

We walk to the car in silence, and I think about Tom's words. The importance of having something solid off the field. What it would take to be more than just a wide receiver. And the idea that Piper already sees that in me.

I think about Piper saying she needs to stand on her own, and how I screwed up the proposal so badly that she probably believes I don't want her.

But I do. God help me, I want her. I want all of it—the banter, the chemistry, the way she challenges me. I want to wake up next to her, fall asleep holding her, and build something real together.

I just have to make her believe I'm worth the risk.

Because Piper Hart deserves a man who does things right. Who plans and romances and actually uses words to tell her how he feels instead of blurting out panic-proposals.

"What are you thinking about?" Tyler asks as we pull out of the parking lot.

"How to win over a woman who thinks I'm a twatwaffle."

Tyler laughs. "Good luck with that."

"We need to make a stop."

He raises an eyebrow. "Where?"

"A jewelry store."

Tyler gapes for a second, but then grins and pumps his fist in the air. "You're buying her a ring."

"I'm buying her a ring." The words feel right coming out of my mouth. "And then I'm going to convince her to marry me. The right way this time."

"Hell yeah, you are." My friend seems almost proud of me, and I'll take it. A hundred times over. "I know just the place. It's in Cherry Creek." He pulls out his phone and types the name of the jewelry store into the GPS. "Let's do this."

Twenty minutes later, I slide back into the driver's seat with an embossed bag in my hand. Inside is a velvet box, and inside that is a ring that isn't flashy or ostentatious. It's an oval diamond in a delicate platinum setting, elegant and understated. The kind of ring a woman wears because she loves what it represents, not because she needs everyone to see it.

It feels like exactly what Piper would want. I sure hope it is.

Because as I point the car west toward the mountains, heading back to Skylark—toward Piper and Ellie and the potential of what we could build together if I can find a way to get there—I realize I don't need the luck Tyler talked about. I just need to stop being afraid of what I want and start fighting for it.

And I've never backed down from a fight in my life.

24

PIPER

"So let me get this straight." Avah points a corner of her turkey club in my direction. "One of your high school besties invited your douche canoe ex-fiancé and his new wife to her wedding because the bitches do yoga together?"

The afternoon sun beats down on us despite the shade from a nearby Douglas fir, and I'm grateful we picked this spot in Town Hall Park. A light breeze carries the scent of pine and wildflowers, offering some relief from the late summer heat. Ellie toddles between us and the tree, her little fists full of treasures.

I glance over my shoulder to where she's happily collecting pinecones from beneath the branches, then back to Avah.

"Can we keep the language G-rated?"

"Can you answer the question?" she fires back.

"Yeah. I texted Christy, and she said she meant to let me know, but there's been so much going on with the wedding planning. She said Marie is *really nice*." The words taste bitter in my mouth, even though I'm trying not to care.

"You have..." Avah flicks her eyes toward Ellie. "...poopy friends."

"It's not a big deal," I say and pick up a chip, only to put it down again. My heart is still doing that annoying pinch thing whenever I think about Bradley and his really nice new wife at Christy's wedding.

"It's kind of a big deal." Sloane places a hand on my arm, the gentle pressure grounding me.

Avah and I had lunch plans today, and I was glad when Sloane said she could join too, and even more grateful that the two of them were up for a picnic in the park across from Town Hall. The grass is soft beneath our blanket, and Colorado's endless blue sky stretches above us. It's the kind of summer day that makes you forget that in a few months the whole landscape will be covered in a layer of snow.

Tucked under the shade of a tree, we're also away from the potentially curious stares of Skylark locals that we'd get at the diner in town. One of the perks of living in a small town is that people look out for each other. The downside to that is people being all up in your business. It's not like I'm trying to hide Ellie. I smile as I watch her squat to examine a particularly large pinecone.

Now that Ian knows about her, Felix has gotten a lot more comfortable taking her out in public. And as if he wasn't popular enough, his vague explanation that he's helping out a friend has melted hearts all over town. It actually seems to have made him even more of a fan favorite, at least with the residents of Skylark.

On the other hand, I get a not-at-all-melty reaction when I explain that I'm working as his temporary nanny while he helps out said friend. I've gotten a few veiled *oh, so you're the nanny* comments, along with some straight-up attitude. *Trying to follow in your sister's footsteps, huh? Worked out pretty well for her.* Sometimes it's a fight not to roll my eyes sometimes.

I hate the innuendos and judgment. For one, they aren't true. But also because it's only going to get worse once my pregnancy is public knowledge. My hand drifts to my stomach, which is starting to show just enough that I've switched to loose-fitting tops.

"I swear I don't care."

"What's up with your pruny face then?" Sloane asks.

"This is just my face," I say with an eye roll. "Ellie, do you want another bite of sandwich?"

The girl toddles over to me with a pinecone in each fist. "Pi cone." She holds out her hand like she's gifting me with a gold crown.

"Oh, this is a perfect pinecone," I tell her sincerely. "I'll treasure it always."

"Always," she mimics, and that one word does something funny to my chest. It makes my breath catch, and my heart squeeze with an emotion I'm not ready to name.

"Pruny," Sloane repeats, her voice knowing.

"You better work on fixing your face, Pip," Avah adds with a laugh. "The Hart sisters are for sure not poker players."

I take a breath. "I didn't get pregnant purposely to trap Felix." The words come out softer than I intend.

"Sweetie, no one thinks you did," Avah assures me quickly.

I shake my head. "Because hardly anyone knows. But once they do..."

"None of us think you did," Sloane says. "And who gives a rat's ass what other people think?"

Avah nods, a strand of shiny blonde hair falling across her cheek. "Your friends are the only ones who matter."

"My high school friends will for sure think it was on purpose." My tone edges toward bitter. "When Christy found out I'm nannying for Felix, she just about demanded I bring him as my date to the wedding so she can post it on social media."

"Hey, it worked for Sadie," Avah says, and Sloane nudges her. "What? I'm not saying it's the same thing, but bringing him to your wedding as her fake boyfriend is how it all started. Why not take advantage of—"

"No." I shake my head emphatically. "I won't fake a relationship with Felix. That's going to be a little awkward given that I'm carrying his child." My hand goes to my stomach again, a protective gesture that's becoming a habit.

"He'd go with you, though," Sloane says gently, "if you need the moral support."

Avah snorts. "Which you shouldn't fu—fudging need when you're going to be at this wedding with people who are supposed to be your lifelong friends."

"You guys are my friends now." I mean it. These women have shown up for me more in the past few months than my high school crowd has in years.

Avah pops a grape into her mouth. "We're a big improvement, too."

"Speaking of Felix." Sloane arches a delicate brow in my direction. "Obviously we've established that you don't hate him like we thought you did."

"Like *I* thought I did."

"There's a thin line between love and hate." Avah looks at me while she's saying the words, but I don't think she's just talking about Felix and me. Something dark flickers across her face before she masks it with a smile.

"Are you going to give us another lecture on how great hate sex is?" Sloane asks with a laugh.

Avah's smile tightens. "I've already told you, I'm not giving that lecture anymore."

Sloane's expression shifts to concern. "Everything okay with the elopement plans? There's still time for a ceremony surrounded by your book club besties instead of some secret self-solemnizing spot."

"We don't want any fuss," Avah insists.

When I first heard about Avah's plan to elope in Colorado with just her and Jonathan, it had sounded like a dream. After all the stress of wedding planning—seating charts, dealing with vendors, nonstop opinions from anyone with a pulse—running off to say vows on a mountainside seemed like the only sane option.

But now something about it feels off. Avah's not someone who shies away from attention, and Jonathan's so focused on his career and reputation, it seems like he'd love an excuse to throw a lavish party. So why the cloak and dagger routine?

"Besides, you know I'm all about the honeymoon, and without wedding expenses, we're going all out in Bora Bora." She does a shimmy. "Really, you guys. I couldn't be happier."

Except she sounds about as happy as someone about to face a firing squad. The forced cheerfulness in her voice makes my chest constrict. There's a beat of silence, and I know Sloane must also be registering how odd our friend is acting.

Avah picks up the container of oatmeal cookies she brought along. You wouldn't guess it to look at her, but Avah's sweet baking game is wicked good. "What's new at the bookstore?" she asks as she offers Sloane a cookie. "And how does it feel to have kicked cancer to the curb?"

"Book sales are solid," Sloane says, studying the cookie she's holding. "But I haven't quite kicked it to the curb yet. I've got another round of meds coming, but—"

"Wait." Avah shakes her head, and I watch the same confusion cross her features that I'm sure is mirrored in mine. "I thought after the stem cell transplant, you were good. Your hair is nearly to your ears now. I mean, I know that's not a measure of health," she clarifies quickly, "but—"

"I've qualified for a new drug trial." Sloane runs a finger through her dark hair, shining in the afternoon sun. "The best part is it's not like chemo. I'm not supposed to lose my hair with this one."

Her tone is thoughtful, but strangely at odds with the bright summer sunshine. Where's a rain cloud when you need it?

"So you're not..." I swallow hard. "Cancer-free?"

She tries to hide her wince, but isn't quite successful. "Not yet. One more round of treatment to go, and then I'm onto my survivorship care plan."

"What do you need?" Avah asks.

"How can we help?" I echo.

Sloane rolls her eyes. "You know Jeremy has everything dialed in." Her brother, a billionaire tech bro, has been at her side for every step in this cancer journey. He doesn't seem to want much interaction with the rest of us, which pisses Avah off to no end. She doesn't like not being in control, and with his seemingly endless contacts in the medical community, plus his deep pockets, Jeremy has been the person Sloane leans on the most.

"I hate your brother," Avah mutters.

"You barely know him," Sloane counters with a smile, as usual entertained by the animosity between her brother and her best friend.

Avah wrinkles her nose. "I know enough to hate him."

Ellie comes back over and offers Sloane a pinecone, as if she can sense the shift in the conversation, the emotion thick around us.

"This is lovely, sweetie. I'm going to put it on my desk where I can look at it every day." Sloane's smile is almost wistful. She's the only one of us, if you count my situation-ship with Felix, who's not with a guy. As far as I can tell, she didn't date much before her cancer diagnosis, and not at all since. Although I'd never ask her directly, I wonder if her treatment has affected her ability to conceive, and whether she might want to eventually.

Ellie grins. "Pretty," she says, and leans in to give Sloan a smacking kiss on her cheek.

A pang of guilt pierces my heart when Sloane presses two fingers to the place where Ellie kissed her. Sadie and Ian are having trouble starting a family, and Sloane might have limited options, while I'm apparently Fertile Myrtle, wallowing in my worry over a circumstance so many people dream of. And even though it wasn't planned, I love this baby already and appreciate how blessed I am that things have gone smoothly with this pregnancy so far. Well, smoothly if I ignore the all-day morning sickness, which seems to be easing slightly.

"Hey, kid, am I chopped liver over here?" Avah waves her hands in the air, clearly trying to lighten the mood. "Do you have a pinecone and a compliment for me?"

It's not as if Avah doesn't know she's drop-dead gorgeous with blonde hair, a killer figure, and more confidence than I've ever seen in one person. But lately, I'm beginning to wonder if her brash and sass might be hiding something. The same way my bluntness and sarcasm do.

"Ya," Ellie says after a minute, nodding like Avah passed some invisible test. Then she heads back to her pile to pick out the perfect one.

"Want to talk more about how your brother is a bossy asshole?" Avah grins as she asks the question, but it's more a baring of teeth.

"I think that's an unwritten rule for tech billionaires," Sloane concedes. "But I can't complain because he's been so supportive during all of this."

"Maybe." Avah makes a show of studying her nails, which are perfectly manicured. She's wearing a long-sleeve turtleneck sweater, which might be lightweight, but seems odd given the temperature today. "But he needs to learn to share."

That makes Sloane laugh. "Jeremy was never good at sharing."

My phone vibrates, and I glance down at the message from Felix.

Felix: You guys good?

The simple question makes something twist in my chest. I tap out a response and hit send without thinking.

Me: Why wouldn't we be?

"What's wrong? You've got that pruny look again," Avah tells me. "You don't want to be a wrinkly hag in your mid-twenties."

Perfect. One more thing to add to my list of concerns. Premature wrinkles.

"She wasn't serious," Sloane assures me.

"If it gets bad, you can do Botox." Avah makes a face like *duh, girl...you know I'm joking.*

Except suddenly I'm not in the mood for teasing. "Listen to what Felix sent me," I say, reading the text aloud. But when I glance at my two friends, neither of them seems offended on my behalf. Frustration bubbles up in my throat. "He doesn't think I can handle Ellie on my own for the day."

"Or," Sloane says slowly, drawing out the word, "he's checking in because he cares."

"Not everything is a judgment on your capabilities, Pip," Avah adds. "Maybe it was with Bradley, but Felix doesn't strike me as the micro-managing type."

I open my mouth to argue, then close it because...yeah, that tracks. And I'm bordering on unhinged when it comes to my doubts and fears and feelings for Felix Barlowe. I don't even think I can blame hormones at this point.

"You said he's doing some sort of NFL team bonding or whatever today," Sloane continues. "It's got to be stressful. Maybe he just wanted to touch base with the person who makes him feel grounded."

The idea that I might be Felix's grounding force, the way he's become mine, has my heart melting faster than a popsicle on a summer sidewalk.

"I didn't think about it like that," I admit quietly.

"Of course you didn't. You were too busy assuming the worst." Avah's tone is gentle despite her words. "But I'm gonna go out on a limb and say the guy who stress-bakes sourdough at five a.m. and researches high-altitude prenatal nutrition actually cares about you for real."

Before I can respond, a pinecone comes flying through the air.

Avah catches it one-handed without even looking, which is both impressive and very her.

"Nice aim, girl," she says, examining it with mock seriousness. "Also, excellent pinecone selection. Ten out of ten."

"Ava catch!" Ellie giggles and launches herself at Avah for a tight hug. "Good grl!"

"Yeah, yeah. Kids love me." Avah's deadpan delivery makes me snort. "They can sense that I'm never going to attempt to feed them vegetables."

"You're going to make a heck of a mother someday," Sloane teases.

The darkness I keep catching glimpses of flickers across Avah's face again, but it's gone before I can pin it down.

Satisfied that she's given each of us the perfect pinecone, Ellie toddles over to me and climbs into my lap. She smells like sunscreen and graham crackers, and as she burrows against my chest, her thumb finds its way to her mouth. She settles in, letting out a sigh that holds so much trust, it makes my throat go tight.

"Aww," Sloane says softly. "Look at you two."

"You look good with Felix's kid in your lap," Avah adds, none of her usual sarcasm in the observation.

The words hit me harder than they should. Ellie isn't Felix's— not really. And neither am I. We're both just temporary pieces in a life he's still trying to decide if he wants.

I want him to choose both of us.

The realization crashes over me with the force of a dam breaking, flooding every inch of me with need. I want to be his. For the three of us—eventually four—to be a family. Sure, it's messy and complicated and nothing like what I planned, but it would belong to me. I want more mornings of waking up to the scent of sourdough and more nights of Felix memorizing every inch of my body.

Most of all, I want to stop pretending this arrangement is

temporary when everything in me is screaming that it should be permanent.

"I should head home to get her down for a nap." I clear my throat when the words come out rough. "It's past her usual time."

As if they're somehow attuned to my inner turmoil, my friends gather the remains of our picnic while I hold Ellie, who's already growing heavy-lidded against my shoulder.

"Do you want a ride back to the bookstore?" I ask Sloane as she hands me the folded blanket.

"I'll walk. It's only a few blocks."

I give her a one-armed hug, mindful of Ellie. "Thanks for being up for an impromptu picnic. I needed this."

"Any time, Pip." She waves as she heads toward Main Street, leaving Avah and me to walk toward the parking lot.

Ellie startles awake when a car horn sounds, then reaches for Avah with both arms. "Ava up!"

"Oh, aren't I the lucky one," Avah says as she settles the toddler on her hip with surprising ease. "I thought you only had eyes for Piper."

"She's an equal opportunity cuddler."

"That's a good quality in an ankle biter."

We cross the park toward where our cars are parked in the small lot beside Town Hall. The afternoon heat shimmers off the pavement, and Avah looks visibly uncomfortable in her long-sleeve sweater.

"I need to get back into the central air." She shifts Ellie to her other hip. "It's too darn hot."

Concern prickles at the base of my skull. "Maybe you shouldn't be wearing a turtleneck in the middle of summer in Colorado."

"Fashion doesn't care about weather," she says lightly, but there's an edge to her voice.

We reach my Jeep, and Ellie pats Avah's cheeks while I dig in the diaper bag for my keys.

"Found them," I say just as the toddler reaches up and tugs at the collar of Avah's turtleneck.

The fabric pulls down before Avah catches the girl's hands, revealing a dark purple bruise on her neck. It's not a hickey. I've seen enough of those over the years to know the difference. Her skin is marred by finger-shaped marks that make my stomach drop.

Avah yanks up the collar and deposits Ellie into my arms with more force than necessary.

"What's going on?" I whisper.

"It's nothing." She focuses on fishing her keys from her purse.

"That bruise isn't nothing, Avs." I place a hand on her arm and step in front of her, forcing her to meet my gaze. "It looks like someone strangled you."

She barks out a brittle laugh. "Geez, Piper. Dramatic much?" She pulls away from me and inclines her head toward Ellie. "Might want to earmuff the kid."

I dutifully cover Ellie's ears with my hands. "Well?"

"Jonathan and I just get a little rough in the bedroom sometimes." She waggles her eyebrows like she's letting me in on some scandalous secret. "It's actually pretty hot."

Everything in me screams that she's lying. There's a tremor in her hands and a forced casualness in her tone that feels wrong.

"Avah—"

"I really need to get back to work." She unlocks her car with a click. "Jonathan's expecting me for a marketing meeting."

Right. Because she's working for her fiancé's financial firm now. Totally enmeshed in his life. And I have a bad feeling about all of it.

"I can help—"

"With what?" There's something fierce in her gaze when it slams into mine again, like she's a wild animal that's been cornered. "You've got plenty to deal with on your own, Piper." She starts ticking off my problems on her fingers. "You're pregnant, unemployed, and living with a man you can't figure out if you love or hate. You're helping to raise a kid who isn't yours. And, oh yeah, attending a wedding with your ex-fiancé and his new wife." Her blue eyes narrow. "Don't invent problems for me because misery loves company."

I take a step back, stung by her words.

Guilt and remorse flash in her eyes for just a second before she locks down her expression. "I'm sorry, Pip. That was...I shouldn't have..." She presses her fingers to her temples. "I'm fine. Really."

She slides into her car before I can respond, the door closing with a decisive slam. I stand there in the parking lot with Ellie, watching the BMW pull away too fast, and knowing that my friend is anything but fine.

"Ava bye-bye." Ellie waves at the retreating car.

"Yeah, Bean. Bye-bye."

But not for long. Avah might have shut me down, and she might be right that I have my own mess to sort through, but I know that look in her eyes. I saw it too many times during my ER rotation. On the faces of women who came in because of accidents but with stories that didn't add up.

On the way home, Ellie falls asleep in the car seat, her stuffed elephant clutched in one fist. I grip the steering wheel and make a silent promise. I might be a hot mess, still trying to figure out how to stand on my own two feet and build a future that's mine, not one handed to me by someone else.

But I sure as hell know how to stand up for a friend.

And whether Avah wants it or not, I'm going to have her back. Because something is very wrong, and I refuse to look away.

25

FELIX

I'M at Ian and Sadie's place Saturday afternoon, sitting on the floor of their family room and watching my thirteen-year-old niece orchestrate the most ambitious blanket fort construction project in the history of the world.

"Uncle Felix, can you hold this corner?" Riva asks, handing me the edge of what I'm pretty sure is their guest bedroom comforter. "We need structural integrity."

"Structural integrity for a blanket fort?"

"It's not just a blanket fort." She rolls her eyes in that way only teenagers can pull off. "This is the official Princess Ellie castle."

The princess toddles over with a throw pillow clutched in both hands, her face serious with concentration. "Fee, help."

"On it, munchkin." I secure the corner Riva handed me under the couch cushion while Ellie adds her pillow in what I can only describe as an interior design statement.

Piper's attending her friend's wedding while Sadie's off doing a private dog training session at some client's house, which is why we're in charge of the castle. I use the term "in charge" loosely, considering Riva is clearly running this operation.

Ian's sprawled on the floor next to me, his back against the sectional, grinning at the controlled chaos. "Remember when we used to build forts like this?"

"Yeah, and Dad would come home and make us tear them down because they were in the way."

"Good times." Ian's tone is dry, but there's no real bitterness there anymore. He's made peace with the fact that our father sucked at actual parenting. Ian's also quick to claim he's defied the Barlowe curse Dad loved to spout on about in great detail. How men like us weren't built for love or commitment. I'm starting to understand my father's legacy is not something I have to haul around like some kind of generational rucksack.

"So." Ian stretches his legs out, crossing them at the ankles. "How'd it go at Grizzlies' headquarters yesterday?"

"Good." I adjust my position so I can see both him and the girls. "The facilities are incredible. Matheson seems like a solid guy."

"Tom's a good quarterback. Smart. Not as good as me, obviously."

"Obviously." I grin. "Might have a smaller ego, though, which is refreshing."

"I earned my ego."

"Russ texted me the other day," I say, keeping my voice casual.

Ian's expression shifts. "What did that asshole want?"

"To wish me luck with the new team. Said he and Ronnie broke up, and maybe we could get together sometime. You know, hash things out."

"Please tell me you told him to kindly go f— himself."

"I left him on read."

Ian laughs, reaching over to fist-bump me. "Well played. Russ and Ronnie are in your rearview mirror, right where they belong."

I'm thirty-four years old, and I still get a kick out of making my older brother proud. Some things never change.

"Fee!" Ellie crawls out from under the blanket fort, her blonde hair staticky like she just shoved her finger in an electric socket. "Come see!"

I make my way to the corner of the fort, then duck my head under the main entrance, trying not to disturb what seems to be a Jenga-type arrangement of couch cushions and approximately five thousand blankets. The inside of the fort is cozy, with a pile of books and string lights Riva pilfered from somewhere creating a soft glow.

"This is amazing, Ellie."

She beams at me, then crawls back out to where Riva's adjusting something on the exterior.

As I settle next to my brother again, I notice him watching me with that knowing look that drives me crazy.

"What?"

"You're down bad."

"I'm not discussing your sister-in-law with you." And I'm certainly not mentioning the ring box tucked in the back of a dresser drawer at Piper's house. Not until I figure out when and how to give it to her. I'm sure it's the right next move, but I still need to convince Piper of that.

"I'm talking about Ellie."

Right. I glance at the little girl who's standing next to Riva, hands on hips like she's the castle's main architect.

"She's a sweetheart," I murmur.

"She is. And you're great with her, Felix."

I don't know what to say to that. I definitely don't tell him that Julie's Aunt Nancy is interested in possibly adopting Ellie. I still haven't gotten back to the attorney, who must think I'm a complete loser for ghosting him when he's finally having success with the task I gave him. I told Tyler I'm going to keep Ellie, and I meant those words in the moment.

But my doubts are a real thing, and I need to figure out my shit before I say anything to my brother, or to Piper. I don't want another round of either of them looking at me like I've failed in some deeply meaningful way.

"Dad, can you help me with this part?" Riva calls from her position near the entertainment center. "I need someone tall."

"That's me." Ian unfolds himself from the floor, joints cracking. "Getting old sucks, by the way. Enjoy your youth while you have it."

"You're thirty-six, bro. Not exactly ancient."

"Tell that to my knees."

He's halfway across the room when the front door opens and Tyler walks in, carrying what looks like coffee and a bag from the bakery downtown.

"What happened in here?" Tyler surveys the blanket explosion with raised eyebrows. "Did someone rob a Bed Bath and Beyond?"

"Ty Ty!" Ellie abandons her pillow mission to run at him full speed. He barely has time to set down his stuff before she launches herself at his legs.

"Hey there, munchkin." He scoops her up, settling her on his hip like he's been doing it his whole life. "What are you building?"

"Fort." Ellie points back at the structure. "Big fort."

"It's massive."

She wiggles to be put down, and once her feet hit the floor, she grabs his hand and tugs him toward the fort entrance. "Come see."

Just like me a few minutes earlier, Tyler crawls partway into the fort, his muffled "Wow, this is amazing" floating out from inside.

The interaction makes me smile even as my heart aches. God, how I wish Troy and Julie were here. But I also love how my people have become Ellie's people. That means something, right?

"I'm surprised to see you," I say when Tyler emerges so that Riva has room to join Ellie under the blankets. "I thought you were heading up to Vail this morning."

He grabs his coffee and settles on the floor next to me. "Mindy's sister lives in Denver. She's getting married next weekend, and apparently there was some crisis with the centerpieces or the tablecloths or whatever. Mindy drove down to help her, which is probably a good thing." He takes a long pull from his cup. "After that workout this morning, I'm more whipped than your protein smoothies."

"Lightweight," I scoff, and he checks to make sure the girls are still in the fort before flipping me off.

"Speaking of whipped," Tyler says as he takes a muffin from the paper bag. "What are you doing here? Shouldn't you be at Piper's friend's wedding?"

My stomach knots again. "She didn't want a plus one."

Ian and Tyler exchange a look. The kind that makes me feel like I'm back in high school, missing some obvious social cue that everyone else picked up on.

"You're letting her do it alone?" Tyler's staring at me like I'm the biggest idiot he's ever met.

"Do what alone? It's her high school friend. She's going to know everybody there."

"Yeah. Including her ex-fiancé and his new wife."

The words slam into me like a hit from my blind side. "What?" Why in the hell didn't Piper mention that to me?

"Her supposed friends haven't exactly been nice to her since she's been back," Tyler continues, and now Ian's nodding along like he already knows this. "She told me they've been making comments about her being your nanny and following in Sadie's footsteps with the whole NFL player thing."

I look at Ian. "Did you know about this?"

Ian holds up his hands. "Sadie mentioned it, but she also told me I couldn't say anything. Piper wants to stand on her own two feet."

I turn back to Tyler. "And how the fu—fudge do *you* know?"

"Because I ask her questions about herself." Tyler's tone is pointed. "You know, like you would do with a person you want to—"

"Message received." The last thing I need is Ty blurting out my ring purchase. There's no way Ian wouldn't spill those particular beans to Sadie. My gaze flicks to him. "I can't believe you didn't tell me."

"What part of figuring it out on her own don't you understand?"

"That's fine and good until one of those women takes her out at the knees," Tyler adds.

A hot band of protectiveness surges through my chest. My heart pounds, my muscles tensing the way they do right before a game. "Nobody's going to be mean to Piper. Not on my watch."

My brother rolls his eyes. "Maybe you should watch more closely, Jon Snow," he teases, but his voice is gentle.

"Exactly." I'm already on my feet. "I have to get to that wedding."

Tyler checks his watch. "The ceremony's over by now, and you can't crash the reception."

"Watch me. Who's going to turn away Felix Barlowe?" I run a hand through my hair, panic starting to set in. "But all my dressy clothes are down in Denver."

"You can borrow a suit." Ian stands, assessing me with a critical eye. "You'll just need to suck in your gut."

I look down at my washboard abs. "I'll do that." I take a deep breath as I think about the question I have for my brother. I guess Piper isn't the only one who has trouble asking for help. "Can Ellie stay here?"

"Of course," Ian agrees like it's no big deal, then turns toward the blanket fort. "Hey, Riva. Want to make twenty-five bucks an hour babysitting for Uncle Felix?"

My niece pops her head out of the fort, blue eyes lit with excitement. "Yes!"

"Yes!" Ellie echoes from under the blankets, even though I doubt she understands what we're talking about.

I stand frozen in place for a moment, as the reality of what I'm about to do explodes through me. I don't care about showing up to a wedding reception uninvited, especially now that I'm part of the hometown team. But what if Piper truly doesn't want me there? The old voices start whispering—the ones that say I'm not enough, that I'll screw this up like I screwed up everything with Ronnie and the two girlfriends before her.

Ian smacks me on the shoulder, hard enough to snap me out of my pointless ruminations. "Bro, are you waiting on a gallant steed for the white knight routine? Let's get you cleaned up."

I follow him upstairs to his bedroom, my thoughts churning. Ian heads straight for his walk-in closet, flipping on the light.

"Stop it," he says without turning around.

"Stop what?"

"Whatever spiral you're going into." He pulls out a dark suit, checking the jacket. "I can hear you overthinking from here."

I lean against the doorframe. "Why didn't she tell me?"

"Because she's twenty-three and trying to figure out who she is without someone swooping in to decide for her." Ian turns to face me, holding the suit.

"I don't want to make her decisions for her."

"You also haven't really let her in." He raises an eyebrow. "You're both so busy trying to be independent and prove something that you're missing what's right in front of you."

"And what's that?"

"You're better together."

"I'm sure as shit better with her."

But I'm also terrified of being found lacking again. How can I try again with a proposal—a real one—when I don't even know that she wants me in her life?

He shoves the suit into my hands. "Stop letting the past dictate your future. Piper needs somebody in her corner right now. Are you going to be that man?"

The question hangs there, and something clicks into place. All this time, I've been so focused on not getting hurt again that I've been holding back. I'm keeping Piper at arm's length while simultaneously wanting to pull her closer.

But she's not like Ronnie, or my other exes.

She's infuriating, brilliant, beautiful Piper. The woman who makes me want to be better. She's carrying my baby and taking care of Ellie and trying so damn hard to stand on her own two feet that she won't ask for help, even when she needs it.

"Hell yeah, I'm going to be that man."

Ian grins. "There's that annoying AF Felix flash. Now take a shower. You need it."

I take a whiff under my arm. Oh, I need it alright.

"And Felix?" Ian waits until I meet his eyes. "Don't fuck this up."

"Super helpful."

"I'm serious. If you hurt Piper, Sadie's going to murder you, and I'll have to help her hide the body."

"Noted."

I head for the bathroom, and twenty minutes later, I'm showered, shaved, and stuffed into Ian's suit. Current wide receivers definitely have different body types than retired quarterbacks. The jacket won't button, and the pants are snug in the thighs, but I can make it work.

I bound back downstairs, where the three of them have Ellie occupied with what looks like a very serious tea party just outside the fort's entrance.

"You look almost presentable," Tyler says, giving me a once-over.

"Thanks. I'll text when I know what time I'm picking up Ellie. Riva, you've got my number if you need anything."

"We'll be fine." Riva waves me off. "Go get her, Uncle Felix."

"Who get?" Ellie asks, looking up from her plastic teacup.

"I'm going to get Piper, munchkin. Be good for Riva, okay?"

"Pi," she says with a wide smile before blowing me a kiss that I pretend to catch, pressing it to my chest. When did catching toddler kisses begin to feel as important as catching the perfect spiral?

Ian walks me to the door. "Go be her hero."

"She doesn't need a hero." The words come out certain. "But I'm hoping she'll take me anyway."

"No one can resist Felix Barlowe," Ian assures me. I hope to hell he's right.

I slide behind the wheel and lock in the GPS for the Skylark Country Club. As I pull out of the driveway, I catch a glimpse of myself in the rearview mirror. I look determined, and maybe a little crazy. For sure like a guy about to crash a wedding.

Perfect.

Because it's time to remind Piper—and everyone else—that she's not alone anymore.

Time to get my girl.

26

PIPER

The ceremony was beautiful but had a generic Pinterest board vibe that makes me think social media has mostly killed originality. White chairs were arranged in perfect rows with puffy tulle bows tied around the backs, and a string quartet played the same songs they probably performed at nine weddings out of ten.

It makes me appreciate even more what Molly is doing at her flower farm. Her bespoke events highlight each couple's individual personality. That being said, I guess Christy's basic-bitch aesthetic fits her to a tee.

I sat in the back row like the coward I am, gripping my small clutch purse with both hands while my childhood friend walked down the aisle in a dress that probably cost as much as my old Jeep. She looked happy. Her groom looked happy. Everyone looked happy. Except me. With a fake smile plastered on my face and sweat pooling in places sweat has no business being, the truth is, I felt a bit stabby through the whole thing.

And I can't even blame hormones.

We've just finished dinner service, and I'm wondering how soon I can duck out of here without anyone noticing. The setting is admittedly gorgeous. The manicured golf course stretches out below us with the Rocky Mountains rising in the distance, their rugged peaks jagged against the fading blue of the late afternoon sky. The sun hangs low above the horizon, painting everything golden. Round tables draped in ivory linens dot the stone patio, and tiny white lights have been strung overhead, ready to twinkle once darkness falls.

It's the kind of scene that should make a person feel hopeful about love.

Instead, I'm quite possibly about to throw up, and not just from the morning sickness that's decided to make an evening appearance.

I stand near the edge of the terrace, one hand resting on the wood railing, trying to look like I'm admiring the view instead of plotting my escape route. My dress, a flowing maxi with a geometric pattern that hides my barely-there bump, catches the breeze, and I smooth it down with my free hand.

"Hey, Piper, why are you hiding?"

I turn to find Morgan Finnegan approaching with two other girls from our high school graduating class. She's wearing a designer dress, her dark hair styled in perfect waves. The softness of the look is at odds with her smile, which is sharp as a knife.

"Hi, ladies." I force brightness into my voice. "You look great."

"You too." I turn the wattage of my grin up a few notches while Morgan's eyes do a quick scan, cataloging every detail of my appearance. "I wish I had chosen my dress for comfort over style."

Ah, yes. Nice one. So original.

"I heard you're working as Felix Barlowe's nanny?" she continues before I can come up with an appropriate response. "That's quite the adventure."

The way she says "adventure" makes it sound like I'm a bank account barnacle.

"Just helping out a friend," I say, keeping my voice steady.

"Right. A friend." Morgan exchanges a look with the other

girls. "I'm sure you're *very* helpful, especially since you quit your job at the hospital."

"Taking a little break to figure out what I want to do next," I answer, trying, and likely failing, not to sound defensive.

"Have you met Marie? She's the sweetest."

"Oh, I'm sure," I agree, and it feels like my cheeks might crack from smiling so hard.

One of the catering staff announces that the newly married couple will be starting their first dance together. Which is a blessing because I'm about to let loose on Morgan and the gang.

"I promised Christy I'd video the dance. Let's catch up later, Pip." Morgan's smile doesn't reach her eyes. "I want to hear all about your...arrangement."

They drift away, and I resist the urge to scream or cry or both. Instead, I turn back to the view, gripping the railing harder.

I'm fine. Completely. I don't need these people. I have real friends now in the book club ladies, who actually care about me for real. And I have my baby. I press my other hand to my stomach, seeking the reminder that I'm not alone, no matter how it feels in this moment.

"There you are."

The deep voice behind me is so unexpected that I actually jump, spinning around to find Felix Barlowe standing there in a dark suit that's both too small and looks way too good on him. Not that it's hard when you're built like Felix, but seeing him dressed up is something special. The jacket emphasizes his broad shoulders, and the crisp white shirt makes his tan skin seem even more golden. His hair is styled but still has that slightly messy quality that makes me want to run my fingers through it.

My mouth goes dry. "Felix? What are you— How did you—"

"I had a sudden urge to attend a wedding." He steps closer, and his scent—woodsy and clean—wraps around me.

"You can't show up at a wedding you weren't invited to." I glance around nervously. People are definitely looking now.

Morgan and her crew have stopped mid-conversation to stare. "What will everyone think?"

His grin is all swagger. "They'll think you have the hottest date here."

A borderline hysterical laugh escapes my throat as heat floods my cheeks. "That's not—"

"Breathe, Hart." He reaches out and takes my hand, his thumb gently brushing over my knuckles and sending sparks up my arm. "I'm here because you're not doing this alone."

My chest nearly cracks open at the simple statement, and suddenly my eyes are burning with tears I refuse to let fall. "How did you know?" I whisper.

"Tyler might have mentioned that your high school friends are assholes." He says it casually, like he's commenting on the weather. "Then I heard that your douchey ex would be here with his new wife. And I thought to myself, 'No fucking way am I letting Piper have all that fun on her own.'"

A watery laugh escapes me. "You didn't have to—"

"I wanted to." His expression softens, and the tenderness in his eyes has my heart doing a series of backflips that would make Simone Biles proud. "Besides, it's a well-known fact that the food at these things is usually top-notch."

"The rubber chicken was mediocre at best."

"Fair. The truth is, I came for the company." He tugs on my hand. "Dance with me?"

"They're just finishing the first dance."

"So there's room on the floor for us."

"Felix—"

But he's already pulling me toward the dance floor, which is a section of the terrace that's been left clear next to the DJ stand near the edge of the patio. A few other couples are swaying along with Christy and her new husband. I try not to notice how all eyes swing to us as Felix pulls me close, one hand settling on my lower back while the other keeps hold of my hand. And my heart.

"This is ridiculous," I whisper, acutely aware of the attention and what people must be whispering behind my back.

"It's perfect. Let's give them something to talk about, Hart." He spins me once, and I can't help but laugh again. "You're having fun. Don't deny it."

"You're insane."

"You've mentioned that before." His eyes crinkle at the corners. "It usually precedes you throwing something at my head."

"Only twice."

"Both times showcased your athletic prowess."

The song ends and transitions into another one, a slow country ballad I don't recognize. More couples join us on the dance floor, and gradually, the attention shifts away from us.

Felix pulls me closer, and I let him, resting my cheek against his chest. I can hear his steady heartbeat and feel the warmth of him through his shirt.

"Thank you for coming," I murmur.

"Thanks for not turning me away." His hand splays wider on my back, and the gesture feels possessive in a way that should probably bother me but doesn't. "How are you doing?"

My throat goes tight. "Better now." I pull back enough to look up at him. "What really made you show up here, Felix?"

He studies my face, his own expression unreadable. "Because you matter to me, Piper. You and the baby. I know you want to prove you don't need anybody, but—" He brushes a strand of hair behind my ear. "Needing people doesn't make you weak. It makes you human."

The tears threaten again, and I blink furiously. "Stupid hormones."

"I'm a big fan of those hormones." He gives me an exaggerated wink. "Especially because they make your boobs huge."

The ridiculous statement pulls another laugh from me, which is exactly what I need as Felix guides me around the dance floor. For the first time all day, I feel like I can actually breathe.

We dance to two more songs before Felix suggests we get drinks. He guides me toward the bar with his hand on my lower back, and I'm hyperaware of the stares we're getting.

"Everyone's looking at us," I mutter.

"We're fucking hot." He sounds unbothered. "Do you want sparkling water or lemonade?"

"Lemonade sounds perfect."

He orders for both of us—lemonade for me, club soda for himself—and we move away from the crowd to a quieter corner of the terrace.

"Piper!"

I turn to find Christy approaching, her wedding dress swishing around her ankles. Her smile is bright and genuine, and for a moment, she looks like the girl I used to know in high school. And despite everything, I'm truly happy for her.

"Christy, congratulations. The ceremony was beautiful."

"Thanks, girl." She pulls me into a hug, and when she pulls back, her eyes go straight to Felix. "So it's true that you're—"

"We're friends," I tell her at the same time Felix says, "It's true."

"Felix Barlowe." He extends his hand with a megawatt smile that's probably gotten him out of a thousand awkward situations. "You must be the bride. Congratulations. You look lovely."

"I—thank you—I just—" Christy giggles then clasps a hand over her mouth. "Piper only RSVPd for one, but of course, we're so happy you're here." She lowers her voice like she's sharing a secret. "We're huge Grizzlies fans. My husband's going to die when he meets you."

"Glad to make his day." Felix's tone is relaxed, probably because he's totally used to people fawning over him. It makes me marvel at the fact that he seems to like that I don't. "Thanks for being cool about me crashing."

"Are you kidding? You have to promise to pose for pics. But

first..." Christy moves to take my arm, then pulls back. "Can we talk for a second?"

Felix releases me after a squeeze to my hand. "I'll go introduce myself to the groom." He inclines his head toward the other end of the bar. "I'm guessing he's the guy in the tux?"

"The one staring at you?" Christy laughs. "That's Derek."

As Felix makes his way toward the groom and his buddies, Christy leads me a few steps away. "Okay, first of all, Felix Barlowe is totally into you. We need to discuss this at some point."

I shake my head. "We absolutely don't. Let's just say it's complicated."

"I'll bet." She takes my hand. "I need to apologize, Pip. I shouldn't have invited Bradley and Marie."

The apology catches me off guard. "It's okay."

"It's not. I've been a terrible friend since you moved back, and I'm sorry." Her eyes are suspiciously shiny. "You deserve better."

My own eyes start burning again. "Thanks for saying that."

"I mean it." She gives me another hug. "And if Bradley says anything out of line, you let me know, and I'll give him the boot. It's my wedding, and I can do what I want."

A surprised laugh escapes me. "I don't think that'll be necessary, but thank you."

"Right. Because you have a date who could kick his ass." She winks. "And then throw you over his shoulder, which is hella hot."

I don't even bother to deny it. We join Felix and the rest of the wedding party, which has gathered around him at the far side of the bar. Guests snap about a thousand photos, and a couple of the guys lament that he's not wearing his Super Bowl rings. This is normal for him, I know, but when his smile begins to look tight at the corners, I make an excuse to pull him away.

Our hands stay joined as we make our way toward one of the empty tables near the edge of the terrace. "Want to sit for a bit?" he asks. "I imagine it's been a long day."

The thoughtfulness of the comment is also hella hot, and I

force myself not to climb this man like a tree right here in front of God and the rest of the wedding guests. "You can tell I'm tired?"

"I pay attention." He pulls out my chair, waiting until I'm seated before taking the seat next to me. "Plus, you keep shifting your weight. Dead giveaway."

"You're very observant."

"When it comes to you? Yeah." He says it matter-of-factly, like it's the most obvious thing in the world.

The sun is starting to set now, painting the sky in shades of orange and pink, and the temperature is dropping. Even in the summer, Colorado evenings can get chilly once the sun goes down. I suppress a shiver, but Felix notices.

"Take this." He shrugs out of his jacket, draping it over my shoulders before I can protest.

The fabric is warm from his body heat and smells like him. I want to burrow in and never give it back.

"Now you'll be cold."

His grin is wicked. "You know I run hot, Hart." He leans back in his chair, stretching his long legs out in front of him. "On a scale of one to ten, how much are you hating being here?"

"I started at a solid nine, now down to maybe a four?"

"I'll take that as a win."

I'm about to respond, when a familiar voice makes my spine go rigid.

"Hello, Piper."

Bradley stands a few feet away, looking like a condescending jerk in his seersucker suit with his Hugh Grant-coded mop flopping over his forehead.

"Bradley." I force my voice to stay level.

His eyes slide to Felix. "Keeping it in the family. What a surprise."

"We're full of surprises." Felix stands, towering over Bradley by a good six inches, but doesn't extend his hand. "You must be the ex-fiancé. I've heard a lot about you. None of it good."

Bradley's face flushes. "Now wait just a—"

"I'm not waiting for anything." Felix leans in, and even though he's smiling, there's something dangerous in his eyes. "Piper dodged a massive bullet when she called off your wedding. Any man who treats a woman the way you did doesn't deserve her. Not for one second."

Bradley's mouth opens and closes like a fish. "You don't know what you're talking about."

"Is that so?" Felix tilts his head. "I don't know why you're talking to her like you two are buddies, but I do know guys like you. The kind of douche canoes who make their partners feel small so they can feel big. As far as I'm—"

"Felix." I stand and place a hand on his arm. "It's okay."

He looks down at me, and some of the tension drains from his shoulders. "You sure?"

"I'm sure." I shift my gaze to Bradley. "I hope you and Marie are happy together, but Felix is right. I dodged a bullet. So thanks for that."

My ex-fiancé's face goes through several shades of red before he manages to stammer out, "Marie's waiting," and beats a hasty retreat.

I watch him go, then look up at Felix. "That was—"

"A little extra?" He winces. "Sorry. I might have gotten carried away with the whole caveman vibe."

"It was a ten out of ten moment." I rise up on my toes and press a kiss to his cheek, not caring who's watching. "Thank you."

His eyes darken, and for a moment, I think he might kiss me for real. But then he smiles and tucks a strand of hair behind my ear.

"Anytime you need someone to tell your ex that he's a douchebag, I'm your guy."

I laugh, feeling about a hundred times lighter than I did when I walked into the ceremony a few hours ago. "Can we go home?"

"I thought you'd never ask," he says with a giant sigh of relief.

He tucks my elbow into the crook of his arm as we head toward the parking lot, and I let myself bask in the contentment I feel at this moment. Maybe I don't have to have it all figured out right now. Maybe it's okay to lean on someone while I find my footing.

Maybe—and this is the scariest thought of all—I don't just want Felix here tonight. I want him here tomorrow and the day after that and every day for the foreseeable future.

"What are you thinking about?" he asks as he hits the button on his key fob to unlock the vehicle.

"How happy I am right now." The admission slips out before I can stop it. "And how much that scares me."

He stops walking and turns to face me, his expression serious. "Being happy scares you?"

I nod. "I've been here before. Convinced things were good, and then—" I shake my head. "I don't want to be hurt again."

"Piper." He cups my face with one hand, his thumb brushing my cheekbone. "I can't promise I won't mess up. I undoubtedly will, because I'm an idiot when it comes to this stuff. But I can promise I'll show up when you need me."

The sincerity in his voice makes my chest ache. "That's a pretty good promise."

"It's the only one I know how to make." He leans down until our foreheads touch. "Is it enough?"

I can hear the faint sounds of the reception as we stand here together—laughter and music and the clink of glasses. The mountains are steady in the distance, and the first stars have appeared in the darkening sky.

And Felix Barlowe is here, wearing a too-tight suit, having crashed my high school friend's wedding just to make sure I didn't have to face it alone.

"Yeah," I whisper. "It's enough."

His smile is brilliant and beautiful and aimed directly at me. "Good. Now let's pick up Ellie and go home."

"Home," I echo, the word taking on extra meaning when it involves the three of us.

Sure, my life is a mess. I don't have a job, I'm living in my childhood home with the father of my baby—who I'm pretty sure I'm falling for—and I'm carrying enough emotional baggage to fill a cargo plane.

But right now, I'm happy, which is also enough.

27

FELIX

I HAVE trouble keeping my eyes on the road on the way back to Sadie and Ian's. Piper's too damn distracting in the passenger seat. She's kicked off her heels and has her feet propped on the dashboard, my jacket still wrapped around her shoulders, humming along to my favorite playlist.

This is what I want. Not the crowds or the cameras or the people who only see Felix Barlowe, new star wide receiver for the Denver Grizzlies. I want quiet drives with Piper singing off-key to Luke Combs, her pink-polished toes on my dashboard, and her hair coming loose from whatever she did to it for the wedding.

I want her.

The idea of opening myself up again is slightly terrifying, but mostly it just feels right. A fractured part of me sliding into place when I didn't even notice I was out of alignment.

The porch light is on as we pull up to Ian and Sadie's house.

"Still doing okay?" I meet her gaze across the vehicle's darkened interior.

Piper nods, then pauses with her hand on the door handle. "Thank you for showing up even though I didn't ask you to."

"My pleasure." Emotion lodges behind my ribs because aren't

we a pair? Both of us so intent on proving we don't need anyone that we can't get out of our own way to let each other in. "But you can also ask."

Her eyes go shiny, and she blinks and looks away. "I'll remember that."

We head up the walk together, and Ian opens the door before we can knock, grinning like an idiot. "How was it?"

"Your suit might never recover from these thighs," I say, earning a laugh from Piper. It feels like I won the lottery every damn time. "How's Ellie?"

"Asleep on Riva with Sadie watching over them in the family room. She actually sat on my lap for our Bluey marathon."

"That's progress," Piper says as we step inside the house.

"I have Beast to thank." Ian shrugs his big shoulders, but it's obvious how happy that progress makes him. "The dog adores me, and I guess Ellie trusts his judgment. I'll take what I can get." He looks at Piper. "You look lovely. I assume my baby brother didn't make too much of a scene?"

"He did alright," Piper says, and I catch the teasing note in her voice.

"High praise." Ian closes the door behind us and then claps me on the shoulder. "No white steed needed."

Piper gives us a funny look before heading to the family room. Sadie is curled up in the armchair with a book. Riva is sprawled across the sectional, Ellie zonked out on her chest with one hand curled into a fist near her mouth.

My heart swells up so big I can barely breathe around it.

"Look who's back," Sadie announces, setting down her book. Her gaze goes straight to Piper, who's still wearing my jacket. "How was it?"

Piper glances at me, then back at her sister. A soft smile tugs at her lips. "It was good."

Sadie arches a brow. "*Good* good, or good as in you survived?"

"I had a great time." Piper's cheeks flush pink. "Once my personal wedding crasher showed up."

"Always the life of the party," I say, moving toward the couch. Ellie stirs slightly at the sound of my voice, but doesn't wake. "Looks like you wore her out, Rivs."

"She asked for you maybe fifty times," Riva reports quietly. "But other than that, easy peasy."

Ian snorts. "She begs for Felix. Meanwhile, Uncle Ian tries to engage, and she looks at me like I'm going to force broccoli on her."

Damn. My brother referring to himself as uncle is powerful in a way I didn't expect. I crouch beside the sofa and focus on Ellie so the adults in the room don't see how close I am to completely losing my shit. "I have a way with the ladies." I smooth back Ellie's hair, and she makes a soft sound in her sleep. "Thanks for watching her," I tell my niece.

"Anytime." Riva shifts carefully, and I slide my arms under Ellie, lifting her against my chest. She immediately burrows into me, her chubby fingers curling into my shirt.

"Hey, Bean," I murmur. "Time to go home."

She makes a sleepy sound that might be my name.

Piper moves to my side, gently tugging Ellie's striped shirt down over her toddler belly. Warmth spreads through my chest at the automatic and innately maternal gesture.

"We should get her to bed," Piper says softly.

"Yeah." I look between Riva, Sadie, and Ian. "Thanks for stepping in tonight."

Sadie waves me off. "That's what family does."

Another hit straight to the feels.

The drive home is quiet with Ellie asleep in her car seat. I'm not even sure she realizes she's doing it, but Piper keeps one hand on my thigh, her thumb making light circles that are both comforting and distracting as hell.

When we pull into the driveway of her little house, she glances toward the front porch light. "Home."

"Yeah." I kill the engine and look at her. "Home."

We get Ellie inside and upstairs without any fuss. She rouses slightly when I lay her in the crib, her eyes cracking open.

"Fee," she mumbles, reaching for me.

"I'm here, sweetheart." I lean down to brush a kiss across her forehead. "Sleep tight."

"Love Fee."

Oh, shit. The words take me apart in an instant. My heart stumbles, my throat tightening until it's almost impossible to speak. "Love you too, Ellie Bean."

She's out again before I finish tucking the blanket around her. I stand there for a minute, watching her breathe and wondering how the hell I thought I could let this kid go. There's no way I can hand her over to Julie's aunt or anyone else when every cell in my body is screaming that she's mine.

I slip out of the room, pulling the door mostly closed behind me. My brain short-circuits for a second when I find Piper waiting for me in the hallway. Having shed the jacket and her heels, she's standing there in just that flowing dress with her hair still pinned up but coming loose around her face.

"Did she go down okay?" Piper asks.

"Out like a light." I take a step toward her. "You tired?"

"Not really." She reaches out and takes my hand. "Come with me."

She leads me down the hall to her bedroom, with its white iron bed frame and fairy lights left over from the girl she once was strung along the headboard. There's a stack of books on the nightstand and a framed photo of Max on the dresser.

Piper closes the door behind us and leans against it. "I want to say thank you."

"You already thanked me."

"Properly." She moves closer, her hands sliding up my chest to loop around my neck. "I didn't realize how much I needed someone in my corner today until you showed up and—"

I kiss her before she can finish. Not because I want to stop her from talking, but because I can't wait another second to taste her. She makes a surprised sound against my mouth, then presses her body flush against mine.

We're both breathing hard when we break apart.

"Are you sure?" I whisper. "You don't have to—"

"Shush, you." Her smile is wicked and sweet at the same time. "Stop overthinking and kiss me again."

So I do.

This time, there's no hesitation. My hands find the zipper at the back of her dress while she works at the buttons of my shirt. Fabric pools at our feet, and then her hands are on my skin, tracing the lines of muscle, her fingertips flicking over my nipples.

"You're beautiful," she murmurs. It sounds strange applied to me, but I'll take the compliment coming from her. I'll take anything she's willing to give.

"Right back at you." I move her toward the bed, my hands skimming down to her hips. She's in a simple white bra and panties, nothing fancy, but she's never looked more perfect. "God, Piper. You're so fucking beautiful."

She moves the covers and scoots back against the headboard, those hazel eyes blown wide with need in a way that will haunt my dreams for years to come if I'm lucky. "Lose the pants, Barlowe."

I grin and comply, kicking off my shoes and shucking the dress pants Ian loaned me. When I'm down to my boxer briefs, I notice her gaze drop, lingering on the undeniable evidence of how much I want her.

"See something you like?" I ask.

"Maybe." She bites her lower lip, a motion that goes straight to my dick. "Come here."

I climb onto the bed and settle between her legs. She reaches behind her back and unhooks her bra, tossing it aside, and my brain momentarily forgets how to form words. Her breasts seem even fuller than the last time, and when I cup one, she arches into my touch.

"Sensitive," she breathes. "Everything's more—"

"Tell me if there's anything you don't like." I lower my head and take one nipple into my mouth, swirling my tongue around the peaked flesh. She gasps, and her hands thread through my hair, which I take as encouragement.

I worship her gorgeous breasts, alternating between gentle licks and firmer suction, until she's squirming beneath me. Then I kiss my way down her stomach, pausing when I reach the slight swell that I can now see and feel.

Our baby growing inside her.

The thought makes my pulse thunder in my ears as I pause to press a kiss just below her navel.

"Are you having second thoughts?" There's a thread of uncertainty under the teasing lilt to her voice.

I look up and find her watching me with wide eyes. "Not even a little," I say, placing my hand over the slight curve of her belly. "This just makes you more beautiful."

She lifts off the bed and kisses me hard, and it feels like she's trying to tell me something she doesn't have words for yet.

I kiss back just as fiercely, then work my way down again, hooking my fingers in the waistband of her panties to drag them down her legs. She raises her hips to help, and when she's bare, I take a moment to savor the fucking perfection spread like a feast before me.

She lets out a husky laugh. "Take a picture, it lasts longer."

"Let me look, Hart." I spread her thighs wider. "I want to see what I'm about to taste."

"Oh," she breathes as I lower my head and drag my tongue through her folds, groaning at what is quickly becoming my favorite flavor—Piper Hart. She's sweet and salty and perfect.

Almost immediately, her hips buck up as she cries out, and I move to nuzzle her inner thigh until she's still again.

"Easy," I murmur against her skin. "This is a marathon, not a sprint."

I take my time, circling her clit with the flat of my tongue, then flicking against it rapidly until her thighs start to tremble. She's already drenched when I slide two fingers inside her, her inner walls clenching around me.

Christ, I could live between her thighs. I slow down just to draw it out and keep her right on the edge with me. If she'd let me, I'd spend hours and even days making her fall apart. There's nowhere else I want to be.

"Felix—oh god—" Her hands twist in my hair, pulling just hard enough to make my scalp tingle. "I'm—"

"Come for me, Piper," I command, then seal my lips around her clit and suck.

Her back arches off the bed as she shatters, calling out my name like it's the only word that matters. I work her through it, gentling my movements as the aftershocks roll through her. Her thighs twitch against my shoulders, and I press a kiss to the inside of one and then the other. The tremors slowly ease beneath my lips, but I don't pull away until her breathing starts to even out and her fingers loosen their grip in my hair.

When I finally lift my head, she's watching me with heavy-lidded eyes and the kind of blissed-out smile that undoes me more than a little. I crawl up her body, loving how thoroughly wrecked she looks with her hair spread across the pillow, lips parted, and a gorgeous flush coloring her chest.

"So fucking beautiful," I repeat, lying back on the pillow next to her.

"Yeah, well, it's your turn," she says, biting that lower lip again as she reaches for my boxer briefs.

I let her strip them off me, and my cock springs free. She wraps one hand around me, and I hiss at the contact. Then nearly lose my mind when she dips her head and takes me in her mouth.

"Piper—" Her name tears out of me.

She hums around my dick, and the vibration shoots straight up my spine. Her tongue swirls over the head, and she takes me deeper, her hand working what she can't reach. It's too good. Way too good.

After a few strokes, I smooth a hand over her long hair then tug her up my body before I embarrass myself. "I need to be inside you."

"As you wish," she says with a wicked smile.

"Fucking *Princess Bride*," I murmur, only to forget my own name as she straddles my hips, positioning herself over me. I grip her thighs as she sinks down slowly, taking me inch by inch. The feel of her wrapped around me is like a delicious, dangerous vise, squeezing the air from my lungs.

"You feel incredible, Hart."

She rocks her hips, finding a rhythm, and plants her hands on my chest for leverage. "Samesies, Barlowe."

I let her set the pace, content to watch her move above me. Her hair cascades over her shoulders, and her cheeks are flushed, pupils almost black with desire. She's the most beautiful thing I've ever seen.

"That's it," I tell her, hands sliding up to cup her breasts. I brush my thumbs over her nipples, and her rhythm falters as she whimpers. "You've got this, sweetheart."

She starts to move faster, grinding against me to chase what she needs. I thrust up and match her pace. The sounds she makes— breathy little moans that get higher and more desperate—drive me to the edge of my own pleasure.

"Touch yourself," I say, my voice rough. "I want to feel you come around me."

One hand slides between her legs, fingers working her clit. I feel them brush against where we're joined, and it takes everything I have to hold on.

Her head lolls back, and I reach up a hand to support her neck.

"So close," she breathes.

"I've got you, Piper. Let go now."

Her whole body trembles when she comes apart, clenching around me so tight, my vision whites out. I follow her a second later, my release tearing through me as I lift off the bed to bury myself even deeper inside her.

And when she collapses against my chest, I wrap my arms around her, holding her close while I wait for the world to stop spinning. Her heart pounds against mine and then gradually slows.

"Still good?" I stroke a palm up and down her spine.

"More than." She presses a gentle kiss to my chest.

We stay tangled together, neither of us wanting to break the spell. Eventually, she shifts, and I slip out of her. Her soft sound of protest makes me smile.

"Come here, Hart." I tuck her body against my side, her head beneath my chin.

She drapes a leg over mine, her hand resting over my heart. "Felix?"

"Yeah?"

"Thank you, again."

I kiss the top of her head. "That was the best fucking thank you in the history of thank yous. You'd better be careful, or you're never going to get rid of me."

She's quiet for so long I think she's drifted off. "That's not the worst thing I've ever heard," she answers finally.

The words sink into me, filling a corner of my heart I didn't know was empty.

"You're going to give me a big head with that kind of praise."

She laughs softly. "You've already got a big head."

"Bigger," I amend.

She snuggles closer, her breathing evening out as her body goes heavy against mine.

I stare at the ceiling while Piper sleeps, thinking about today. I should be terrified by the way she's snuck past my defenses and wound herself around my heart with that particular combination of sweetness and sass. Three women have wrecked me. The last one did it with my best friend, in my own bed, and I was down so fucking bad I didn't see it coming. I swore I was done with everything about commitment. No more handing someone the knife and waiting for them to use it.

My dad's voice is still in my head, even now. *Don't let 'em see you bleed, boy. That's how they know where to cut.*

Piper's not like that, but I don't know if I'm ready for this. Can the misshapen parts of my heart stretch far enough to hold everything she deserves?

Yet with this woman curled up in my arms, all I can seem to feel is something dangerously close to hope.

For her, I want to try.

28

PIPER

I **WAKE** up to sunlight peeking through the edges of the curtains and the warm weight of Felix's arm across my waist. For a moment, I lie still and listen to his breathing. I want to memorize this moment.

I could get used to this.

The thought would have sent me into a rumination spiral a month ago, but this morning I'm okay letting it just feel right. Like I might be done running because I've found something—someone—worth standing still for.

I love Felix Barlowe.

I admitted it to myself last night while he was tracing patterns on my shoulder in the dark, and now in the soft light of morning, it remains true. I love his terrible jokes and his sourdough obsession and the way he looks at Ellie like he'd go to the moon and back for her. The way he makes me feel like I can be both independent and vulnerable enough to let someone hold me.

"You're thinking too loud," he mumbles against my neck.

I smile. "How do you know I'm thinking?"

"Your breathing changes." He turns me to face him. "Plus, you get a cute little line between your eyebrows."

"Wrinkles are not cute."

"Yours are." He kisses the spot in question. "What's going on in that clever brain, Hart?"

I could tell him. The words are sitting on my tongue. Instead, I tilt up my face and kiss him, slow and sweet, trying to communicate what I'm feeling without saying it out loud.

When we break apart, his eyes are dark and his mouth curves into a smile that feels like it's just for me.

"Good morning to you, too," he says.

"Morning." I trace the line of his jaw. "What time is your workout with Tyler?"

He groans. "Nine. It's leg day. I'm thinking about canceling."

"Don't be a wuss, Barlowe."

"Wuss my ass." In a flash, he's on top of me, pinning me to the mattress in the most delicious way. His arms cradle my head, the heat of him sending need spiraling through me. "I'd rather get in a workout right here." He leans in and nuzzles my neck.

I laugh, but it quickly turns into a moan thanks to the way he's nipping along my jaw. "I'll be here for your cardio workout later."

"Promise?"

"Promise."

"What if I like morning cardio?" he asks, the words tickling my skin as he presses his erection into my belly.

"I guess I'm due for a workout," I agree with a grin.

The monitor on my dresser crackles, and the sound of Ellie babbling to herself the way she does upon waking fills the room.

I groan softly. "The bean has other plans."

He smooths my hair away from my face. "Nighttime cardio is good, too." He kisses me again, like he can't help himself, then rises from the bed.

We move through the morning in a way that already feels familiar. He makes coffee and pours me a juice while I get Ellie up and changed. We all crowd into the kitchen together, Ellie in her highchair, smearing yogurt on her face, while Felix toasts sourdough, and I cut up fresh fruit.

Felix hasn't promised me anything or made any grand declaration. But the ease of us—the way we fit so effortlessly—it's too good to be one-sided. I have to believe he feels it too.

He laces up his training shoes after breakfast, kisses me goodbye like it's the most natural thing in the world, then crouches down to Ellie's level as she whips up something in her play kitchen. "Save me some food, okay?"

"Fee go?"

"I'll be back soon."

As she throws her arms around his neck, his handsome face softens. His eyes meet mine over her blonde head.

"I'll be back in a couple of hours," he says as if I need the reminder.

"We'll be here."

I should say it now. I love you. Three simple words.

But he's already out the door, and it's just me and Ellie in the quiet house. She runs over and lifts her hands in the air. "Up."

"Alright, Miss Bean." I hoist her onto my hip. "What should we do this morning?"

"Blocks." She points toward the living room where her toys are stacked in one corner. We're well on our way to creating a block tower that defies the laws of physics and my architectural skill level, when the doorbell rings.

Ellie's head whips toward the door. "Fee!"

"Not Felix, baby." I set her down and stand, brushing off my leggings. Probably a delivery.

I pull open the door and find myself face-to-face with a stranger.

She's maybe mid-fifties, with dark hair cut in a neat bob that curls under at her jawline. She's wearing pressed khakis and a lavender cardigan that looks expensive. Something about her stiff posture makes me instantly nervous.

"Hi," I say, trying to keep my voice friendly. "Can I help you?"

The woman's eyes flick past me into the house, and her face lights up. "Oh, is that Ellie?"

I turn to find the girl toddling toward us, her hand reaching for my leg. She latches onto my pants and peers up at the stranger with those wide brown eyes.

The woman puts her hand to her mouth. "She looks just like Julie did when she was small."

My stomach drops, the hair on my arms standing on end. "I'm sorry, who—"

"Nancy Harmon." She extends her hand, and I shake it automatically. Her grip is firm. "I'm Julie's aunt. Her mother's sister."

For a second, I can't process the words. It's as if she's speaking a foreign language.

Julie's aunt, which makes Nancy Harmon Ellie's great-aunt.

"I—" My mouth is dry. "Did Felix know you were coming?"

"Not exactly." Nancy's smile is apologetic. "His attorney reached out to me a few weeks ago. I'll be honest, the news was overwhelming. It took me some time to return his call." She looks at Ellie again, and there's something raw in her expression. "But once I did, I couldn't wait for Felix to have time for an official meeting. I flew in from Charlotte late last night and drove here this morning. The attorney gave me the address."

I bend down and scoop Ellie into my arms, holding her against my chest like a shield. "I don't understand. The attorney gave you this address?"

"He wanted to coordinate a time for me to meet Ellie, but he mentioned he was having trouble reaching Felix." She glances past me into the house. "Is he here? I'd like to meet him, as well."

"He's not." My heart is pounding so hard I'm surprised she can't hear it. "He'll be back soon."

Nancy nods, and there's a hope mixed with nervousness in her expression that makes me instantly trust her. "I know showing up unannounced is unusual. But my sister and I were estranged for years, and I hadn't seen Julie since she was about Ellie's age." Her voice cracks. "I didn't even know she'd passed until Felix's attorney contacted me."

Blood rushes to my head like a freight train. "Can you just—" I step back from the door, arms tightening around Ellie. "Can you wait here for a minute?"

She inclines her head. "Of course."

I close the door too quickly to be polite and carry Ellie into the kitchen. My hands are shaking as I grab my phone from the counter.

"Pi, 'k?" Ellie pats my cheek, and I realize I'm scaring her.

"I'm okay, sweetie." I force a smile. "Everything's okay."

What a damn lie. Things are very much not okay.

I dial Felix's number, and he picks up on the first ring.

"Hey, Pip. What do you need?" His voice is breathless, like he's mid-set.

"I need you to explain why you didn't mention Nancy Harmon to me."

Complete silence on the other end of the line.

My voice shakes when I continue. "Because she's standing on my porch wanting to visit her great-niece."

"Fudge." The word is G-rated but still comes out like an expletive.

"No." My laugh is sharp. "Fudge you, Felix. You better get back—" I almost say home, but the word sticks in my throat. This is my home, not his. "Get back here right now."

I end the call before he can respond and hold onto Ellie, trying to breathe through the panic rising in my chest.

The attorney tracked down Ellie's great-aunt, and Felix didn't tell me.

What else hasn't he told me? Well, that he loved me. And now I know why. Because he's not planning to stay. Why would he be willing to let Ellie go if he was?

I can't fall apart right now.

I carry Ellie back to the door and open it. Nancy's still there, like she's willing to wait all day.

"I'm sorry," I say, although I'm not sure what I'm apologizing for. "Please come in."

Nancy steps inside, and I close the door behind her. She looks around the space at the scattered toys, the coffee table covered in board books, the corner of Ellie's play kitchen just visible in my kitchen.

"You have a lovely home," she says.

"Thank you. It was my mother's." The words come out automatically. "Can I get you something to drink?"

"Water would be wonderful."

Nancy follows as I move into the kitchen, and Ellie watches her with wide eyes, a thumb creeping toward her mouth.

"I see so much of her mother in her," Nancy says softly. "The shape of her eyes and the little cleft in her chin." She breaks off. "I'm sorry. This must be so strange for you."

"For both of us." I pass her a glass of water with a hand that's steadier than I feel. "Felix should be here soon."

"I really didn't mean to ambush anyone." Nancy takes a sip. "I know I should have waited for the attorney to set up a proper meeting. But I've been thinking about Ellie ever since I got the call. I had to meet her. My sister and I hadn't spoken in over twenty years when she passed. I missed everything."

"Oh." I don't know what else to say. This woman has every right to want to know her great-niece. But Felix should have told me. And given that he didn't, I can't help but assume the worst about his intentions.

Ellie squirms in my arms, and I set her down. She immediately grabs her favorite stuffed animal from the stuffy basket next to the sofa.

"El'phant," she announces, holding it up.

"That's a very nice elephant," Nancy says with a watery laugh.

Ellie considers this, then toddles over and holds the toy toward the great-aunt she doesn't even know.

"Oh." Nancy crouches down. "Is this for me?"

"El'phant," Ellie repeats, more insistent this time.

Nancy takes the stuffed animal as if the girl has gifted her the Hope Diamond. "Thank you, sweetheart. What's your elephant's name?"

Ellie babbles something incomprehensible and pats Nancy's knee before moving toward the block tower again.

When Nancy looks up at me, tears shimmer in her hazel eyes. "I'm sorry. I promised myself I wouldn't cry."

I grab a tissue from the box on the counter and hand it to her. "It's okay."

"I always hoped Ellen and I would reconcile someday." Nancy wipes her eyes. "That I'd get to know Julie again when she was older. I never imagined this."

The front door bursts open, and Felix strides in, hair damp with sweat and a wildness in his eyes I've never seen before.

"How did you find us?" His voice is tight.

"Felix," I cut in before Nancy can answer. "This is Ellie's great-aunt, Nancy Harmon, who was sent here by the attorney you hired. The same attorney you've apparently been ignoring."

He runs a hand through his hair but doesn't deny it.

"Fee!" Ellie squeals, abandoning her blocks and racing toward him as fast as her little legs will carry her.

Felix lifts her into his arms, and she immediately wrinkles her nose. "Stinky Fee."

He laughs, but there's no joy in it. He presses a kiss to the top of her head, and I notice how sad his smile is, like he's already bracing for a loss. Then he sets her back on the floor, and she returns to her blocks like this is still the ordinary day I was so pleased with earlier.

Nancy holds out a hand, and his giant one engulfs hers. "It's good to meet you in person."

"You too." He doesn't sound like he means it. "I wish the circumstances were different."

"So do I."

I watch them size each other up. Two strangers bound together by a little girl who doesn't understand any of this.

"I think we should talk," Nancy says when the silence stretches a beat too long.

Felix's gaze flicks to me. I want to run. I want to grab my keys and drive until I'm so far away that my heart can't feel the connection I have to this infuriating man. Instead, I plaster on a smile that says everything's fine. I'm fine. We're all fine.

I gesture toward the living room. "Let's sit down."

Ignoring the awkwardness of the situation, we arrange ourselves with Nancy on the armchair and Felix and me on opposite ends of the couch.

Ellie's oblivious to all of it, happily playing with her toys like her life isn't about to change again. But my heart is breaking, because everything has changed.

And Felix didn't trust me enough to warn me it was coming.

29

FELIX

THE SOUND of the garage door opening is like a gunshot in the quiet house. I watch through the front window as Piper's car backs out of the driveway and disappears down the street. As far as I can tell, she didn't look back.

"Pi, bye-bye," Ellie says, her small hand pressed against my chest. She'd gotten a kiss on the cheek and a promise from Piper that she'd see her later. Me? I got exactly nothing. Not even eye contact.

I deserve worse.

"We'll see her soon," I tell Ellie, but the words are ash in my mouth. Because I'm not sure that's true.

Piper told Nancy she was going to her sister's to give us time to talk about whatever we needed to work out. The implication being that she wasn't part of that "us" anymore. That she'd stepped back across whatever line we'd been drawing and then erasing for the past month.

"Ellie dog," Ellie says, her face crumpling as she burrows against my chest. She knows Piper went to Sadie's, which means seeing Beast, who Ellie has decided is her personal property despite all evidence to the contrary.

"We'll go see Beast later," I promise, then glance at Nancy, who's watching us from the living room with an expression I can't quite read. "If Sadie will let me in the door," I say for Ellie's ears only, though from the look on Nancy's face, she caught it anyway.

Sadie warned me not to hurt her sister. And I didn't intend to. But here we are—another item on the growing list of ways I've screwed up with Piper.

"Julie loved to snuggle just like that." Nancy dabs at the corners of her eyes with a tissue. "I'm old enough now not to regret most things in life, but I wish I'd mended the fences between my sister and me."

I shift Ellie to my other hip, searching for the right words. "Would you mind sharing what caused the estrangement?" I don't want to pry, but something about the question feels important.

Nancy shakes her head. "Julie's mom and I each had our issues. We didn't grow up in a happy home, and we both got involved with drugs and alcohol." She rolls her eyes. "But I'm embarrassed to admit our falling out was over a man. Not Julie's father, although he was a real piece of work, and I wasn't sad when I heard he went to the great beyond. It was a guy we both knew in high school. My sister and I were only a year apart in age. We reconnected with him after Ellen's divorce. She called dibs." Her laugh is hollow. "Only, I was pissed at her—some dumb sister fight—and I slept with him. She caught us and all hell broke loose. We both said things we shouldn't have. I think Julie was around three or four at the time. That was it. We never talked again."

Ellie's gone heavy in my arms, the way she does when she's getting tired or overwhelmed. I ease back down onto the couch, letting her settle against my chest.

Nancy continues, her voice softer now. "I tried to patch things up when Ellen was diagnosed with ovarian cancer. It was terminal from the start, and Julie was in college at the time. Ellen had moved away after our fight. It wouldn't surprise me if she told her daughter I was dead." She pauses, looks at me. "But I reached out anyway."

"And?" I prompt when she doesn't continue.

She shrugs. "I showed up on her doorstep, much like I did today. Maybe that should've been a lesson I learned. Unlike your Piper, Ellen had no problem turning me away. Told me I was dead to her and I better not try to reach out to her daughter after she was gone." Nancy's voice cracks. "So I didn't. When I first heard from the attorney, I thought maybe Julie had initiated the contact herself. Then I realized..." She bites down on her lower lip as if she's working to compose herself. "I know I should have waited to hear from you, and now I've caused a lot of trouble for you with your woman."

I can't help my snort. "Piper is very much her own woman." The fact is, she doesn't belong to me just because I want her to or because I'm the father of her baby or because we've built something fragile and tentative over the past few weeks. She's independent and stubborn and so determined to prove she can handle things that sometimes I think she'd rather break than lean on someone else.

But I want her to lean on me. To be mine in all the ways that matter. Not because of the baby, though that's part of it now, but because of who she is. She makes me believe there's something on the other side of my career that's worth showing up for. And Piper is worth fighting for. Even if she doesn't realize it yet.

I guess I don't really have anything to prove on the field anymore, but I do have something to prove to Piper if she'll give me another chance.

First, I have to get through this conversation with Nancy.

"I'm sorry I didn't follow up the way I should have, but I need you to know I'm keeping Ellie." The words come out firm and final, just the way I feel. "I get that my attorney explained it a different—"

Nancy holds up a hand. "I saw your love for Ellie the moment you walked in the door." She nods at the girl, whose eyes have drifted closed. There's a little ribbon of drool slipping from her open mouth as she sleeps against my chest, and my heart clenches at the sight of her so peaceful and trusting. "If you'll let me, I'd still like to be part of her life."

She lifts her hand again before I can respond. "I'm not a big football fan, despite growing up in the land of the SEC, but I know who you are. I need you to know that I'm not interested in your money."

I appreciate that more than she probably realizes. Most of the women in my life, starting with my mom and every one of my ex-girlfriends, wanted a piece of whatever I could give them. Now I'm ready to throw money at the women in my life who actually matter, and they don't want it. Life's got a sense of humor, I guess.

"I'm glad you're here for the right reasons, because it's important for Ellie to know her mother's family." I pull the sleeping girl closer. "But I'm also her family now, and I won't let Troy and Julie down."

"Ellie is lucky to have you," Nancy says gently, then yawns and covers her mouth. "Sorry about that. I flew in late yesterday and didn't get much sleep overnight. I'm staying at a B&B just outside of town. My flight goes back in two days."

I draw in a deep, solid breath, grateful to have one part of my life on track. Baby steps and all that. "Then we'll make the most of it."

During the next few minutes of conversation, she explains that after everything with her sister, she got clean and eventually married a great man. They never had kids of their own, but he's a retired pilot, so she has flexibility with her travel. She shows me a photo on her phone of him in a captain's uniform, gray at the temples, smiling at the camera. He looks like good grandpa material.

After she yawns again, we both stand, and Nancy drops a soft kiss on Ellie's sleeping head, the gesture so tender it makes my throat tight. She gives me a small nod, squeezes my arm, and I walk her to the door, promising to call her later.

Because right now I've got a woman to win back.

I grab my phone from where I left it on the kitchen counter. There's a missed text from Ian that was sent five minutes ago.

Ian: On my way over. Called in reinforcements.

My first instinct is to message back and tell him I don't need help. I can handle this on my own. I've been handling my own shit for most of my life. The younger brother of the perfect Playmaker who was determined to prove myself without relying on anything except my ability to catch a football.

But the truth is, I could use all the help I can get.

I carry Ellie upstairs to the small office Piper converted into a makeshift nursery. It barely fits the crib, but Ellie couldn't care less. Her eyes barely flutter when I lay her down.

"I'm going to fix this, munchkin," I whisper. "I promise."

By the time I get back downstairs, Ian is letting himself into the house, followed by Eric and Chase, their expressions landing somewhere between understanding and disappointment. I've earned the latter.

"Jake's in New York meeting with his publisher," Eric says, as if I'm due an explanation for why all of my new gang hasn't shown up.

"He's gonna want a full report," Chase adds. "Everything is fodder for an author."

Speaking of fodder...

"Hold that thought." I race back upstairs, pull open the dresser drawer that holds my socks and briefs, and return to the kitchen carrying the velvet box. "Just so you know I'm not a complete fuckwit, I bought a ring in Denver the other day. I want her to marry me. Not because she needs me or because of the baby, but because..."

I break off, the words sticking in my throat.

"Because you love her, dip shit," Ian says. His voice is matter-of-fact, like he can't believe it's taken me this long to pull my head out of my ass. Join the club, bro.

"Because I love her," I repeat.

Saying it out loud to these guys feels real. Right. It doesn't make me weak, like my dad tried to convince me. No one—not the least of whom Piper—is sharpening their sword, ready to take a swipe at my unguarded heart.

It's the opposite, in fact. She makes me want to be better and stronger. Not for football or my career or any of the bullshit that used to matter. Better for her and Ellie and our baby. The people who matter most.

Eric cocks a brow. "Well, let's see how you did."

I flip open the box, and the simple oval diamond catches the light from the kitchen window, sparkling in an understated way. If a four-carat diamond can be called understated.

Ian's blue eyes crinkle as he studies the ring before glancing up at me. "That isn't exactly the kind of flashy drip Felix Barlowe has made his calling card."

"No shit, Sherlock." My tone is straight-up defensive because I'd like to punch my brother right in the nuts. "I picked out something *Piper* would like. She's fucking beautiful just the way she is. That woman—my woman—doesn't need any—"

I break off when Ian pulls me into a tight hug, still holding onto the velvet box like I'm cradling a caught ball in the end zone. "Well done, Felix." He pulls away and cups my face between his giant mitts, clapping his palms against my cheeks. "You figured it out."

Oh. He approves. Okay, then. Let's fucking go.

"Hell, yeah, I figured it out." My voice is a little trembly. Could be I'm developing sympathetic pregnancy hormones.

"It's perfect," Chase says.

"She's gonna love it," Eric adds with a laugh. "Assuming you don't screw up the proposal the way you did last time."

I wince. "About that. I need to do this right. I want to propose right here. This house…" I gesture around us. "It's her childhood home, and Sadie raised her here. Honestly, I've felt more at home in this house over the past few weeks than I have anywhere in years."

The three of them nod like they're picking up what I'm laying down.

"You could go big." Eric gives me a slow wink. "I hear secret garden themes are a thing for NFL players."

I shake my head. "Much respect to my man in KC, but I'm done with secrets. That's half of what got me into this mess in the first place." I set the ring box on the counter. "Besides, Piper would see right through some elaborate production. She'd know it wasn't me."

"So what *is* you?" my brother asks. I have a feeling the great and powerful Playmaker already knows the answer, but I'm going to get there on my own.

I massage a hand over the back of my neck thinking about the past month. "I don't want something ostentatious. Part of why I fucking fell for her is that Piper makes the ordinary moments feel special. She doesn't need grand gestures. I want it to be real."

"What about wildflowers?" Chase asks quietly. We all turn to look at him. "There are acres in bloom at the farm. Molly says they're the perfect mix of delicate and resilient."

Hats off to the quiet cowboy with his mic drop moment. Delicate and resilient describe Piper perfectly. Strong enough to keep going after losing her mom as a kid, soft enough to love a little girl who isn't hers, and brave enough to make the decision to keep our baby even when her life was falling apart.

"That's exactly her," I say.

Chase reaches around to pat himself on the back. "I'm kind of an expert on women, just don't tell Molly I said so." We all laugh, and then he continues, "I'll head back to the farm and call her on the way. We'll bring back enough flowers to satisfy every bee on the planet."

He turns for the door. "Wait," I call out. "I also need a dog."

Ian snorts. "You're going to pick out a dog for the woman who wants to make her own decisions about everything?"

"Good point." I scrub a hand over my face. "I need a stuffed dog that can represent getting one together. Based on how much she adored Max, committing to a dog might mean more than the actual ring. But, yeah, she gets a say."

Three sets of eyes flick to the overflowing basket of stuffies visible through the doorway to the family room.

"I don't want to use one of Ellie's. This is for Piper."

"I'll run to the toy store in town," Eric offers.

"Buy every breed of stuffed dog they have." The idea builds momentum. "Hell, all the animals in the store. If Piper decides she wants a pet giraffe, I'll find a way to make that happen."

Eric grins. "Now you're cooking with peanut oil."

I turn to Ian and voice the question that refuses to stay buried in my chest. "What if she doesn't come back?" The words come out raw in a way I hate but can't seem to help.

"She'll come back," Ian says. "I'll call Sadie and tell her the plan—"

"No." I move toward the counter. "I'll call Sadie. I want to ask her permission to marry her sister."

"Dude." Chase points a finger at me, then shifts to a thumbs-up. "Getting Sadie in your corner. Pro move."

"Agreed," Eric adds.

I grab my phone and immediately see a missed call from Piper. Several texts, too. I didn't unmute it after Nancy left and I saw Ian's message.

The texts are general variations of the same theme.

Piper: Call me.

Piper: Are you around?

Piper: Felix?

The last one was fifteen minutes ago.

I pull up voicemail, my stomach dropping to my toes as Piper's voice fills my ear, shaking and hesitant in a way that makes my blood run cold.

"Hey, um, sorry to bother you. I know you've got a lot you're dealing with and...well..." A ragged inhale. "I started cramping, and there's some blood. Sadie's driving me to the hospital, but I was just wondering if you could..." She trails off. "Never mind. I'll call you later with an update. Don't worry about me."

Don't worry about me.

The phone nearly slips from my grip.

"What is it?" Ian's voice sounds far away.

"Piper." The word comes out strangled. "She's bleeding and cramping. Sadie took her to the hospital."

The room goes still.

"Something's wrong," I manage, my chest constricting, the air suddenly too thick to even draw a breath.

A moment later, I feel the solid weight of Ian's hand on my shoulder, grounding me so I don't come apart. There's no time for that.

"It's going to be okay," he says.

"You don't—"

"No," he admits. "But you have to keep it together for Piper."

Fuck yeah, I do.

"What do you need?" Eric asks quietly.

I look toward the stairs, where Ellie is sleeping peacefully, completely unaware that the woman we both love to the moon and back might be in trouble.

"Can you stay with Ellie?" My voice sounds hollow. "She should nap for at least—"

"However long it takes," Ian tells me. "I've got her. You know where you need to be."

"We're here, too," Chase says. "Whatever you or Piper need."

Eric nods. "We'll wait to hear before we do anything else."

The proposal plans. Wildflowers and stuffed animals. All of it suspended now, hanging in the balance along with everything we stand to lose.

I grab my keys with shaking hands. None of it matters without her.

Ian's right. I do know where I need to be—at Piper's side, for as long as she'll have me.

Without another word, I race past all three of them and out the door.

30

FELIX

THE HOSPITAL SMELL hits me as soon as I clear the ER's automatic doors, and my stomach churns hard enough that I have to pause just inside the doors to get my bearings. My heart is pounding so hard I can feel it in my throat. Skylark Community Hospital is relatively small, but it felt like miles from the parking lot to this moment.

"Felix." Sadie stops pacing when she sees me. Her voice is tight, and she looks like she's been running her hands through her hair for the past hour. "She's still in the exam room. They haven't told me anything yet because I'm not—" She waves her hand in frustration. "She went back on her own about twenty minutes ago."

"Is she okay? Is the baby—"

"I don't know." My sister-in-law's eyes are red-rimmed. "She tried so hard to stay calm in the car, but I could tell she's scared. If something happens to this baby—"

"I'm going to get to her." I grab Sadie's shoulders, to steady myself as much as to comfort her. "No matter what, we're going to get through this."

"You better mean that." There's a warning in her voice, but

also a soft thread of approval. "She loves you, Felix. Even when you're a complete idiot, she loves you."

"Not half as much as I love her." I give Sadie a quick hug that I hope conveys everything I can't say right now, and charge toward the information desk. The young woman behind it has pink hair, matching cotton-candy-colored scrubs, and is snapping her gum like she's getting paid per pop.

"I need to see Piper Hart." My voice is rough but sounds steadier than I feel.

She looks up from her computer, her eyes narrowing slightly as she assesses me. "Are you her husband?"

"I'm going to be." The words tumble out before I can think about them. "I'm her person. She's mine. And I'm the father of her—"

"Holy shit, you're Felix Barlowe."

I turn toward the new voice. A man in his fifties with wire-rim glasses and a completely bald head that gleams under the fluorescent lights has appeared behind the desk. His expression vacillates between professional concern and the kind of starry-eyed recognition I'm used to.

"I am." I manage a smile despite the terror clawing at my insides. "And I've got two fifty-yard-line tickets to the Grizzlies' home opener if you get me to my woman in the next thirty seconds."

The girl with the pink hair looks between us, clearly shocked. "Doctor—" she starts, but he shakes his head.

"What's the patient's name and room number?"

"Piper Hart," I supply.

"Exam room four," the receptionist adds. "But—"

"I've got this, Holly. Buzz him in."

She looks reluctant, her hand hovering over the button like she's not sure whether to follow protocol or her boss. Finally, she does what the doctor says, and the security door clicks open.

He leads me down a hallway lined with partially closed doors.

The walls are painted a pale yellow that I'm sure is meant to be calming, but does nothing to relax me amid the beeping of monitors and quick, solid footfalls on the linoleum floor.

He stops in front of a metal sign that designates room four. "Here it is." He turns to face me. "For what it's worth, you don't have to—"

"You're getting those tickets," I tell him. "Club level if I can swing it."

He claps me on the shoulder before heading back the way we came. I watch him go, then turn to face the door, hand hovering over the handle.

Piper Hart threw a shoe at my head a month ago and made me fall in love with her in the weeks after. She's the mother of my child, and the person who makes me want to be better than I ever thought I could be. She's alone in this room, quite possibly scared out of her mind, and I'm the reason she's in here.

Not directly, maybe. But the stress of the past few weeks, the uncertainty about us, the way I've handled Ellie...

This is on me.

I take a breath, then another. I'm not selfish, although I can definitely be bullheaded and stubborn. More than occasionally obtuse when it comes to matters of the heart. But I know how to love. Or I'm damn well ready to figure it out at least. If Piper will give me another chance.

I push open the door, and my knees nearly buckle when I see her in the hospital bed. Her eyes are closed, her face pale against the white pillow. A wire trails from under the thin hospital gown she's wearing, connecting to a monitor at her bedside. The steady beeping of the machine fills the room, and I cling to that rhythm like a lifeline. Steady has to be good. For both of them.

As if sensing the weight of my stare, her eyes flutter open. For a second, I'm lost in the pale hazel shade that's become my favorite. When they focus on me, I see surprise flash across her face, followed by a flicker of tenderness that nearly buckles my knees all over again.

"Hey," I whisper, my voice so thick it's barely recognizable. "Are you okay? Is the baby—"

She smiles, and it's like the sun breaking through clouds. Her hand moves to rest on her stomach in a protective gesture I've seen her do a hundred times.

"The baby's fine. Strong heartbeat." She points to the screen, where a small number pulses steadily. "They want me to stay hooked up for a little while longer to keep monitoring the vitals, but the doctor thinks it was just a mix of dehydration and..." She pauses, then grimaces slightly. "Stress."

The relief that washes over me is so intense I can't keep my feet under me anymore. I stagger forward and drop to my knees beside her bed, reaching for her hand like it's the only thing keeping me anchored to the earth.

"I'm sorry." The words scrape out of me. "I'm so sorry, Piper. Sorrier than you'll ever know for putting you through this."

"Felix—"

"No, let me finish. Please." I press my lips to her knuckles, then look up at her. "I'm keeping Ellie. I made the decision in my heart the moment I got the message from the attorney saying he'd tracked down Julie's aunt. Giving her up was what I thought would be best for her, but I was wrong. She's mine. Ours." I swallow hard. "At least, that's my hope. You were right about all of it. Troy and Julie picked me for a reason, and I'm going to spend every day trying to be worthy of that little girl and their faith in me."

Her brow furrows with confusion. "What about Nancy?"

"We talked, and she knows Ellie is staying in Colorado with me. I want Nancy to be part of her great-niece's life, but Ellie is my daughter now. Ours, if you'll have us."

A tear slips down Piper's cheek, and she swipes at it with her free hand. "Stupid hormones," she mutters. "Men hate it when women cry."

Despite everything, I feel the corner of my mouth quirk up. "We've talked about this. You are well aware that I cry at every sappy Super Bowl commercial. Remember the Budweiser one with the Clydesdale and the puppy?"

"You're ridiculous."

"I mean it." I squeeze her hand tighter. "I'll supply all the tissues you need, Hart. But I hate that I made you cry. Most of all, I hate that I gave you a reason to doubt my feelings. I should have told you sooner, and hope to hell it's not too late." I stare into her eyes, hoping she can see everything she means to me in mine. "I fucking love you, Piper Hart."

She makes a sound that's half laugh, half sob. "Felix—"

"I love that you're beautiful inside and out. I love that you're stubborn as hell and refuse to let anyone take care of you, even when you deserve it. I love that you have amazing aim when you're throwing shit at my head. I love that you have the patience to read *Chicka Chicka Boom Boom* on repeat even though it's the most annoying book ever."

"I'd argue for *Moo, Baa, La, La, La,*" she says with a soft laugh. "But we can agree to disagree."

"That's fine with me," I tell her and turn her hand to press a kiss to the center of her palm. "Because you're my favorite person to disagree with. My favorite person, full stop."

She's really smiling now, but I can see the doubt warring with hope in her eyes. She's been hurt before and doesn't trust easily, and I've given her plenty of reasons not to trust me.

"If this is about the baby—" she starts.

"It's about you and me. The baby is part of it now, absolutely. I already love our kid more than I ever dreamed possible, and I haven't even met them yet." I shift closer, and my knees protest against the hard hospital floor, but I couldn't care less. "It's also not about me taking care of you because I think you need rescuing.

I want the honor of taking care of you because I already know it will be the best thing I do with my life. Better than any catch or contract. You, Piper. You're my Super Bowl ring."

She snorts and wipes at her cheeks again. "That's the cheesiest line ever."

I shrug. "Yeah, well, I'm not great with words. I know exactly what to do with a football. Ask me to talk about my feelings, and I'm basically an idiot with one too many concussions." I take a breath. "But it's all true. I understand if you need time. I've broken your trust, and the truth is, you're more than capable of handling life on your own. I've seen—"

Piper shakes her head, and for a terrible gut-wrenching moment, I think she's going to tell me to leave. But then I notice that the tears shining in her eyes don't look like sad ones.

"You big, beautiful idiot." She links our fingers together. "It's taken me way too long to figure out, but I don't want to do it on my own, either. I had to prove I was strong, and I thought that meant not needing anyone. But real strength—real love—means opening up and being willing to stand *with* someone. To lean on them when you need to, and be steady for them when they need you."

"Any chance I'm up for that part?" My voice cracks embarrassingly.

"You're the only one I want in it." Her smile feels like every Christmas morning I never got as a kid, all rolled into one. "You're my rock, even when I thought what I wanted was to hurl one in your direction. You're Ellie's person, and you'll be that for our baby, too. I love you, Felix." Piper laughs, the sound bright and clear in the sterile hospital room. "So damn much, and definitely forever. Now get up off your knees before you hurt something. You're no spring chicken."

I start to stand, then feel my eyes widen as I remember the ring box I shoved into my pocket as I listened to her voicemail. At the time, I put all plans of proposing out of my head. The only thought in my brain was getting to Piper as fast as humanly possible. But here, on my knees beside her hospital bed, feels like exactly where I'm supposed to ask this beautiful, strong, stubborn woman to spend the rest of her life with me.

"About that," I say slowly.

Her eyebrows draw together. "About what?"

I reach into my pocket and pull out the velvet box, loving the way her breath catches as she notices.

"I wanted to do this right," I tell her. "I had a whole plan, sweetheart. Wildflowers from Molly's farm, because they're delicate and resilient, just like you. Stuffed dogs from the toy store, because I want us to pick one out together. There was talk of a giraffe. I wanted to turn the family room into something special for you."

"Felix—"

"I know we're in a hospital room that smells like antiseptic, you're hooked up to a monitor, and I'm pretty sure I smell like last week's trash thanks to twenty terrifying minutes of anxiety sweat..." I flip open the box, and the oval diamond catches the light from the fluorescent bulbs overhead, glimmering despite our sterile surroundings. "But the best things in my life haven't been planned. You. That night in Denver. Ellie. This baby. None of it expected, and all of it exactly what I need."

Piper's free hand trembles as it covers her mouth, fresh tears streaming down her cheeks. God love hormones.

"What I'm trying to say," I continue, my own voice raw, "is that I don't want to wait for the *right* moment. Every second with you is perfect enough for me. So, Piper Hart, will you marry me? Will you let me spend the rest of my life proving I'm worthy of you and Ellie and our baby?"

For a long moment, she just stares at me. Then she pulls her hand away from her mouth and says, "Yes."

"Yes?"

"Yes, you giant oaf. Yes, I'll marry you."

The grin I feel splitting my face actually hurts, but I couldn't stop it if I tried. I slide the ring onto her finger, and it fits like it was meant to be there. Then I push myself to my feet and lean down to give her a kiss filled with every promise I intend to keep.

When I pull back, Piper scoots over in the narrow hospital bed, tugging at my hand. "Climb in, Barlowe."

"Uh, that bed was not made for two people. Especially when one of them is my size."

"I don't care. Get in."

I should probably argue. There are about fifteen different reasons why it's probably against hospital protocol. But when the woman I love gives me a command, I do it.

I toe off my shoes and carefully climb onto the bed beside her, arranging myself until I can pull her to my chest. I already know she fits perfectly, like we were designed to occupy this exact space.

"This is not comfortable," I complain, even as I skim my lips across her forehead.

"Tough." She nestles closer, her hand resting over my heart. "You're stuck now."

"Like glue."

We lie there in comfortable silence while the beeping monitor provides a steady soundtrack. I can feel her heartbeat against my ribs and the slight swell of her stomach where our baby is growing strong despite today's scare. Outside the window, the Colorado sky is just starting to turn golden, as if the lightness in my heart is painting it.

"Felix?"

"Yeah?"

"What kind of dog do you think we should get?"

I let out a laugh and kiss her again, breathing in the smell of her shampoo. "Whatever kind and as many as you want. I was serious about the giraffe, too."

I feel her smile. "Definitely a rescue. One that needs all the love we have to give it."

"That sounds perfect."

Another stretch of silence.

"Hey, Hart?"

"Mmm?"

"I'm never letting you go. You know that, right?"

She tilts her head up to look at me, her eyes full of an emotion that looks a lot like forever. "Back at you, Barlowe."

I tighten my arms around her, careful of the wire, and let myself believe it. Neither of us is perfect. We're going to fight and make mistakes and probably drive each other crazy on a regular basis. But lying here in this too-small hospital bed with the woman I love, our baby's heartbeat steady on the monitor beside us, I know one thing for certain.

I wouldn't trade this imperfectly perfect love for anything in the world.

EPILOGUE
PIPER

COLORFUL BOUQUETS GRACE every table beneath the white tent, and I catch myself pressing a hand to my chest as if I can hold onto this moment. Two weeks ago, Felix surprised both of us with his proposal in a sterile hospital room. Tonight we were married surrounded by our siblings, friends, and Molly's fields of wildflowers, which feels exactly right for what we're building together.

The ceremony was simple. My sister cried while Ian subtly swiped at his cheeks, pretending he wasn't misty-eyed. Ellie threw flower petals with the enthusiasm of a botanical firecracker. And Hopper—the three-legged rescue mutt Ellie calls Hoppy— watched from his spot next to Felix under the arbor like the dignified gentleman he pretends to be when he's not stealing socks from the laundry basket.

Now the intimate reception is in full swing, string lights twinkling overhead as the summer sun dips toward the mountains. Although Felix and I wanted something casual, my sister and our book club friends insisted that the evening also needed to be special. Someone—probably Sloane—connected a speaker to a playlist that's heavy on country love songs and light on anything that requires actual coordination.

"Mrs. Barlowe." Felix's voice is warm against my ear as he takes my hand and pulls me toward him. "Dance with me."

"I'm not sure my feet can handle another round." I wince and then smile up at him. "Heels were a mistake."

"Let me help free your poor, beautiful toes," he says and drops to his knees, lifting each of my feet to slide off one shoe and then the other, tossing them into the grass.

I sigh in relief, then laugh at the whoops and whistles his behavior elicits from Eric and Chase on the far side of the tent. "I think you just like me barefoot and pregnant," I tease as he stands and slides his arms around me.

"I like you full stop, wife," he clarifies as my new husband cups my cheek with one hand and presses a delicate kiss to my lips.

Husband.

The word sends a flutter through my chest every time I think it. His dark hair is mussed from Ellie's hands after she demanded to take part in our first dance as a family perched on Felix's shoulders.

"I got that vibe," I tell him, smoothing down a particularly wild lock, "since most grooms wait longer than two weeks to drag their brides to the altar."

"Most grooms don't have a season starting at the end of the month." His palm splays across my lower back, warm through the lace of my dress. "Besides, I seem to recall someone being pretty enthusiastic about the timeline."

"I was delirious with post-proposal euphoria on top of pregnancy hormones."

"Well, I'm just straight up happy." His voice drops, soft and certain. "And I don't think I'm alone in that."

It's not a question, but I answer anyway. "You make me happier than I ever thought I could be."

His smile lights up something behind his eyes that I've come to recognize as purely Felix—the golden retriever heart that keeps showing up no matter how many times life has kicked at him. "Good. Because I have plans, Hart. Big ones."

"It's Barlowe now, technically."

"You'll always be Hart to me." He pulls me closer, and I rest my cheek against his chest, breathing in the woodsy scent of his soap mixed with the cooling air of evening. "My stubborn, beautiful, takes-no-shit Hart who holds mine in the palm of her hand."

Across the dance floor, I watch our friends and family also enjoying our celebration. Sadie—the other Mrs. Barlowe—with her head thrown back, laughing at something Ian just whispered into her ear, while Molly leans into Chase near the cake table. Riva is trying to teach Molly's twins, plus Iris and Jake, an elaborate dance routine that has Taylor and Eric grinning widely as they cheer on the group. Avah catches my eye and raises her champagne glass in a toast, Jonathan's arm draped stiffly around her shoulders. I do *not* like that guy, but every time I voice my concerns to Avah, she brushes them aside. Their elopement is happening before the end of summer, and I'm not giving up.

But tonight is about being happy. And speaking of happy...

I smile at Ellie, who's sitting at the edge of the dance floor, legs splayed wide, Hopper sprawled at her feet. Her flower girl dress is streaked with icing, and her wispy curls escape the careful work Sadie did this morning. She's chattering to the dog like he's her most trusted confidant.

My heart expands until it feels too big for my chest, pressing against my ribs like it's trying to make room for everyone I love. I'm kind of getting used to the sensation, and I definitely like it.

"I got a call from the landscape company earlier," Felix murmurs against my hair. "They're installing the sandbox and playset on Monday." I hear the smile in his voice. "I might have gone overboard with the slide situation."

"How overboard?"

"There are three of them, all at different heights, which I think is for developmental purposes."

"Developmental purposes." A laugh bubbles up from deep in my chest. "Nice."

"Also, the nursery wallpaper samples arrived. I narrowed it down to seventeen options."

"Seventeen?"

"Down from thirty-three. I'm showing restraint."

I pull back to look at him, this man who declared last Christmas that he didn't want children and now has nursery wallpaper samples and sandboxes and a whole heart full of love he's been waiting his entire life to give.

The bump is barely visible under my flowing white dress, but his hand finds it anyway, palm warm and protective over the life we created. "How do you feel?" The teasing fades from his voice, and awareness shoots up my spine at the tenderness that replaces it. "It's been a long day."

"It's been a perfect day, and I feel good." I mean it. The cramping and bleeding that sent me to the hospital were scary, but my most recent doctor's visit confirmed that our baby is healthy and strong, growing exactly as they should be. "I feel *perfect*, actually."

"Fee! Pipey!" Ellie's voice carries across the dance floor, and we both turn to see her running toward us, Hopper hobbling along behind her on his three legs. "We dance!"

Felix scoops her up in one smooth motion, settling her on his hip while keeping his other arm around me. I lean in to kiss her cheek, loving how she smells like vanilla frosting and the lavender soap I used for her bath this morning. Her small hand pats my cheek, then Felix's, as if confirming we're both real and here and hers.

"Ellie dance," she announces. "Hoppy, too."

"Hoppy's a great dancer," Felix tells her with a grin as the dog circles our feet.

The three of us—four, counting the baby—sway together as the sun finally slips behind the mountains and the string lights take over. Ellie rests her head on Felix's shoulder, her eyes heavy with the exhaustion of a toddler who's had the best day of her short life. Felix presses a kiss to her temple, then turns to brush his lips against mine.

"I love you," he says, quiet enough that only I can hear. "All of you. More than football, more than anything I've ever loved in my entire life."

"Even more than your sourdough starter?"

"Don't push it, Hart."

Laughter catches in my throat as emotion wells up. At the start of all this, I was terrified of needing anyone, convinced that being strong meant standing alone. I was certain that if I let Felix in, I'd be setting myself up for the kind of hurt I'd felt when Bradley shattered everything I thought I wanted.

Real strength, I've learned, is trusting someone with your whole messy heart and believing they'll hold it carefully. It's swaying on a dance floor with a sleepy toddler and a three-legged dog, and building a life with the mountain of a man who sees the sharp edges I use to protect myself and loves me anyway. Felix softens those edges, and maybe even loves me more because of them.

In a few days, we'll move into the Denver house that's become ours instead of just his. I helped choose the living room furniture and the artwork for the walls. We've already filled Ellie's room with books and toys and the kind of chaos that comes with a two-year-old who knows she's loved. I don't know yet what I'll do about work—whether I'll go back to nursing or try something new—but for the first time, that uncertainty doesn't feel like failure. It feels like possibility.

We might argue about wallpaper patterns and which takeout place is best. Felix will probably buy a whole bunch more stuff we don't need for the baby, and I'll pretend to be annoyed while secretly loving every ridiculous purchase. We'll have hard days and sleepless nights and moments where we wonder what the hell we're doing.

But we're also going to be happy, even when it's messy and imperfect and nothing like what either of us planned.

Ellie's eyes have drifted shut, her breathing slow and steady against Felix's neck. Another slow ballad plays as the reception continues around us. There's laughter and conversation and the clink of glasses raised in celebration. Sadie catches my eye across the dance floor. She mouths "I love you," and I mouth it back, grateful beyond words for the sister who raised me. Who gave me roots and wings and the courage to find my way here.

Felix pulls me closer, our daughter tucked between us, and I let myself sink into this moment. He's my husband, and this is our family. It's the life we're choosing, one imperfect day at a time.

"Hey, Barlowe?" I whisper.

"Yeah, Hart?"

"I'm really glad you're my person."

His smile is brilliant and beautiful and aimed directly at me, the same way it was the day he crashed a wedding to make sure I didn't have to face it alone. "Back at you, sweetheart. Right back at you."

I HOPE YOU LOVED PIPER & Felix. Up next in The Skylark Series is Someone To Keep. Here's what's in store for Avah & Jeremy: She just watched her whole life go up in flames. He's a socially awkward billionaire who considers "friendly" a four-letter word. A fake dating scheme, one bed, and zero chance they're not falling for each other.

Keep reading for a sneak peek and coming to a bookshelf near you on April 16th!

SNEAK PEEK
SOMEONE TO KEEP

Avah

I should have left after the first hit.

The metallic taste of blood in my mouth makes me wince, but it didn't start this way. It never does. Because of what I'd seen and who I am, I figured I had asked for it and maybe even deserved it. How pathetic and ridiculous. I reduced myself to a cliché after years of watching my mother do the same and hating her for it. Now I'm no better. All because I've never been anything more than nothing in the first place, which landed me here.

Landed is the right word.

I'm sprawled on the floor of an overwater bungalow at Solstice House, the fanciest resort on the island of Bora Bora, and the coffee table has a beveled glass edge that hurt like a bitch when I caught it on my way down. I shouldn't be noticing that even the hardwood planks smell like tiare, the ubiquitous Tahitian flower that's everywhere in the resort, but my brain keeps serving up that detail like it's trying to distract me from the main event.

When I lift my fingers to touch my throbbing temple, they come away red.

"Damn, baby. You've got to be less of a klutz." My fiancé picks

275

up his phone with the hairline crack across the screen and shoves it into the pocket of his linen pants. Jon's voice holds that mix of annoyed and dismissive I've come to know so well. "And don't ever try to grab something away from me."

As I stare up at him, my chest cracks open, way wider than the fractured phone. It's not my heart, which has been slowly calcifying for months. This is the thing I keep in a locked box, the truth I've been hiding behind excuses and rationalizations, just like my mother used to.

He hit me, although he's careful, and the bruises can typically be hidden by long sleeves or turtlenecks.

Yeah, this is a pattern, a no-good, rotten, very bad dynamic. But I'm finally ready to let the truth out into the light, even if it hurts worse than my pounding head.

"I'm not a klutz." I stand up and smooth a hand over the front of my floral dress, ignoring the blood I feel dripping down my face. "You're an asshole. An abusive one. This was a mistake, Jon. All of it."

We were supposed to get married on a mountainside in Colorado a week ago—just us and an expensive photographer. God forbid I have a real wedding where people might see behind the carefully constructed veil I've draped across my life. Then a wildfire broke out in the area, and instead of pivoting to another location like normal people, Jon suggested we do the honeymoon first and get married when things were back to normal.

That should have been a sign. The universe set our wedding plans on fire, and I just went with it.

Jon stops halfway to the bathroom. He was probably going to get a washcloth so we could smooth this over like we always do. First there's the explosion, then the apology he doesn't mean, then the part where I convince myself it won't happen again or that I asked for it somehow. His dark eyes are glazed over thanks to the two bottles of wine he drank at dinner, mostly on his own. At some point, I stopped drinking more than a glass, as if one of us being in control of our faculties could manage the chaos. Not so much.

"I'm not marrying you." My voice is a lot steadier than my pulse. "Our honeymoon is over as of right now."

He turns to face me, and the glint in his eyes makes my breath hitch. I've spent two years pretending our relationship was just intense, that we had the natural friction of two strong personalities. I was lying to everyone, mostly to myself.

"You can't walk away, Avah." A muscle tics in his jaw. "What will people think? What will my father—"

"Not my problem." I want to call him a douche nozzle or a cockwaffle. Among my friends, I'm Avah-on-the-spot with vulgar insults that land like a comedic punch. Only my dickhead fiancé lands the real kind, and I've learned to tamp down my brashness to keep the peace.

And while I'd like to tell him to fuck right off, I need to get out of here first. My purse and phone are on the bathroom counter where I left them when I was psyching myself up for a seduction that could distract him from whatever work shitstorm had put him in a dark mood mid-dinner. My passport is tucked into the safe in the bungalow's closet. Everything I need to make my escape is behind the man who just backhanded me hard enough to make me see stars.

But I know how to survive impossibly shitty situations. In his own twisted way, my father taught me that. When the FBI showed up at our Connecticut McMansion and my whole world turned upside down, I learned that sometimes you walk out the door with nothing and get yourself right on the other side.

"If you leave," Jon says, "we're done." I hear the menacing promise in his voice but have zero fucks to give about the future in this moment. As long as the future means I'm free of the cage I've let him keep me in for far too long.

I almost laugh at the absurdity of his threat when I want to be done more than I want my next breath. Instead, I incline my head like this is anywhere near a rational conversation. "Promise?"

"Fuck you, Avah."

"Never again, Jon."

I don't think about my purse or phone or passport as I exit into the tropical night, my bare feet silent on the walkway that connects our bungalow to the main resort. For a moment, I brace for footsteps behind me and Jon's hand as it closes around my arm to drag me back inside. But that's not his MO. He's never had to chase me down before, not when I stayed willingly and convinced myself that the next time would be different.

He'll make me pay for this eventually, but that's a problem for future Avah, and that girl is going to want to throat punch present me. I'll take it.

I lift the hem of my silk maxi dress and use the fabric to wipe the blood from my face. It's going to ruin the dress, a small sacrifice when I've just blown up my entire life.

A soft breeze flutters my hair, and I keep one hand on the railing as I move forward, listening to the gentle lap of water against the wooden pilings beneath the walkway. Music drifts toward me from the main beach, along with the low hum of people enjoying paradise with cocktails and laughter instead of split temples and a shattered future. Exhaustion takes hold, and I sag under the weight of keeping up the lies my life is built on for so long.

The sand is cool under my feet when I get to the beach and sink onto one of the resort's teak lounge chairs. The stars out here are different from how they appear in my hometown of Skylark, Colorado. They're closer, like you could reach up and touch them if you just stretched far enough.

I'm twenty-eight years old and basically an orphan. My father is in federal prison for defrauding elderly people out of their life savings. My mom fled to Florida the day after my high school graduation. She taught me to duck and flee and that playing the part of a bitch is the best defense against people asking questions that I don't want to answer. The engagement ring on my finger is now just a souvenir from my self-hate era. I should have left the first time he grabbed my wrist hard enough to bruise.

I should have left a lot of times.

A shooting star streaks across the sky, but it's gone before I can fully register the magic. Mom used to say that wishes were for suckers. The only thing that matters is what you can take with you when you go. But she also stayed way longer than I did, so maybe her advice isn't worth much.

I close my eyes and make a wish.

Please don't let me become her. Please let me be okay.

When I look up to the sky again, the stars blur, and I realize I'm crying. God, I hate tears. But if there was a time to give in to weakness, it's probably here alone on a beach in the South Pacific with no phone and no money and a man who isn't going to take this gracefully waiting back in our room.

I'm tired of pretending and managing and being the version of Avah Harris that everyone expects—the sharp-tongued bitch who always has a comeback and never lets anyone see her bleed.

Fat lot of good that did. And I close my eyes and let the darkness take me.

PREORDER AVAH & Jeremy now.

ABOUT THE AUTHOR

USA Today and Top 5 Amazon Bestselling author Michelle Major writes swoon-worthy stories full of heart, heat, and guaranteed happily-ever-afters. When she's not dreaming up romance, you'll find her hiking the trails (or avoiding housework) in her home state of Colorado.

Connect with her at www.michellemajor.com or come say hi on Instagram and Facebook.